Imperfect

by

Lauren Shiro

Vanilla Heart Publishing
USA

Imperfect
by Lauren Shiro

Copyright 2014 Lauren Shiro

Published by: Vanilla Heart Publishing
www.VanillaHeartBooksAndAuthors.com
10121 Evergreen Way, 25-156
Everett, WA 98204 USA

ISBN-13: 978-069223-24-84
ISBN-10: 0692232486

10 9 8 7 6 5 4 3 2 Second Edition

First Printing, June 2014
Printed in the United States of America

Imperfect

by

Lauren Shiro

Table of Contents

Dedication and Acknowledgements

More Great Books by Lauren Shiro
Lauren Shiro Author Bio and Photo

Dedication

To Will & Kim:
for being my rocks & confidants in some of my darkest hours.

Thank you!

Acknowledgements

To my Grandparents: For always believing that I have talent and need to be a writer. Your unwavering faith and love in me is the greatest treasure!

To Chelle: Thank you so much for believing in me, and my writing. None of this would have been possible without you, and your help. My books exist because of you, and I am the writer that I am because of you. Thank you for encouraging and inspiring me. I am forever indebted to you!

To Kimberlee of Vanilla Heart Publishing: I want to thank you as well for believing in me and my writing. I doubted myself, but you never doubted me. Thank you for your patience and guidance as I re-entered the world of fiction writing. Thanks for taking a chance on me, and supporting me in this endeavor. You are more than a publisher, you are a great friend!

Chapter One

Carol had anticipated this day for years. Just lso many college students, the day she could legally drink was a great rite of passage in her life.

Marlene, Carol's roommate, along with other friends and fellow students, had planned a wild night for their typically reclusive friend. Carol knew it would be a long, unpredictable night despite her early class. Carol didn't care, though. She never went out and never partied. Her social life typically consisted of long nights with her textbooks. She deserved this one night to live it up.

At around seven, there was a thunderous pounding on Carol's dorm room door. Wearing makeup and nice clothes for a change, Carol opened the door. A herd of people stood in front of her, some of whom Carol didn't even recognize. She didn't mind. This was her night. Tonight was her night to live, to laugh, and to enjoy.

"Surprise!" Everyone shouted, but the surprise was on them. Marlene was floored to find Carol wearing an uncharacteristically soft, delicate, slightly ruffled black blouse and a cute asymmetrical black skirt. This was Marlene's first time in four years seeing Carol in anything other than a tee-shirt and jeans. Her outfit confirmed her ownership of this night. Carol grabbed her winter coat and purse and the crowd left to go paint the town.

Marlene had decided on the evening's venue. Since her roommie was openly gay, Marlene led the crowd to the best lesbian bar in town: City Girls.

Carol's troops wasted no time in splurging on shots, beer and a variety of hard alcoholic beverages. Carol, normally introverted, drank the shots and other intoxicating spirits; it didn't take long for her to become inebriated.

Alexandria, a 24-year old local, watched the loud, raucous group and quietly chuckled to herself. She went to City Girls tonight to people watch and she certainly got an eye-full.

Suddenly, Carol got off her bar stool to go to the ladies' room. Carol tripped over her own two drunken feet and began to fall forward. She saved herself by slamming her hand on the table in front of Alex. Embarrassed, Carol slowly pulled herself up to find the dark beauty smiling back at her. With skin like rich, dark chocolate, eyes that were beautiful, tranquil, bottomless pools, and neatly braided jet black hair, Alexandria took Carol's breath away. The two paused and the world around them melted away as they intensely stared at each other.

"Sorry," Carol weakly whispered. Mortified that she had made such a fool of herself in front of this stunning woman, Carol hastily stumbled to the ladies' room.

Carol leaned onto the sink and held on to it with all her might in fear she might fall over again. She took in a few deep breaths as she stared at herself in the mirror. Carol's beauty was her simplicity. She had brown hair to her shoulder in a simple style, but there was a special charm to it. Her skin was fair and delicately painted with tiny freckles. Her face seemed plain, but it was brilliantly symmetrical. The very tip of her nose turned upward in a playful manner. Her deep brown eyes sparkled like jewels. She had a slight gap in between her front teeth; Carol was embarrassed by it, but her father had always compared her to model Lauren Hutton. He told his beloved daughter that the imperfection made her unique and beautiful. Carol sighed thinking of her father's words. She pushed the faucet on for cold water and took a few handfuls to sip with the unrealistic hope she would miraculously sober up. She really wanted to go back and talk to that gorgeous mahogany queen. Focusing on her father's words telling her that she was pretty, Carol mustered up the courage to go back out and speak to the woman who currently occupied every thought in her mind.

Carol took a step slowly and then stepped again. She focused on each step and she walked back out to the bar, this time with a bit more grace.

As she turned the corner, she saw the beautiful black woman still sitting at the table. Carol's crowd hadn't even noticed her absence.

Alexandria happened to look up at just the right moment, and saw Carol carefully approaching her. Alex's dark eyes lit up and she smiled a big, beautiful, wide smile at the birthday girl.

Carol carefully sat across from the intriguing woman. "Hi,"

she said feebly. "I'm so sorry about before. I normally never drink, but today's my twenty first birthday."

Alex began to laugh lightly. "It's ok. I understand." Her voice was smooth and rich. Carol was becoming more intoxicated on this woman than she was on the alcohol. "I'm Alexandria. My friends call me Alex." The dark beauty extended her hand to Carol.

Carol grasped her hand. Alex's skin was soft and as smooth as silk. "I'm Carol," she replied. "My friends call me Carol," she joked as she gently shook Alex's hand. Alex couldn't help chuckling at Carol's wisecrack.

Suddenly, a large wave of cheers and shouts sounded from the bar. Both Alex and Carol looked over. Carol's group was intently engaged in a drinking game. The team of people who had come with her were busy celebrating, having completely forgotten the cause of the celebration. They did'nt appear to be slowing down either. It didn't matter though, Carol was enjoying this quiet time with Alex more than anything. Alexandria's company was an exceptional birthday present for Carol.

Alex stole a glance at her watch. "Well, it was nice meeting you."

Carol looked up at Alex, startled.

"It's 11:30 already. I need to go."

"I should go too. I have an 8 o'clock class," Carol replied.

"Do you want a ride home?" The question was unexpected. Carol wasn't sure if she should trust this woman she had just met. Whether alcohol induced, or caused by infatuation, she accepted the offer.

The two ladies quietly left City Girls and walked to Alex's white Camry. Alex opened the door for Carol. Even in her drunken state, Carol thought about *A Bronx Tale*, and quickly unlocked the door for Alex.

"Thanks," Alex winked as she got in. "So, where to, birthday girl?"

Carol blushed. "I live at the Martin-Haagen dorm at the University."

"Yes, ma'am," Alex enthusiastically answered. "What are you studying?"

"I'm a computer science major with a history minor."

"That's an unusual pairing."

"I know. I'd love to be an historian," Carol admitted, "but I know I'd have a better career in computers."

"Smart plan. I'm impressed."

"Thanks." Carol blushed again. "What about you?"

"I'm a paralegal."

"That's really interesting," Carol said sincerely.

"It's ok. It's a living." Alex pulled up to the front of Carol's dorm. "Well, I guess we're here."

"Oh," Carol said, surprised that the trip had seemed so quick – too quick. "Thanks." She began to open the door.

"Wait," implored Alex. Carol turned to look at the striking woman again. "Did you get what you wanted for your birthday?"

Carol paused for a moment. "Yeah – I spent my birthday with great company," she answered flirtatiously.

"How about something sweet for your special day?" Carol looked at Alex, puzzled. Alex slowly leaned in and gently kissed Carol. Her lips were warm, soft, and inviting. It was the sweetest birthday present Carol ever had. Slowly, Alex pulled away and the two women just smiled at each other. Alex took Carol's hand and placed something in it. "Here's my card," she said tantalizingly. "Feel free to call me – *any* time."

Carol sat in the car staring at this amazing woman. "Thanks," she quietly replied. Reluctantly, she opened the door and slowly stepped out.

"Happy birthday," Alex called through the open door. Her smile seemed endless now. Carol gleamed back as the car door closed.

Carol watched Alex pull away. This was definitely Carol's best birthday ever. She looked forward to seeing Alex again.

Chapter Two

A week passed by since Carol met Alex. Carol desperately wanted to call her, but her inhibitions held her back. Now it was Valentine's Day and Carol was spending it alone, studying as usual.

Carol looked over the words in her textbook about servers, hardware, CPU's, and other endless computer terminology when she was startled by a knock on her door. All of her floor-mates knew she'd be studying.

Carol wondered who was at her door.

She opened the door hesitantly. Before her stood Alex, radiant as ever in a beautiful red dress that contrasted nicely against her dark skin. Alex held a dozen roses and handed them to a dumbstruck Carol. Slowly, Carol's face began to reflect the bright, beautiful smile and glow from Alex's face.

"It's a good thing your friends like to talk," Alexandria said.

Carol just stood there silently for several minutes. Finally she said softly, "I've wanted to call…"

"I heard," Alex laughed. "Now, are you ready to go?"

"But – I'm – you…"

"Oh, just put those books away, and come with me already." Alex jokingly commanded Carol.

Carol simply laughed and walked out of her dorm room with her stunning companion.

Alex drove them to her apartment. It was the ground level of a house and she had her own driveway. It seemed to be a nice, quiet place to live. As they entered, Carol was greeted by candles lit all over the apartment. The dining room table had two tall pink taper candles glowing beautifully. Rose petals surrounded the two places settings on the table. It was the most beautiful, romantic picture Carol had ever seen.

Alex grabbed Carol's hand. "C'mon, it's ok." Alex led Carol into the cozy apartment. Carol heard smooth jazz music playing in the background. Alex had tended to even the most minute of details. "Sit," Alex quietly said.

Carol sat herself at one of the elegant place settings at the long, rectangular, wooden dining room table without saying a word.

"Ever have Riesling wine?" Alex asked.

Carol shook her head no.

"It's my favorite. I have a major sweet tooth so I even like my wine sweet. It's very light and fruity. I think you'll like it." Alex sounded like a wine expert as she poured the two glasses. "So," she said setting the glasses down and sitting across from Carol. "Tell me about yourself. Not that your friends haven't already told me a lot. You have them to thank for this by the way."

"What do you mean?"

"Well, I had this all planned out, but all I had to go on was your first name. I drove back to your dorm in the hopes that I would somehow find you. Thankfully a group of people were just heading out of your dorm as I pulled up."

"Marlene," Carol whispered.

"Is that your roommate?"

Carol nodded.

"Well, thank God. She saw me and came right up to me. She asked me if I was the 'incredible Alexandria' that you met at City Girls last week. I told her I was anything but incredible, but my name is Alexandria."

Carol giggled quietly.

"Anyway," Alex continued to ramble. "She asked me if I was there to get you. I said yes, but only if you didn't have other plans. So then she laughed and said your plans were a hot date with your books. She told me all this stuff about how quiet you are, you take classes every term, even during school breaks, you rarely date, blah blah blah. So please explain to me how a cute and obviously very intelligent girl like you isn't living it up during your college years."

Carol silently stared back at her companion. How on Earth would she even begin to explain everything? "It's – uh – complicated," she said softly in the hopes that it would satisfy Alex.

"Well, that's ok. We'll start with the simple stuff. And we'll do that over dinner." Alex stood up and walked into the kitchen. She returned with two heaping salad bowls. "Caesar salad ok?"

"Oh yeah – great. Thanks," Carol sheepishly answered. Carol felt so awkward next to this beautiful, elegant, graceful, articulate, boisterous woman. Her ambitious attitude and her positive personality was all too irresistible for Carol. Alex was so intriguing and inviting to Carol. She wanted to be wrapped up in the light and beauty of this woman. She wondered what she had to offer Alexandria. What did Alex see in her? She felt lacking compared to Alex, yet there was an incredible comfort and safety she felt with her. Carol had never felt so at ease before – not even with her own family.

"Ok," Alex started in again. "So, explain the computers and history thing to me."

"Well, like I said, technology is constantly changing, improving and becoming more and more of a cornerstone to all businesses. There's steady work there, but I love history, always have."

"Really?" Alex cocked her head to the side; she was intrigued.

"My dad was really into history. Since I'm an only child, I spent a lot of time with him when he wasn't working. He loved me like a daughter, but treated me like a son. He'd read me historical stories and books. We watched a lot of historical movies together. He taught me a lot."

"That is so sweet," Alex soothingly commented. "Is he proud that his little girl is a history minor?"

Carol looked down at her salad. She pushed a few pieces of lettuce around the bowl before answering. "My father died almost four years ago now." Her bottom lip began to quiver.

Alex reached out and placed her hand over Carol's. "Oh, I am so sorry."

Carol heard the sincerity and compassion in Alex's voice. Slowly, she looked up and her eyes locked with Alex. "Thanks," her voice was shaky.

After a few quiet, awkward moments, the conversation started up again and the two made small talk during the rest of Alex's delightful dinner.

Carol found herself laying on Alex's couch with her head resting in Alex's lap as Alex continually ran her fingers through Carol's soft brown hair. Carol felt as if she was in heaven. It felt perfect. Carol couldn't feel more comfortable or content.

"By the time I had graduated high school, I had kissed and briefly dated three girls. I just kind of knew," Carol began. "I decided it was important that I told my folks before I went off to college. So, one night – just a few weeks before I left for school, I decided to tell them."

"Uh oh," Alex mumbled.

Carol sighed heavily. "I don't know what I expected, but it didn't go well. It got nasty pretty quick. Dad, as usual, was trying to keep the peace between my mother and me. We never had a great relationship, and my coming out just made it worse."

"So, anyway, mom started screaming. I was crying, and Dad couldn't fix any of it. He tried. He tried so hard to understand me and to keep my mom cool."

"I wasn't trying to piss my mom off any more, but it seemed that she refused to accept that her one and only daughter was gay. I refused to take it back, to deny who I really was – am. My mother's inability to accept me and my refusal to pretend to be something I'm not just escalated everything to an all out shouting match.

"My poor dad tried so hard to let me be me and to comfort my mom at the same time, but it just wasn't working. Mom was calling me all kinds of horrid names. He told her to stop, but she wouldn't. I was just crying so hard – I was inconsolable and you could just see how much that broke his heart. It all became way too much for him. So he said he was gonna go for a ride on his motorcycle to clear his head."

"Was that normal for him?" Alex's voice was soothing and reassuring to Carol.

"When things got out of control, yeah. Mom's so overbearing and bitter. Dad's bike was his sanity.

"He was going to leave," Carol's voice cracked. "I begged him not to go – not to leave me. My dad was my best friend – my savior. I didn't want to be left alone with my mother." Tears began racing down her face. "He told me he wasn't leaving me. He said he'd be gone for just a few minutes. He looked at me and said, 'it's gonna be ok, kiddo.' Those were the last words he ever said. We got a call a few hours later. Dad was killed in an accident while he was riding. Some asshole who was driving a big SUV wasn't paying attention..." Carol began to sob so much that she could not speak.

"Oh honey," Alex tried to comfort her by rubbing her shoulders. "I'm so sorry," she whispered.

After several minutes of uncontrolled weeping, Carol was able to compose herself enough to continue. "My mother blamed me for Dad's death. She blamed me for a lot of things and she just added dad's death to the list. I guess I was just too evil in her eyes. In a way, she was right. Had I not come out, he wouldn't have left - or gotten killed. So, she kicked me out of the house that night and hasn't spoken to me since. I can't say I blame her." Her crying started up again.

"Sssshhhh. Don't say that. It's not your fault." Alex paused. "You do know it's not your fault, right Carol?"

"I don't know," Carol blurted out between tears.

"It's not. What happened is horrible and I am sorry for that. But, it's not your fault, Carol. I promise you that."

Carol wept uncontrollably for the next few minutes until she couldn't cry any more. "So," she blubbered, "I went to school and I've just buried myself in my studies. I took classes even during school breaks like Marlene said. I had nowhere else to go. So I stayed on campus all day, every day. I took classes I didn't need just to stay busy. Studying and working so hard also helped me to not think of the pain of Dad's death, or the cruelty of mom's words. It helped and I'm graduating Magna Cum Laude so the work's been worth it." Carol took a deep breath.

Unsure what to say, Alexandria decided the conversation needed to change direction to ease Carol's pain. "So, how did last week happen, then?"

Carol chuckled through her sniffles. "Marlene and I met at Freshman orientation. We've actually been roommates since day one. She and her boyfriend, Brad, are always out. It's one reason we get along so well. She's never home and I'm always home. Kinda funny how that worked out."

"She insisted that I go out for my birthday. She said 21 was way too important to miss. I figured one night out wouldn't kill me. Marlene knew about City Girls and she's straight. She decided that was the best place for me to spend my big day and the rest is history."

Alex laughed as Carol wiggled in to cuddle with her.

"Hey, what time is it?"

Alex looked over her shoulder to see the big digital clock on the oven behind her. "2:38."

"Oh shit," Carol mumbled. "I should go." As she sat up, she noticed a snow storm had started some time earlier. The snow was falling heavily. "If it keeps up like this, classes might be canceled," Carol thought to herself. She looked up to Alex for an answer.

"You want me to bring you back? I will if you want."

Carol sighed. Not once in four years had she ever played hooky from school and classes might be canceled anyway. "No," she finally decided. "But I promise I won't be a burden."

"You're no burden. Girl, I'd love it if you stayed."

Carol turned to the beautiful Alex, confused. Alex saw the confusion in Carol's eyes. She slowly leaned over and tenderly kissed her.

"You have got to get over this," Alex said. "I invited you here for a reason. You're beautiful, intelligent, sensitive – you're different, Carol. In a good way. I really want to know you better."

Carol still looked puzzled. Alex placed her hand on Carol's face as she leaned in to kiss her again. This was a longer, softer kiss. There was emotion in this kiss. It was passionate, yet tender. Finally after several moments of pure bliss, Alex slowly pulled away. Carol finally opened her eyes. They sat in silence, visually studying each other.

Finally, Carol broke the silence. "I, we, should get some rest."

"Ok. I'm sorry to say, this couch isn't comfortable to sleep on."

"Actually," Carol stammered, "I was wondering – ummm, can I sleep next to you?"

Alex's eyes grew wide and bright. "Of course!" She stood up and held out her hand. Carol placed her hand in Alexandria's and stood up. They walked hand-in-hand to Alex's bedroom.

Alex pulled back the thick, warm duvet and bed sheets. Carol crawled in underneath all the warmth and soaked it in. Alex followed suit. She pulled herself right behind Carol and placed her arms around her. Carol had never felt so safe, or so wonderful, as to just lay in Alex's arms. Quickly and comfortably, the two slipped into sweet sleep.

Carol woke to hear Alex on the phone.

"Yeah, they plowed right behind the Camry. It's almost all the way up to the bumper. I'm going to have to shovel so I can get out, but there's just no way..." She paused for a moment. "Yeah, I know. I'm sorry about that. Dave has a truck, he could probably cover for me." Alex waited while the person on the other end rambled. "Ok, that sounds good. Thanks." She finally hung up.

Still wearing her clothes from the night before, Carol tiredly entered the kitchen.

"Morning sunshine," Alex said as she gently kissed Carol on the forehead.

"Morning," Carol replied, still rubbing her eyes.

"You sleep ok?"

Carol paused for a moment and looked at Alex with a beautiful smile. Carol felt safe with Alex. After a moment, she said, "yeah. Yeah I did."

Alex smiled back. "Good. I've got coffee going and I wanted to see what you'd like for breakfast."

"Oh, I don't want to be a bother."

"Carol, please. You are anything but a bother. I'd love to cook for you. Would you please let me do this for you, Carol?"

Carol sheepishly nodded.

"Good. Now, what sounds good to you? Are pancakes alright?"

Carol was dumbstruck once again. She nodded since her ability to speak was gone.

Imperfect

"Alright then," Alex said exuberantly. She started getting all of the ingredients and tools from around the kitchen. Every movement she made seemed perfectly choreographed to Carol. Before Carol even knew it, Alex had the pancakes on the griddle.

Later that day, Carol once again found herself lying on the couch with her head in Alex's lap. Carol was enthralled by this new and incredible feeling.

"Oooh, this is my favorite part," Alex said as the pair watched The Princess Bride. Buttercup had just been reunited with Wesley. She told him she thought he was dead. "Not even death can stop true love," Alex whispered right along with the movie as Wesley promised to Buttercup.

Carol smiled a big smile. This moment was so heavenly, so endearing. This moment was perfect.

After watching the rest of the movie with the expected twists, turns, laughs, gasps, and pure enjoyment Carol reluctantly pulled her head from Alex's lap and stretched out. She looked behind her. According to the clock, it was almost four in the afternoon.

"This has been really amazing, but I really should get back to the dorm."

"You do realize tomorrow's Saturday, right?" Alex asked.

"Well, yeah. But I have to study and..."

"Say no more my little bookworm," Alex teased.

The couple grabbed their coats and Alex took Carol back to the dorm.

Not wanting to leave the warmth of the car, Carol said, "This has been incredible. Thank you."

Alex smiled back. "You're welcome. The feeling is more than mutual." Alex stopped for a moment, if nothing else to stall Carol from leaving. "You wanna come over next weekend?"

Carol silently fought herself. Her studious side said no, but there was a stirring in her heart that told her she could not decline this woman. "Yeah, ok. Ummm - I mean, I may need to study some."

"So bring your books with you. That's fine."

"Thanks," Carol smiled. Feeling brave, Carol leaned over and delicately kissed Alex. "I can't wait." She slowly got out of the warm car and into the frigid winter air. She and Alex smiled at each other through the windshield, until Alex had pulled away completely. Impervious to the cold thanks to her new found joy with Alex, Carol slowly sloshed through the snow into her dorm.

As expected, her dorm was empty. Marlene was out with Brad and wouldn't be back until Monday. In silence, Carol cracked open her books again and studied as best she could, though she couldn't stop thinking about the up-coming weekend.

Chapter Three

Carol sat waiting anxiously. She kept checking the clock. Time was not moving fast enough. Every Friday afternoon, Carol was distracted in class. Her bags were packed and sitting at her feet, reminding her of her weekend plans. She prayed for time to speed up so she could spend time with Alex again.

This was their third weekend in a row together. Although Alex was a fun and attractive distraction, she made sure that Carol spent time studying as well.

Carol daydreamed of resting in Alex's strong, yet gentle arms. She imagined Alex's glorious laugh: it was highly contagious. Carol felt at home in Alex's apartment. Alexandria was a very gracious, hospitable, and considerate girlfriend. Although it was very early in the relationship, Carol knew that she and Alex shared something extremely special.

Class was finally over. Carol put her books in her bag quickly, grabbed her over-night bag, and left Mason Hall as quickly as possible so she could be with Alex again.

As soon as she stepped out, Carol saw Alex's car. Carol put her bags in the back seat, climbed in, kissed Alex, and the couple were off for another weekend retreat of romance.

"Did you bring any nice clothes?" Alex asked on the way home.

"No, honey. Should I have?"

"I made a last minute reservation at Cucina. I thought we were way over due for a real date."

Carol smiled and blushed. "I've heard the food there is really good."

"It's great. I really think you'll like it. You can borrow something of mine if you want."

"Oh – Ummm - Ok," Carol agreed.

When they arrived at the apartment, Alex led Carol back to the bedroom. Alex picked out a white satin button-down blouse and black pencil skirt.

"I'll go change in the bathroom. Take whatever you want," Alex offered.

Carol stood in front of the closet stupefied. It was full of beautiful and expensive clothing. Finally, she picked out a dusty rose colored dress. Carol closed the bedroom door and changed. After a few minutes, she stepped out into the hallway.

Alex heard the door and came out into the hall to see her. The dusty rose color complimented Carol's fair skin beautifully. The dress hung somewhat loosely on Carol's slight curves. Although Carol didn't fully fill out the dress, she still looked radiant. Alex was beaming with pride and joy as she looked at her date.

"You look beautiful."

Carol chuckled uncomfortably, and flushed. "Thanks."

Alex stepped forward grabbed her shy date's hand and the two left for dinner.

Two hours later, the couple returned full and happy.

"Thank you so much," Carol said. "It was a fantastic evening."

"You are more than welcome," Alex answered as they sat on the couch and both kicked off their shoes. "You made tonight very special for me." Alex affectionately placed a hand on Carol's delicate face.

The two leaned in and shared an exquisite, gentle kiss. It was warm and tender, almost like their previous kisses. This time was different though. Carol let her guard down. She didn't hold anything back.

Their amazing moment continued. As Carol allowed herself to open, the kiss became increasingly warm and passionate.

The kiss was so treasured and so incredible that neither Carol nor Alexandria could contain themselves any longer. They both knew that what they shared was something very special.

After several sweet and tender moments, they paused for a moment to stand. Hand-in-hand, they walked into the bedroom.

Alex walked behind Carol and kissed her neck and shoulder. Her lips were soft and warm on Carol's sensitive skin. Carol leaned her head back and closed her eyes in pure ecstasy. The feelings she was experiencing were astounding.She felt safe, she felt loved, she felt beautiful. Carol felt as though she was flying in the heavens.

Alex carefully unzipped the back of the pink dress and it quickly plummeted to the floor. Alex's hands and lips lightly wandered all over Carol's delicate, lily white body. She followed Carol's dainty curves. Her dark hands were hot and smooth. They felt like velvet on Carol's soft skin.

Wanting more, Carol quickly turned around and embraced Alex. It felt wonderful to hold her so tightly.

Carol held Alex's face with both of her hands as she kissed her with soft, warm lips. Carol carefully unbuttoned the white blouse. Within moments, the shirt floated to the floor behind Alex.

Alex began walking forward with Carol stepping backwards in perfect unison as they continued their fiery kiss. Alex unzipped her skirt and stepped out of it, while still caressing Carol.

Carol reached the bed and lay down. Alex kissed her alabaster beauty lovingly and crawled on top of her.

They continued to explore each other. Soon both women were baring their bodies and their souls. They were naked and uninhibited. There was a beautiful entanglement of black and white as the two women melded into each other.

Alex's hands tenderly caressed Carol's small chest and slowly made their way down her pale body. Unrestrained Carol couldn't get close enough to the beautiful Alex. She pressed herself into her, and savored every inch of Alex's sweet and stunning body. It was magnificent; it was wild; it was emotional.

Her first time in the throes of passion, Carol exclaimed "I love you" to Alex.

"I love you too," Alex gently whispered as she kissed Carol on the ear.

The couple continued to share in their newly declared love for an impeccable eternity.

After sharing such passion they laid intertwined, lightly running their fingers over each other's beautiful body. Alex could see there was fear in Carol's eyes.

"You ok, sweetie?"

Carol tried to hide her insecurities. "Yeah, fine."

"Sweetheart, it's ok. What's wrong?"

Carol looked away. "It's just that you're so beautiful. You're so perfect. And everything I touch falls to shit. I just – I don't want to do that to you." Carol finally looked back up at Alex and her eyes welled up with tears.

"Honey, I love you. What happened with your dad..."

"It's more than just my dad," Carol's voice cracked as she cut Alex off.

"I don't care. Carol, there is something so beautiful, wonderful and genuine about you. You're an incredible woman. I've never told anyone that I loved them - especially after just a few weeks. But you – you're different. You mean so much to me already. I want to be with you."

Carol was crying.

"And sweetie, I'm not perfect. Far from it. We all have shit and baggage from our pasts. I worked hard – extremely hard – to have everything you see."

"All the more reason I don't want to ruin your life."

"Oh stop it, Carol. Do you love me?"

Carol nodded.

"And I love you. That's all that matters. You can't ruin my life, I'm sure of it. What else could have happened that would even have you saying shit like this in the first place?"

Carol sighed heavily. "I – I don't want to talk about it right now. Can I just lay in your arms?"

"Of course," Alex answered tenderly. "I love you.

"I love you too," Carol said as she wrapped herself in the warmth and comfort of Alex's arms.

Alex lay quietly watching her lover sleeping. She wished she could understand the pain that Carol carried in her heart. "I love you," she whispered and softly kissed Carol on the shoulder. "Nothing will ruin this. Remember, not even death can stop true love." Her words were spoken quietly, but the power behind them was amazingly strong.

Carol stretched as she walked into the hall. The smell of fresh brewed coffee woke her.

"Hey lover," Alex greeted her with a quiet, tender tone.

"Hey." They shared a quick morning kiss.

"You sleep ok?"

"Yeah. You?"

"Perfect, 'cause I was next to you," Alex beamed.

Alex and Carol decided to go to all the antique stores in town. It was a fun way for the couple to spend the day together. They never stopped holding hands throughout the entire day.

By dinner Alex decided to say what had bothered her all day. "Carol, honey, I'm worried about you."

"I'm fine," she replied as she took a bite of Alex's roasted chicken.

"Let me tell you something."

"Ok?"

"Carol, my life isn't perfect. It hasn't been. It never will be. Life with you is a lot better and I know you won't, you can't, ruin it."

"No one has a perfect life, Carol. No one. Not you; not me; no one. Here, let me tell you a story."

"My mom was a single parent. She raised my brother and me by herself. My father left her when he found she was pregnant because he never wanted kids. So my mother worked multiple jobs while trying to raise a set of twins. My brother, Byron, and I did the best we could to be good kids. We went without a lot, we didn't beg our mom for expensive toys of clothes. We understood the situation.

"It didn't take long for the bills to pile up. It was really hard on her. She tried so hard, but she had no help. She had no family or friends that could help. Mom was all on her own. With no skills and no education, my mother felt she had no choice but to put herself on the streets. She became a prostitute.

"At first, it was ok. Byron and I would be sleeping when she'd leave the apartment, so we had no clue what she was doing. But then, somehow, the kids at school found out and they teased the hell out of us. I was so angry. No one had any right to talk about my mother like that. I refused to believe what they said and I refused to let them see just how much their teasing hurt me. I started to act real tough. I beat up kids when they talked about my mom. I became a bad kid real quick.

"My mom had been on the street for quite a few years. When Byron and I were ten, my mom got pregnant from a 'John.' Nine months later, my sister Candace was born.

"Then I got even angrier and hurt. I was angry at my mom for doing what she did; I was angry at her for getting pregnant and I was angry at all the kids for making even more fun of us. Because mom was working so hard, and now had another baby, I also felt very unloved. I felt invisible and unimportant to her. I felt like I didn't mean anything.

"By the time I was twelve, I was a straight up alcoholic. When Mom would go out to 'work,' I'd go into her liquor cabinet and drink myself into childhood oblivion. I hadn't even hit puberty, but I was hitting the bottle really hard!

"By fifteen, I was still drinking. I had been smoking pot for a few years and I even started to mess around with snorting cocaine. Poor Byron had to raise Candace, try to help my mom and handle my shit.

"I didn't care whether my actions hurt anyone else. I was so engulfed in my own pain that I couldn't see past myself. I give a ton of credit to Byron and Candace for putting up with all that. The family was under such a strain to begin with and I only made it worse. I caused fights, stress, and just added to all of our problems.

"The family tried to help me. They really did. They tried tough love. They tried soft love. They tried everything they knew and then some.

"I went through rehab three times by my 21st birthday.

"Then, Byron offered me a deal."

Carol looked at Alex perplexed as to what kind of deal he could have offered his sister at such a young age.

Seeing Carol's confusion, Alex interrupted herself. "Oh wait, I should backtrack and tell you that he had already been working full-time since he was sixteen. He worked as a grunt laborer for a contractor after school. He saved every penny he could for the family. He worked on weekends, all summer long, you name it. After high school, he started doing contracting on his own. He never went to school. He just worked.

"He offered to send me to paralegal school if I promised to call him every day and let him check my house whenever he wanted for drugs and alcohol. At that point, I was sober for…three months, I think. I was so desperate to have a good, normal life. I agreed without reservation."

"I still have to call him every day."

"But we drank wine on Valentine's." Carol accidentally interrupted Alex.

"Yeah, we did. I called him and told him that I wanted to have some wine with dinner, for you. He told me I was allowed to have two glasses, and no more. I had a glass and a half.

"And, if you remember back to City Girls, I didn't drink at all. I just had soda pop.

"While I was in school working towards my paralegal certification, my mom got into a bad car wreck. She nearly died."

Carol gasped.

"I promised Byron as a return gift to the family, I'd pay for mom to be in a nursing facility when I graduated and started working. The timing was right. She was hospitalized for so long and went through so many surgeries that I graduated just about the same time she was released from the hospital and sent to the facility.

"So, every month, I pay for Mom's care. It's a payment I don't mind making, the one bill I'm proud to pay. It's the least I can do after nearly destroying my family.

"My point is this, sweetie, you're only responsible for your own actions. Anything in your past is over with. Don't let it hold you back from living now. My family has forgiven me and we have great relationships with each other now. We've moved on from all that pain. You need to move on from all your past pain as well."

Carol sat quietly and one tear made its way down her delicate cheek as she watched Alex speak. "I – I love you." Moved by Alex's story and strength, it was all Carol could say.

Chapter Four

The semester was moving along quickly. Carol found a good balance between studying and spending time with Alex. Their relationship continued to blossom. For the first time, Carol was actually happy with her life.

One Saturday afternoon, the couple cuddled while watching a baseball game, a sport they both thoroughly enjoyed.

"Ya know," Carol chuckled. "This is ironic:watching the Cardinals play. When I was a kid I always told my father I was going to be the first female professional baseball player."

Alex laughed heartily. "Oh really? Did you have a team you wanted to play for?"

"The Cards, of course. Ya gotta go for the home team. How could I not want to play for St. Louis?"

Alex's laugh got louder.

"My dad and I played ball in the backyard. My dad was so awesome. He was always so positive and encouraging. He didn't want to dash my dream by telling me just how not athletic I actually was." The two roared in laughter. "Thankfully, I figured it out pretty quickly on my own."

Alex pulled Carol in tightly and squeezed her. "Well, I don't care that you're not playing for the Cardinals. You still hit a home run with me."

Carol broke out into hysterical laughter. "Did you come up with that all by yourself?"

Alex looked at Carol. "What?" Her eyes glistened with happiness.

"That was cheesy, but I love you anyway." Carol teased her.

"Oh, thanks!"

They both started laughing. They didn't have a care in the world. They both snuggled in even closer, cuddling as warmly and sweetly as possible. They enjoyed each other and the game for the remainder of the afternoon.

A little more than a month before school's end, Alex decided to approach Carol about her post-graduation plans.

"Hey sweetheart?"

"Yeah, babe," Carol replied as she towel-dried her hair, walking out of the bathroom.

"I have a question for you."

"Ok, shoot."

"Well – um, sweetie. I was just – I was just wondering what you were gonna do after school was done."

"Well, I'm lining up lots of job interviews."

"I meant where you are going to live."

Carol stopped in her tracks. The towel hung limply from her hand and her hair was a disheveled mess. "Oh. I don't know. I hate to admit it, but I haven't really given it much thought. I really should start looking for a place."

"Carol, would you consider moving in with me?"

"What? Really? Are you sure? Wait, I don't know..."

"Yes, I'm sure. I know it's a big step, but we're happy. We love each other. I don't see a reason to."

Carol's brown eyes were wide and showed confusion, fear, and elation all at the same time.

"Do you want to?" Alexandria quietly asked.

"I'd love to, but..."

"But?"

"But, I don't know. I just don't want to disappoint you. Like, what if you get sick of me, or something."

"Stop that. It's not gonna happen. Let's just do it."

"Are you sure?" Carol's eyes began to well up with tears of joy.

"Of course."

"Ok then." Carol smiled through the tears. She never imagined that Alex would open her home and her life to Carol in this way. The acceptance and love she felt from Alex was staggering.

Carol's final semester was going quickly. She was ranked second in her class. Only two weeks remained before graduation when she came back to the dorm room to find Marlene moving the last of her belongings out.

"So, you really are doing this, huh?"

"Yeah," Marlene sighed. "Brad got this incredible offer in Kansas City. He couldn't turn it down, and – well, I think he may be the one. I just have to go with him."

"What about you? What about these last few weeks of school? What about nursing?"

"I've worked it out with my instructors. I'm still graduating; I'm just not going through the ceremony. I'm sure I can get a nursing job easily. Besides, his work is way more important than mine. Plus, once we get married, I'm sure we're gonna have kids and all. So my dreams are whatever his dreams are. And let me tell you, this offer is definitely a dream come true for him."

"Wow. You must be so excited."

"I am." Marlene glowed, but Carol could feel the apprehension.

"Well, here's my e-mail address and Alex's address. Keep in touch, ok?" You've been an awesome friend and roommate."

"Here's my info," Marlene said as she quickly scribbled it on a piece of scrap paper. "Maybe you and Alex can come to the wedding."

"That would be awesome." The two young women hugged. Carol sincerely hoped that she and Marlene would keep in touch, but somewhere deep in her gut she knew this would be the last time she would see her friend.

Tearfully, they bid each other farewell. Carol watched as Marlene walked away down her own path in life.

Chapter Five

Carol was nervous as she waited in line. She played with her sleeves, not knowing what else to do. Finally, everyone began moving forward. Like a herd of cattle, everyone just followed the person before them, Carol included.

There was quite a crowd. They all applauded as the students proceeded out. Carol had hoped she could find Alexandria, but the mob was too thick to recognize any faces.

Like all university graduations, there was the customary pomp and circumstance, endless speeches, and the scorching, humid summer heat. It seemed an endless process, but finally the class of 1997 was graduated.

Most of Carol's belongings had already made their way into Alex's apartment, but the two packed up the last few tidbits to make Carol's move in with Alex official.

"Hey, sweetie," Alex called to Carol.

"Yeah?"

"What's your game plan for work?" Alex already knew the answer, but she needed to hold the conversation again.

"Well, I'm meeting with Dawson Networking next Wednesday. That one's looking very promising. Plus, I was going to make follow up calls on all the others on Monday. There's like ten, I think."

"Hmmm," Alex started. "If you have an interview on Wednesday, we're gonna have to figure out a way for you to get there. I can't take off from work so you can use the Camry."

"I know," Carol quietly replied. "Maybe I'll come across a cheap car in the weekend paper or something. I'll figure it out."

"Ok," Alex said as they carried the last few boxes out to the Camry.

As Carol was about to sit in the car, she noticed there was a card on the passenger seat addressed to her and marked to be opened on her graduation day. She opened the envelope. It was a congratulatory card with a very sweet saying on the front. Slowly, she opened the card to read the inscription on the inside.

Dear Carol,

Congratulations on graduating from college! We are all very proud of you. We are so sorry that we were unable to attend, but please know that you are in our hearts.

We consider you a part of our family. Again, congratulations to you, our "daughter." We all love you and are very proud of you.

Love,

Mr. & Mrs. Baker, and of course, Ed

Carol began to cry as she read the letter. A check slid out of the card, and fell into her lap. The myriad of emotions consumed Carol and the tears fell harder.

"You ok?" Alex asked.

"Yeah. Ed was my best friend in high school. His family took me in after my dad died," Carol sniffled. "Mrs. Baker was more of a mom to me than my own mother was even before Dad's death. I was at their house all the time. I could talk to Mrs. Baker when my mom would start shit with me."

Carol sighed as she thought of the painful memories from her childhood. "My mom was always very disappointed in me my entire life."

"She wanted lots of kids, but only had me. She found out when she was pregnant with me that she had placenta previa. It gave her a lot of complications, and then I was a preemie. I was a sickly kid."

"I think my mom blamed me for all of that. And because of all the complications with me, she couldn't have any other children. That was completely devastating for her."

40

"Plus, my parents spent so much on medical bills because of my premature birth and medical issues. She blamed me for that, too. She would tell me it was all my fault we didn't have this, or couldn't do that."

"Even as a kid, I felt terrible that I had caused so much strife. I would do whatever I could to try to make it up to her somehow, but nothing worked. Nothing I did was ever good enough."

"Even my school grades...I could have gotten an 'A' on a test, and she'd be on my case about why I didn't get an 'A+.' Anything and everything I ever did was always scrutinized."

"She was angry with me a lot. She was angry with me over every little thing. She was always yelling at me. Needless to say, we never really had much of a relationship."

"I remember the first time I went to Ed's house, I was amazed at how warm and inviting Mrs. Baker was. She was so nice. We could talk, she'd praise my work. She was so different. We fast became friends. Ed's mom was really the mother and role model I never had. I was so close with everyone in that family. I've always treasured them."

"This just really means a lot to me."

With a sympathetic nod, Alex understood the emotions that Carol was experiencing. The ride home was silent, except for Carol trying to compose herself.

As they pulled into the driveway, there was a bright cherry red 1967 Pontiac GTO with a black hardtop parked by the apartment entrance. There was a large, white bow on top.

Carol Gasped. "What is that? It looks like – like – it looks like my dad's old car."

"Congratulations," Alex whispered. "This is our gift to you from my whole family and me. It's our way to congratulate you for graduating."

"What?"

"You said you had always dreamed of owning a car like your dad's. You need a car, so we decided to get you a car. Well, not just any car. This is your father's car."

Carol simply stared at Alex. "But, how?"

"Byron called your mother. She's had it all this time, but she wasn't using it. Byron made her a good offer. She had no need for the car and she had no reason to turn down the money. It was a win-win situation."

"But," Carol tearfully interrupted, "my mother would never let me have something like this."

"We figured. That's why we did it this way. Your mom doesn't know Byron. He didn't tell her where it was going. That's none of her business. So, as far as your mom knows, some random black guy bought the car."

Carol cried. The emotion of this day, of this gesture, was so much. She got out of the Camry and ran to the GTO.

Tenderly, she touched the car as if she was touching her father again. The metal was hot from the summer sun. The lines, the curves, the feel were all familiar. She felt the soul of the car as her hand gently caressed it. Unable to contain herself, Carol opened the door and sat in what used to be her father's seat. The interior smelled like him. Carol inhaled deeply, hoping to somehow take in her father's soul. The steering wheel was comfortable. The shifter brought a sense of peace and normalcy.

Carol had this feeling to pull down the visor. A faded picture of her with her father landed on her lap, looking up at her. Walter, Carol's father, looked young and bright. Carol looked small and pale. Carol estimated she was about four or five in the picture. Through her tears, Carol saw she was holding her father's hand in the picture.

Carol wept. No longer able to keep the tears from flooding her face, she allowed herself to be swept away by emotion.

"You ok?" Alex's voice was quiet and compassionate as she gently placed her hand on Carol's knee.

Carol nodded, unable to speak. The couple stayed as they were while Carol wept from the depth of her soul. It was an indefinite amount of time, but it was a cherished moment for each woman. Finally, Carol's crying slowed down.

"You ok?" Alex repeated.

Carol nodded, and then rose. Alex held her.

"I just can't believe this. Thank you so much." Carol paused to sniffle and wipe the tears away. "And I just love you so fucking much."

Alexandria smiled as she continued to hold her lover. "I love you too," she whispered. They held each other for a minute. Suddenly, Alex caught a glimpse of the shifter. "Hey, this is a stick. Can you drive it?"

"Yeah," Carol answered brightly, though her face was still soaked.

"How'd you learn to drive a stick?"

"This car. My dad taught me."

"Can you teach me?"

"Absolutely." There was a light in Carol's eyes that Alex hadn't seen before. Carol had been reunited with her father and was sharing this incredible moment with the love of her life. This was the greatest gift and the greatest day of Carol's young life.

Chapter Six

"Well, Carol, I must say that your knowledge as a new graduate is more than impressive. Plus your academic record is fantastic. I think you'd make an excellent addition to our team." Greg Dawson was a short, middle-aged man. His hair was grey, but thick. A mustache matching his hair in color and thickness lay above his top lip. There was warmth and gentleness in his brown eyes.

This was the opportunity of a life time and Carol was thrilled by what she was hearing. She would be one of three head computer technicians at Dawson Networking. The pay was great. A lot of hard work and dedication to the company would be involved, but Carol's instinct told her this was the right job. "I would be honored," she responded.

"Sounds great. Let me introduce you to some of your co-workers." Mr. Dawson led Carol out of his office and into the main work area. Seated a large table were two men, each working on computers. "Will, Paul... I'd like to introduce you both to Miss Carol Mathers, our newest team member."

Will was the first to get up. He was dark skinned African-American man. He stood around six feet tall, wore his hair extremely short, and had a slight mustache and goatee. He was handsome. He was clearly older than Carol by about fifteen years.

"Hi, I'm Will Peterson." He cheerfully greeted her. He had a warm, sweet voice.

Just looking into his light brown eyes, Carol could see that his spirit was bright and boisterous. From watching him work at the table, Carol could clearly see that he was a hard worker and very focused, he also seemed to be a fun and happy person. He shook Carol's hand with enthusiasm.

Imperfect

Slowly and reluctantly, Paul rose. Paul was younger than Will. He was a tall, fairly muscular blonde man with emerald green eyes. Despite his good looks, he gave off an aura of anger and bitterness. His negativity colored his appearance. He glared at her. "A , Greg? Are we really that hard up?" He snorted.

Uncertain of how to react to his statement, Carol forced a laugh, and extended her arm to shake his hand. With a look of disgust, Paul reluctantly returned the salutation.

Feeling incredibly uncomfortable, Carol turned to Dawson to change the subject. "So, Monday? 8 am?"

"Sounds like a plan, kid."

"Thank you, Mr. Dawson."

"Please, call me Greg."

"Ok. Thank you, Greg." Carol left the office feeling as if she was on top of the world.

As Carol pulled up for her first day of work, she saw Will and Paul talking in the parking lot. She pulled up close to where the men were standing. Her heart raced at the idea of her first day of work, real work. Carol got out of the GTO and went up to talk with her new co-workers. "Hi guys."

"Hey, nice ride." Will said.

"Thanks."

"A red GTO? Looking for attention, huh?" Paul asked bitterly.

"Actually, it was a gift, my college graduation gift. It was my father's car. He was the original owner. He always treasured this car. I'm so thrilled that I have it now. It means a lot to me."

Paul huffed at Carol's response and led the trio into the building.

"Don't worry about him," Will whispered to Carol. "Just do your job and do it well. He's an ass, but he's a good tech. Just focus on the task at hand and you'll be fine."

"Thanks." Carol smiled. She appreciated his comforting advice.

Reassured by Will's kindness and guidance, Carol knew that she would do well here. She took a deep breath telling herself that all she had to do was let Paul's comments roll off her back.

She felt excited as she entered the building with Will. Her first day held so much hope, opportunity and possibilities.

It was a sunny, warm late Sunday morning. Carol and Alex sat in an empty parking lot in the GTO. Alex was getting nervous.

"You'll be fine, babe. I'll talk you through this. It's not that difficult, I promise. You'll be driving this stick like a pro in no time."

There was fear in Alex's deep brown eyes as they got out, walked around and switched places in the car.

"Ok, so the first thing I want you to do is to feel comfortable with the stick."

Alex looked at her companion puzzled.

"Go on, put your hand on the shifter." Carol gently encouraged her. Nervously, Alex placed her hand on the shift knob. Carol lightly placed her hand on top of Alex's. "Ok, I want you to know where each gear is. This is first," she instructed as she moved the stick into first gear. "Second," their two hands slowly guided the stick into second. Carol guided Alex's hand into each gear. "Third... and reverse."

Oh, ok."

"Now this is neutral," Carol explained as she moved the shifter between gears.

"Ok?"

"Now just go through all the gears until you get used to the feel."

Alex struggled to put the stick back in to first, this time without Carol's hand. After a few minutes of fighting, Alex finally put it back into first gear. "Ok, first." She pushed the shifter down. "Second." She followed the pattern Carol had just shown her and spoke as she hit each gear, "third... reverse."

"Good! Now, put it into neutral."

Alex was unable to put the car back into neutral, so Carol pushed it in for her. "Feel how loose that is? Feel the difference between how neutral feels versus being in gear."

Alex fiddled with the shift. "Oh yeah. I can feel that." Slowly, she got used to it. Repeatedly, Alex went through all the gears and was soon able to put the car in neutral and then back again into gear. After a while, it was obvious that Alex was beginning to feel comfortable, and even familiar, with the stick. A large smile blossomed on Alex's face as her confidence grew.

"Great, honey. Now, we're gonna turn the car on and actually get you driving it."

The large smile quickly disappeared from Alex's face, and the expression of fear from earlier replaced it. "Oh dear God!" Alex muttered in fear.

"It'll be fine. I'm gonna teach you the way my dad taught me."

"Ok?"

"Alright, so first push in the clutch and turn the car over. If you don't, we won't get anywhere."

Hesitantly, Alex did as she was told.

"Ok, good. See, that part was easy."

"Yeah."

"Now, just let up on the clutch ."

"Huh?"

"Don't do anything, but take your foot off the clutch really fast."

"Uh, ok." Nervous and confused, Alexandria again followed Carol's orders. The car slightly jerked and then stalled. "Oh my God!" Alex screamed.

Carol laughed. "You're fine. That's what's supposed to happen. Now you know the worst that could happen. It's not so bad, is it? Anyway, now put the clutch back in and start the car again."

This time with a bit less apprehension, Alex started the car.

"Great! Now, shift into reverse."

Alex anxiously looked at Carol and then went through the gears. "One... two... three... reverse. Ok, I'm in reverse. Now what?"

"Go backwards."

"What?"

"Go backwards."

"You have got to be kidding!"

"No, seriously. Slowly let up on the clutch as you begin to accelerate."

Concentrating on every tiny movement her feet made, Alex tried. She started off alright, but then the car stalled again. Alex cursed under her breath.

"It's ok," Carol reassured her. "Try again."

Frustrated, Alex tried again. Focusing even harder, she was able to get the car moving in reverse this time. "Hey, I did it!"

"I knew you could. Now, slow back down to a stop and do it again."

Alex repeated the pattern. Again the car moved backwards, somewhat smoothly. Nervously, she followed Carol's every direction. Carol had her repeat the pattern countless times. With each attempt, Alex's comfort and confidence increased. The more Alex drove, the smoother the ride became. It didn't take long for her to drive in reverse perfectly.

Carol had Alexandria repeat the same movements to go forward. Again, Alex struggled with coordination at first. After repeatedly moving the car forward, Alex was doing better.

The last part of the lesson was shifting from gear to gear. Alex had a little difficulty going from first to second to third, then back down to first again.

Late morning turned into early afternoon, then mid afternoon. Except for a few stalls, Alex quickly grasped the concept and the coordination of driving the GTO.

Just when Alex's confidence peaked, Carol's pager beeped loudly.

Carol looked down to see who was paging her. "Oh, I think that's Will. I completely forgot it's my first weekend on call." Carol paused a moment to think. "You know what? This is actually perfect timing. You can drive me home and then I can go on the call."

"What?"

"You'll be fine. Home is what? Maybe two miles from here? Just think it through like you've been doing here and you'll be fine."

"Oh no. No, no, no. I can't do this."

"Oh stop, Alex. You'll do great, I know you will. Now, let's get a move on so I don't leave Will waiting."

Alex shot Carol a dirty look. Then very slowly, and cautiously, an extremely nervous Alex drove them home.

Once they returned home, Carol called Will. "Hi Will."

"Hi'ya Carol. I got a call. It should be an easy one, but I'd really like to have you come and get some field experience with me."

"Ok, sounds good. You want me to meet you at the office, and then we'll head out together?"

"Sure, sounds great. See you in a few."

"Honey," Carol called out to Alexandria. Alex was sitting on the couch drinking a large glass of iced tea trying to calm her nerves from the drive home. "I have to go. Will said it should be a simple call, so I'll be back soon, ok?"

"Ok," Alex called back.

"I love you."

"Love you too."

Alex then heard the roar of the GTO's engine again. As she heard Carol drive away, Alex was impressed by Carol's mastery of such a beast. The GTO was a car that Alex now both feared and respected.

The following weekend was sunny, hot, and humid. Saturday was the perfect day for an long drive in the country. Carol and Alex decided to go out of St. Louis and drive around aimlessly on the Missouri country roads. The sun beat down on the couple in the car. The windows were rolled down and thick, sweltering, summer air blew all around them.

Once they found a quiet, secluded road, Carol had Alex take over driving to help her feel more comfortable. The lesson from last week stayed with Alex and she was driving the GTO well.

Trying to get Alex to feel even more at ease, Carol turned on the radio. She had it set to the classic rock station. Her timing was perfect, just as she turned on the radio, Pink Floyd's Another Brick in the Wall started. The two women looked at each other with huge smiles.

"Turn it up." Alex prompted. She loved classic rock music. Her mind was focused on the music and she was driving the muscle car well. Alex wasn't even paying attention to the car: it had quickly become second nature. She was having too much fun singing with Carol. With the radio blasting, the two sang along, "We don't need no education! We don't need no thought control!"The pair sang their hearts out to the .

Carol and Alex laughed enthusiastically. They didn't have a care in the world. The bright sun, the warm summer air and the music brought them endless joy. Their fun and joyous moment was multtiplied when All Along the Watchtower began to play.

"I Hendrix!" The women shrieked at each other in sync.

"There must be some kind of way out of here said the joker to the thief. There's too much confusion, I can't get no relief."

As the song played, the women sang louder and louder, enjoying every moment, every note.

The pair couldn't stop laughing and smiling as Alex drove them with no particular destination in mind. Their faces were as bright as the summer sun that was watching over them. This was the perfect afternoon. They had been dancing and singing in the car endlessly, when the familiar guitar intro to Stairway to Heaven began to play. This was the perfect ending the perfect day.

The two young women were nearly screaming the entire epic song at the top of their lungs.

Finally the last verse came and they sang with all their might. "And if you listen very hard the tune will come to you at last. When all are one and one is all to be a rock and not to roll. And she's buying a stairway to heaven."

They looked at each other in surprise and excitement. They each adored the classic, but neither of them expected that the other knew the lyrics to the landmark marathon song.

Their entire afternoon had been electrifying. Their day had been full of fun and laughter. The young couple had just created phenomenal memories. Their bond deepened and strengthened as they were driving and singing on an endless summer afternoon. Best of all, Alex had truly mastered the GTO's stick shift.

As Carol was getting ready for work the following Monday, Alexandria called out to her.

"Yeah, babe?" She called back as she walked out of the bedroom, trying to place an earring.

"Did you ever do anything with that check from the Bakers?"

"Oh shit! No, I completely forgot."

"You really need to do something with it, and fast."

"Yeah, I know. You know what? I'm going out on a field service call today, so I'll find a bank on the way back and just start a new account using the check."

"That sounds good," Alex replied.

With check in hand, Carol left for the day.

Thankfully the apartment wasn't far from the office. Carol arrived on time.

"Carol," Greg called out just as she walked through the door.

"Good morning, Greg. What's up?"

"How come you didn't go to Bosworth's over the weekend?"

"Bosworth's? There was a call? When?"

"Yes. Saturday," he said sternly. "And you know you're supposed to be going out to assist on all the field service calls."

"Yeah, I know. I never got a page though, Greg."

"You didn't?"

"No, sir. I would have gone. Paul was the tech on call, right?"

"Yeah."

"Maybe something happened, I never got a page from him. I'd say go check with him, see what happened."

Carol followed Greg as they went to find Paul. He was working on a server at the main work station when the two approached.

"Paul?"

"Yes, Greg?"

"Paul, did you get the call for Bosworth's?"

"On Saturday? Yeah, why?"

"Did you go?"

"Of course. Why? What's going on?" Paul looked confused.

"Did you page Carol?" Greg's demanded.

"No."

"No? Why the hell not? You know she's supposed to be assisting on all field service calls." Greg was irritated with Paul.

"Well, I just didn't think it was worth it. I mean come on, I'd have to page her and then wait for her to show up. And to top it off, I'd have to wait for her to work on a job I could have done in thirty minutes. It just seemed like unnecessary."

"Paul, you know how things work around here. You have to have Carol join you on all your field service calls. I'd really like to get her out there on her own, but not until she's been out a few times with you and Will. Don't you ever pull a stunt like this again. Do you understand?"

Paul approached his boss and turned him so their backs were towards Carol.

"Greg, look. She's young and a girl. It's well-known that girls are not as good as male technicians."

"Paul, that's bullshit. This girl's GPA alone could kick your ass. Now cut the shit and be a damn professional."

"Fine," Paul answered. He turned to Carol. "I'm sorry Carol." His apology was insincere. "I'll have you come out with me next time."

"Thanks, Paul." Carol extended her hand to shake his to show that she harbored no resentment towards his sexist attitude. Paul did not reach out or shake her hand. Instead, he walked away.

"Carol, I'm so sorry." Greg apologized for real.

"Greg, it's not your fault. No worries."

Greg sighed a sigh of relief and smiled at Carol.

Knowing that time was limited, Carol quickly changed the subject back to the work at hand. "Am I still doing that full set up with Will today?"

"Yeah. Go catch up with him and have a good day, kid." Greg patted Carol on the shoulder.

"Thanks, Greg." Carol smiled back and walked off to find Will.

Greg saw much more than a talented IT tech in Carol. He saw a wonderful person and he was thrilled to have her on his team.

Carol and Will drove back to the office after their field service call. Carol's hand was in her pocket and she touched the check she had shoved in there earlier that morning.

"Hey, Will?"

"Yeah?"

"Do you mind if we stop at a bank? Is there one on the way back to the office?"

Will paused to think of the route as he drove them back. "Oh yeah. There's a Missouri State Bank. Is that ok?"

"Yeah, that's fine. I'm sorry to bother you. I just need to open an account. I have a check that I have to deposit."

"Sure, no problem. You want me to grab some food while you're doing that?"

Carol hadn't even thought about eating. It was 2:30 in the afternoon., this would probably be the only break they got for the day. "Sure," she agreed.

Just a few minutes later, Will parked. Carol walked into the bank, check in hand. She was about to open her first bank account.

Will ran to the sandwich shop next store to grab them their belated lunch.

They met back at Will's car and ate their lunch on the remainder of their drive home.

Chapter Seven

It was a cold, rainy, grey winter day. The summer had come and gone in the blink of an eye and Thanksgiving was now here. The naked trees loomed ominously over everything. Crunchy, dead brown leaves covered the ground. There was frost on top of the leaves and light rain trickled down from the sky. The thick, round clouds rolled around the sky. It was a bleak and uninviting day. Carol wasn't concerned with the weather nor the Thanksgiving holiday though. Today she would meet Byron and Candace, Alex's family, for the first time. Making a good impression was first and foremost in her mind.

Carol stood in front of the mirror adjusting her burgundy sweater and black pants. She knew she looked beautiful, yet she still fidgeted. No matter what she did, she just didn't feel as if it was enough.

"Honey, what are you doing?" Alex asked as she re-entered the bedroom.

"I want to look good for your family."

"You'll be fine. Byron and Candace will love you. Just relax."

Carol sighed. They would be her family now; she feared the same rejection from this family that she had received from her own mother. Wanting to change the subject and ease her mind a bit, Carol turned to Alex. "We should take the GTO, babe."

"Huh? Why? It's not great weather, Carol. I don't trust that thing on the slick roads."

"I know it's not the best for bad weather. But since Byron bought the car for me, I think he deserves the right to see what he purchased."

"You want to?"

"It would mean a lot to me and I think he'd appreciate the gesture as well."

"Ok, we'll take the GTO. But you're driving. I'm not trying to drive that thing in this weather."

Carol laughed. "That's fine, sweetie. Are you ready to go?"

"Yeah. Are you?"

Carol huffed. "I guess so."

They went out into the dismal November weather. It was a bit of a drive over to Byron's house. Carol carefully and expertly handled the three-hundred-plus horsepower. Not once did the car slip or slide on the cold, wet roads.

Arriving at Byron's house, Carol's heart began to pound. She prayed that this Thanksgiving was the first of many that they would all spend as a family.

At the front door, Carol's heart jumped when Alex rang the doorbell. Carol's nerves were completely inflamed.

Suddenly, a large man opened the door. Byron was as big as he was tall. His size reminded Carol of William "The Fridge" Perry. His skin was dark and his hair was thick, but his eyes were gentle and warm.

"Hey B!" Alex exclaimed as she gave her twin brother a hug. "Byron, this is Carol. Carol, this is my brother, Byron."

"Hi," Carol said timidly.

"Nice to meet you." Byron's voice was smooth, deep and velvety. "Come on in," he let them come in from the ugly weather. "Hey A, Candace is in the living room. Why don't you go visit with her. I want to talk to Carol for a minute."

"Ok." Alex said and she disappeared.

"Carol," Byron started. "It's nice to finally meet you."

"It's nice to meet you too, Byron."

"I have to be honest; I wasn't expecting a white girl."

"Oh," Carol said shocked. "I'm sorry," she said automatically.

"I'll admit I'm not thrilled that my sister is dating a white girl. But, I'm also not thrilled that she's gay."

Carol stood looking back at the large man, unsure of how to respond.

"Look, I can't change the color of your skin. I can't change your sexuality or hers. But I will tell you this, if any one ever hurts my sister, they will have to answer to me."

"Byron, I can understand your concern for your sister. It's bad enough to deal with racism, but to also battle prejudice against gays – I get it. I know you only want the best for her and being gay in today's day and age isn't the safest thing especially here in the Midwest. It's not as if we're in New York or Los Angeles where people are more open-minded. People tend to be traditional around here. I understand completely, Byron. I live it every day, too.

"I promise you though, I will never hurt Alex. I love her; I adore her. She means everything to me. I would never – could never do anything to hurt your sister. I just want to protect her and give her the best life possible too."

"Thank you, I appreciate that."

"And I need to thank you for my father's GTO. Let me know how much it cost. I'll gladly pay you back."

"No, no. It's a gift. I don't want you to pay for it. I know it means a lot to you. Alexandria explained it all. You're more than welcome."

"I drove it here. I thought you might want to see it," said Carol.

"You know what? I would really like that," Byron answered with a smile. He grabbed an umbrella and Carol led him out to see her most prized possession.

They walked around the red car. They didn't take much time admiring the muscle car though, it was too cold and dreary.

"That's a beautiful car," Byron said as they re-entered the warm house. "Your father kept it in immaculate condition. It looks great, Carol."

"Thanks," Carol paused. "Thank you so much for getting it for me, Byron."

With a gentle nod, Byron said, "you're welcome." Byron took Carol's jacket and hung it up. "Now, let's go inside. You can meet our little sister, Candace."

"That would be great!"

Imperfect

They walked inside the cozy, inviting house and found Candace and Alexandria talking and laughing. As Carol and Byron entered the room, both Alex and Candace turned towards them. Candace's face dropped dramatically.

"Hi," Carol said weakly as she approached the young girl. "I'm Carol. You must be Candace. It's nice to meet you." Carol stopped in front of Candace and shook her hand. Candace's handshake was weak and limp.

"Hi," Candace said coldly. Carol walked over and sat next to Alex.

"Does anyone want anything to drink?" Byron offered.

No, thank you. The girls said in unison.

"Dinner will be in about thirty minutes."

Byron sat down along with his sisters and Carol. They all stared at each other in awkward silence.

In a desperate attempt to break the tension, Carol spoke. "So, I have to ask, who came first? Alex or Byron?"

As if the setting hadn't been awkward enough, everyone stared at Carol after her question. Several more moments of stares and silence passed.

"You're kidding, right hon?" Alex asked.

"Uhhh... no, I'm not. Why? Am I missing something obvious? What am I not getting?"

Alex turned to Byron. "B, I swear, she's actually very intelligent."

Byron merely laughed.

"What?" Carol said as she laughed.

"Sweetheart, think about it. Alexandria, Byron, Candace. A – B – C. We were named in order. When Mom found out that she was having twins, she called us Baby A and Baby B. It was easy for her. Even though we're fraternal twins, she decided to keep it that way and I was named Alexandria and Byron was named Byron. When Candace came along, it just seemed suiting she had a c name."

Carol watched as all three siblings all laughed. "No way," she exclaimed.

"Yes," Alex said between laughs. "It's true, honey."

"Wow. I'm sorry," Carol tripped over her words.

The group all smiled and laughed warmly, but then the unease set in again.

Feeling as a complete outsider, Carol once again tried to start up conversation. "So, tell me more about yourself, Candace."

"I'm fourteen. What do you want to know?"

"Well... what's your favorite subject in school?"

"English."

"English? Really. That's interesting. Why do you like English the best?"

"It's easy," Candace snapped back.

"Oh, I see." Carol was once again defeated in her attempts to get to know this family. "What do you want to do? Do you want to be a writer or something?"

"I don't know." Candace's answers were short and rude.

Watching Carol flounder like a fish out of water, Byron stood up. "Hey, Carol, could you help me with dinner?" He asked.

"Sure," Carol said. The two went into the kitchen.

"I'm sorry," Byron whispered. "Candace is struggling with the fact that her older sister is a lesbian. With all the crap that happened with Alex when Candace was young, they never really had a typical sister-type relationship. Since Alex's sobriety they've begun to build a relationship, but this still hurts Candace." Byron pulled a large turkey out from the oven.

"I can understand that. Alex told me about all that. I know it was bad. I'm sorry if I'm making things worse."

"It's not you, Carol. You're not making things worse, I assure you. If it wasn't you, it would be whoever that girl would be. That's just the way it is. She just has a lot of adjusting to do. It's a lot for a kid to take in."

Byron was being very kind and accommodating to Carol despite his initial reservations. Carol appreciated his gentleness.

"I can imagine. It sounds like she had a lot to deal with in her young life." Carol replied.

"You just have to imagine how much Candace has seen in her fourteen years. And now she sees her sister with a girl - a white girl, nonetheless. Candace hasn't had an easy ride."

"I know. I'd really like to get to know her and help build more of a feeling of family."

"You will. It's just going to take some time." Byron's voice was gentle. Carol looked up at him and smiled warmly.

"Could you take this out to the dining room?" Byron handed Carol a platter of steamed vegetables.

"Sure."

Carol brought out the vegetables. She helped Byron set the rest of the table as well. Within a short while, the foursome were gathered around a dinner table that overflowed with food.

"Carol, in our family we all say grace stating what we're thankful for." Byron explained. "I'll start.

"Dear Lord, thank you for allowing us to come together as a family yet again. Thank you for providing us with such a wonderful dinner. Thank you for bringing Carol here. May this be our first of many Thanksgivings together as a new family."

"God," Candace spoke next. "Thank you for all the wonderful food. Thank you for my wonderful brother and sister. And... uhhh... thank you for Carol, too."

"Lord, I want to thank you for my amazing family," Alexandria was third. "Thank you for all the love and support they have given me over the years. Thank you for allowing us to all come together today. Thank you for my wonderful Carol and for allowing us the opportunity to welcome her into our family today."

Carol wanted to say an eloquent prayer, but she was nervous now that it was her turn. Prayers – anything relating to God or religion – were not a regular part of Carol's life. "Ummmm... God, thank you so very much for everyone who is here today. Thank you for Byron's hospitality and selflessness. Thank you for Candace's youth and intelligence. Thank you for Alex who is the light of my life. Thank you for giving me the opportunity to be a part of a family again. Thank you for my father's car and for these wonderful people who made it happen. Thank you for my new family."

Then all four said, "Amen."

After an amazingly succulent dinner, Carol stood to clear the dishes.

"Hang on Carol," Byron said. "We save whatever we can and bring it to our mom in the nursing facility."

"Oh, I am so sorry."

"That's fine, honey, you didn't know," Alex said standing up. "B, you got the big foil trays?"

"Yep. In the kitchen, usual spot."

Alex went into the kitchen and quickly returned with several large foil trays for food. Quickly, the group of four began dishing out the remaining turkey, stuffing, vegetables, fruits, and pies into the large trays. When the trays were full, Alex and Candace covered all the trays.

"Hey, Carol," Byron called from the front door. "You're blocking me. Can you move the car?"

"Do you want to just take the GTO? There's plenty of room."

"You sure?"

"Yeah, why not?" Carol smiled at the thought of driving her new family in her car.

"Ok, that sounds good to me."

The group loaded up Carol's muscle car with food in the trunk and then they all piled in. With Byron's directions, Carol drove them all to the facility.

Everyone's hands were full with the trays as they walked into the nursing facility.

"Oh hi Byron, Candace and Alex." A nurse greeted the group. "Happy Thanksgiving!"

"Happy Thanksgiving, Erin," Byron smiled back.

The four went up the elevator to their mom's room on the fourth floor.

Alexandria gently knocked on the door. "Hey Mom," she said quietly. The four entered the room. Mary, Alex's mother, was in a hospital bed and another nurse was sitting with her. They looked up to see four bright faces smiling at them.

"Hi, kids." Alex's mother's speech was slurred, but her excitement and happiness was undeniable. The kids placed the trays on a bench seat in the window of the room and all sat around their mother.

"Mom, this is my girlfriend, Carol." Alex introduced.

"Hi," Carol said kindly as she gently held the elderly woman's hands.

"Hi. Nice to meet you." Her face was horrifically disfigured, yet the beauty that was once there was still obvious. Her eyes were bright and warm. The resemblance she shared with her three beautiful children was visible.

"Here's Thanksgiving dinner, Ma." Byron said.

"I'm sure she'll love it. She just took her medications. She's been waiting for you," the nurse said. "I'll go grab some dishes."

"Get a bunch so we can share it with as many patients as possible - ya know, the usual routine." Byron offered as the nurse stood up.

"Thanks," the nurse said. She left, and returned in a few minutes with several plates.

"What would you like, Mom?" Alex asked her mother.

"Everything." A little drip of drool came cascading out of her mouth. Alex quickly and quietly dabbed her mother's face.

Byron dished out fruits, vegetables, turkey and stuffing for Mary. Candace made plates for the other patients. Once all the food was gone, Candace began distributing the extra plates to patients on the floor.

"I'm so happy to see you," the matriarch said to Alex as the nurse fed her.

"I'm happy to see you too, Mom. I love you so much."

"I love you too," her mother's reply was garbled as she spoke with a mouth full of stuffing.

After handing out the extra dinners, Candace returned and the family spent some wonderful, sentimental moments together.

Carol enjoyed watching the family members interact with each other. Despite the pain of the past, they all loved each other. These moments were endearing to Carol.

It didn't seem to take long for the day to slip away. When it came time for her kids to leave, they each gave Mary a tremendous hug.

"Bye Mom. I love you."

"I love you too, Candy."

"Bye, Ma. I love you. I'll see you next week, ok?"

"Ok, Byron. I love you."

"Bye, Mommy. I love you."

"I love you, Alexandria."

Carol bent down to hug Alex's mom as well. "Bye, Mrs. Whetherby. It was so nice to meet you."

"It was nice to meet you too. You be a good friend to my Alexandria, ok?"

"I sure will."

Smiling with teary eyes, each person said, 'I love you' as they left Mary's room.

As they left the facility, Carol felt the love. Holidays had never held such emotion to her. The love and closeness in the Whetherby family was astounding. Carol cherished the memories they created today. This was the most special, most wonderful Thanksgiving Carol ever had.

Chapter Eight

The holiday season was in full swing. Carol was amazed at how quickly this year had flown by. Both Carol and Alex fought for the bathroom mirror as they put their make-up on.

"Your first company Christmas party!" Alex beamed.

"Yes, dear," Carol retorted sarcastically.

"Oh come on, it's fun. I'm excited for you."

"I'm sure it'll be nice, but it's not like it's a milestone in my life or anything." Carol nudged Alex with her elbow and they both laughed.

"Well fine, little miss bah humbug!" Alex said, nudging Carol back. They continued to laugh and tease each other as they finished polishing their looks.

They grabbed their coats, got into the Camry and left.

When they arrived at the restaurant, Greg saw Carol and waved her over. As the two women walked over to the table, and Alex was visible to Carol's co-workers, everyone's surprise was obvious.

"Did you tell them about me?" Alex whispered in Carol's ear.

Carol turned around and whispered back to her. "They know I have a significant other named Alex, but I'm wondering if they just assumed I was talking about a guy named Alex. Oh well. That'll teach them to assume!" The two women laughed with each other as they approached the table.

"Hi everyone," Carol said. "This is my girlfriend, Alex. Alex, this is my boss Greg. Over there is Paul, and this is Will."

"Hi." Alexandria said nervously.

"Hi there!" Greg said. "This is my wife, Susan." Susan was a slender, regal-looking woman. She had warm, bright, beautiful light blue eyes that sparkled from the lights. She matched Greg well. She had grey in her hair and she wore it with great dignity and elegance.

"This is my wife, Robyn," Will said. Robyn was a stunning dark beauty. She had flawless skin, deep, dark eyes, and an incredibly curvaceous body. Carol and Alex sat next to Will and Robyn.

Everyone shook hands. The girls sat down.

Paul seemed removed from the group and lacked a dinner companion. After Alex and Carol were seated, he seemed to pull away even more.

Greg, Susan, Will and Robyn were more than gracious. The three couples all talked and laughed, and seemed to get along well.

Will and Carol talked non-stop. They hit it off since Carol's first day. They were more than just co-workers, they were friends.

"Computer technicians," Robyn said to Alex.

"I know. They're a crazy bunch," Alex joked.

Robyn smiled brightly at Alex. The two African-American women had a quiet understanding and respect for each other.

Robyn continued speaking with Alex, "What do you do, Alex?"

"I'm a paralegal."

"Oh, what an interesting job! I bet you get to experience some amazing court room dramas."

Alex laughed lightly. "Yeah, we do on occasion."

"What about you? What do you do, Robyn?"

"I'm a second grade teacher."

Alex's eyes lit up. "That must be so much fun."

"Yeah, it is. I'm lucky this year. The kids are good. It can be exhausting at times, but it's not terrible.

"I work with kids all day. At the end of my day, I want a normal, adult conversation. But instead, I come home to another kid: Will."

The two women laughed.

"I'm so sorry," Alex responded. "That's why I have her," she said facetiously.

Robyn laughed. "But is she all computers all the time?"

"To some extent she is. She does love all that electronic crap."

"We should start a support group for each other, wives of computer technicians!"

Alex let out a loud laugh. Robyn was fun and cordial. She absolutely adored the fact that she considered Alex to be a fellow computer tech's wife. The inclusion really touched Alex. She reached into her purse and grabbed a business card. "Here," she said handing the card to Robyn. "Let me know when the sessions start." The two started laughing again.

The holiday party dinner went late, both Carol and Alex had a wonderful time despite their tiredness.

Carol felt like she bonded with Greg, Susan, Robyn, and of course, Will. Carol was starting to see that they weren't just co-workers. They were an extended family.

The following night was Alexandria's company's holiday party. Ironically, Alex's law firm was holding their party at the same restaurant Carol and Alex had been at the night before with Dawson's Christmas party.

As they started walking out the door, Carol and Alex looked at each other. It was another late night.

As they entered the restaurant again, Alex found her co-workers sitting at a table on the opposite side of the building.

"Well, at least there's some variety," Alex said in jest as they approached this table. "Hi, everyone, this is my partner, Carol."

"Hi," everyone at the table greeted Carol.

"Hi," she replied.

"Honey, this is one of my bosses, attorney Lisa Ludlow. Over there is my other boss, Frederick Kepwick. This is Dave, the other paralegal, and his partner, John. Nancy, our receptionist, couldn't make it."

"Hi," Carol said to each of them as she shook their various hands.

Carol and Alex split up and each sat on either side of Dave and John. Dave was a cute, waif of a boy. He didn't look to be much older than Carol. He had wispy, blonde hair and bright blue eyes. His boyfriend John was tall, lean and very handsome. He had jet black hair, and stunning olive skin. He, too, looked young. He looked like he might have been of Hispanic or Italian descent.

"Well, she's a cutie!" Dave said to Alex in a high-pitched voice, slapping her wrist. He was a rather stereotypical flamboyant young gay man.

Alex laughed and blushed. "Yeah, she is. That's why I keep her around!"

Carol laughed, knowing Alex's sense of humor well. Jokingly, she replied, "Gee, thanks honey! I'm so glad it's only superficial and not anything like we actually love each other."

The two couples all laughed heartily.

Carol and Alex both felt that it was nice speaking to a gay couple for a change. They felt much more at ease. There was an acceptance and understanding with Dave and John that Carol and Alex had not had with other couples like Will and Robyn. There was neither prejudice nor any awkward moments. It was pleasant to converse with a couple who understood the trials and tribulations Alex and Carol faced daily. Although the conversation was light, there was a silent understanding between the four. These were people that Carol and Alex both wanted to surround themselves with more often.

"So, how long have you two been together?" John asked as he turned to Carol.

"Just under a year," Carol answered quietly.

"Awe, young love!" Dave exclaimed.

"Oh stop, Dave! I remember when you and John first got together. You got to start somewhere." Alex countered. It was clear that they had fun joking around in and outside of work.

"How long have you two been together?" Carol inquired.

"Two years," John replied.

"Two years and four months," Dave corrected his beau.

"Careful, Alexandria. I can see it now. That's going to be you soon," John teased.

The two women laughed.

"Two years and four months seems so far away, and yet I can't wait to spend every moment possible with her!" Carol said, her youth and optimism at their highest.

"Oh, you are simply adorable!" Dave proclaimed.

"Thanks," Carol blushed.

The two couples continued to laugh and talk the evening away. It was another long night, but the company was wonderful and fun.

Carol and Alex thoroughly enjoyed the two holiday parties and looked forward to seeing more of their new friends.

Christmas day finally arrived. Carol and Alex were excited while they waited for Byron and Candace to come over. This would be their second time together as a family. Carol was thrilled at the idea of opening her home to her new family.

"Do you want to do our gifts now, or later?" Alex asked.

"I figured we'd wait till they get here," Carol answered. "Unless you got me like lingerie or something!" The two laughed.

"No, I was just curious. We can wait. I'm just so excited. It's our first Christmas together!"

Carol smiled brightly as she looked at Alex. "The first of many, baby." She said gently. "I love you."

"I love you too."

The couple embraced tightly and then shared an extraordinary, loving kiss.

After several tender and sweet moments, they began to get the house decorated and ready for Alex's family.

Later that afternoon, around three o'clock, Candace and Byron finally came over.

"Merry Christmas!" Byron tried to imitate the stereotypical Santa voice as he entered the girls' apartment.

"Merry Christmas, B." Alex said, hugging her brother tightly.

Carol was next to hug Byron. "Merry Christmas."

Candace came in carrying two bags. "Thanks for the help, bro." She snickered. "Merry Christmas, Alexandria." Candace paused for a moment. "And you too, Carol."

Carol hugged the young girl. "Merry Christmas, sweetie."

Candace looked up at Carol with a puzzled look.

Alex then led Byron and Candace and they all sat in the living room.

"Does anyone want any snacks or anything to drink? We have warm apple cider, non-alcoholic eggnog, milk, and soda."

"No thank you, Carol," Byron said.

"I'll have some eggnog," Candace said.

"You got it." Carol replied warmly.

Carol came out with a big glass of the thick, creamy drink for Candace. "Here you go."

Candace glanced up at Carol. "Thanks," she mumbled.

"Ok, present time." Alex could not contain herself any longer.

"Sis, no matter how old we get, you're still like a little kid when it comes to Christmas." Byron laughed. Byron reached into the bags Candace had brought in and began distributing presents.

Carol handed him a large box in return. "Everyone have something?"

The girls all answered, "Yes!"

"Ok, then. Let the paper fly."

The family tore into their neatly wrapped presents.

Alex held up a beautiful bright blue sweater. "Thanks, Byron. I love it."

Carol got a gift card to a book store. "Oh, this is great. Thanks."

"They specialize in historical books, Carol. Alex told me you'd like that."

"I love it. Thank you, Byron."

Candace held open a box with a fountain pen. "Thank you so much, B. This rocks."

Byron opened his present last. It was an espresso maker. "Wow, this is really nice. Thanks, A; thanks, Carol."

"You're more than welcome, Byron. Alex told me how much you love coffee." Carol said as she smiled.

Carol stood up and passed out more gifts. She gave one to Candace and one to Alex.

Candace opened her present first. There were two leather bound journals and a gift card to a book store. "Wow, these are really nice." Candace paused for a moment. "Thanks, Carol," she said quietly but sincerely. Candace got up, walked over and hugged Carol.

"You're very welcome, sweetheart." Carol answered softly during their embrace. She felt that the barrier that had once separated them had finally been broken down.

Alex opened her box tentatively. She found a delicate Christmas ornament that read, "Our First Christmas." It had Alexandria's and Carol's names on it. Alex's eyes began to well up with tears. "It's beautiful. Thank you baby."

"You're welcome, sweetheart. There's more. Keep looking."

Alex dug through the tissue paper. Inside was a beautiful, clear heart-shaped paperweight that said, "Alexandria and Carol – Always and forever - 2/7/97." Alex couldn't fight back the tears.

Carol walked over to her and held her. "I love you," she whispered.

"I love you too." Alex replied tearfully. The two smiled at each other.

Still crying, Alex got up and grabbed even more presents. She handed one to Candace and one to Carol. "I'm sorry, B." She sniffed back the tears. "That espresso maker was a bit more expensive than we originally planned."

"Alex, it's totally cool. I'm just glad that we have you for another Christmas."

Candace opened her present first. She screamed with delight. It was a book by her favorite author. Then, she pulled it out of the box to find another book by the same author. "Oh, Alexandria, thank you so much!"

"You're welcome."

Carol opened her present. She went through the box. She gasped when she saw a stunning gold necklace with a heart pendant covered in diamond chips. Carol's jaw dropped and her eyes began welling up with tears. She was now the one crying. "It's unbelievable! I love it. Thank you so much, honey." Alex leaned over to Carol and they tenderly kissed. It was a sweet, soft, wonderful kiss. The love they shared was undeniable at that moment.

Carol put the necklace on right away. It glistened against her fair skin.

"My turn!" Candace shouted, ending the tender and loving moment between Alex and Carol. Candace got up and rummaged through the bags she carried in. She handed a card to each person. They each thanked Candace as they received their card.

"Carol, we have a tradition in the family," Byron stated. "We each read our cards from Candace out loud. I'll start.

"Dear Byron, thank you for being the best big brother ever. I don't know what I'd do without you. You are the rock of our family and I love you very much. Merry Christmas. Love, Candace." Byron paused while he turned to Candace. "Thanks, Sis." Byron squeezed his little sister.

"Dear Alexandria, it's great spending another Christmas with you. I'm glad you're my big sister. You never stop inspiring me to keep going. I love you. Merry Christmas. Love, Candace."

Alex got up and hugged her sister. "Thank you, C. I love you so much, little sis."

Nervously, Carol opened her envelope and began to read the card. "Dear Carol, Merry Christmas. I'm not sure what to write, but I hope this is your first of many Christmases with my family. You seem like a great person and I hope that I can spend some time with you as my new sister-in-law. Welcome to the Whetherby family. Love, Candace."

The tears that had only just stopped moments earlier, started up again. "Thank you so much, Candace." Carol got up and hugged the young girl tight. "I'm honored to be your new sister-in-law."

Alex and Byron both beamed as they watched Candace and Carol.

After a few quiet moments, Alex stood up. "Well, let's eat. Carol helped me make a ham and we have all kinds of veggies and goodies," she said enthusiastically.

The family all got up and went to the dinner table. They enjoyed a delectable dinner. Carol and Alex had done well. The first Christmas as a family was going well. The conversation was light, happy and warm.

Carol felt as though she finally belonged and that this was indeed her family. It was precious and inviting. This was more than a Christmas dinner. In a way, this was a family reunion. It was a memory to be treasured by all.

Chapter Nine

Carol spent her entire ride home from work on her cell phone planning an anniversary surprise for Alex.

Somehow the past two years had flown by. It all happened so incredibly quickly.

Carol and Alex were still like young lovers. They were so happy together. They fit each other well and they had built a great life together.

When Carol walked into the apartment, she was more than surprised to see Alex sitting on the couch talking to a greyhound that stood in front of her looking as perplexed as a dog could look. Alexandria quickly looked up when she heard Carol enter.

"Surprise!"

Carol looked at Alex; then at the dog; back to Alex; back to the dog; and then at both together. She was stunned.

"Come on Sugar," Alex softly said as she led the dog to greet Carol. "Carol, this is Sugar."

"Uh...hi Sugar. Alex, what's going on?"

"Well, you've been talking about getting a dog for a while and we both wanted to rescue a dog if we got one. So, Sugar's your anniversary-slash-birthday present."

"Thanks." Carol said sincerly. She and Alex hugged each other tightly. To outsiders, it might have seemed a strange gift. To Carol and Alex, getting a dog together was a very precious moment.

Carol knelt down to meet the newest member of the family. Lightly, Carol ran her delicate hands over the dog's short but soft fur.

Sugar was a fawn colored greyhound, with a white chest. Carol paused as she pet the dog. Sugar was a unique name, though the dog looked more like brown sugar. "Sugar, huh? Where'd you come up with that?" Carol asked Alex.

"Sugar was her racing name, actually. The rescue group just kept it. She's only a year and half old. If you don't like it..."

"No, I do. I thought it was really cool, truthfully." Carol stood up and smiled at Alex.

"I'm glad you like it. And her," Alex said quietly.

"I love her name. I love her. And most of all, I love you." Carol's face was bright with joy.

On Valentine's Day, Carol treated Alex to a romantic anniversary. Balloons and a large, exotic arrangement of flowers in an exquisite crystal vase were delivered to the apartment. Alex felt so spoiled by Carol's gesture. It was amazing to be treated like a queen by her white beauty.

That evening, they shared a quiet, romantic dinner at a newly opened restaurant in town.

The dinner was elegant, and the couple stared into each other's eyes. Their love had not faded in the least over the past two years.

"This is magnificent. Thank you, sweetheart," Alexandria said to Carol.

"You are more than welcome, my love. These past two years have been amazing. You are the greatest thing that ever happened to me. I love you so much."

"I love you too."

The couple continued to indulge in the fabulous food, and left the restaurant holding hands like young lovers.

When the pair returned home, they found Sugar staring at the balloons and trying to play with them by pulling on the ribbons and bouncing the balloons on her nose. Carol and Alex laughed so hard, their eyes were tearing. Their family was unquestionably complete. It was a moment of pure joy. These were the moments they had only dreamed of when they first thought of getting a dog. They both felt as though their lives were complete.

Smiling at each other, they decided to leave the dog to her new balloon game for the evening, and walked into the bedroom.

Carol came up behind Alex as she was undressing, and began kissing her neck, and running her fingers through Alex's thick, black hair.

"Oooh, sweetie." Alexandria moaned. "That feels good."

"Good, that was the plan," Carol seductively replied. She continued to kiss and caress every soft inch of Alex.

Alex finally turned around to face her and the two then began kissing passionately. Their excitement was just as sweet and sensual as the first time they had made love.

They spent the night pleasing and loving each other until the wee hours of the morning.

February twenty fourth was one of the few fortunate days that Carol came home just a few minutes after Alexandria.

Carol was about to greet her partner when she heard the answering machine playing as she entered.

"Hi Carol, this is Sandra Baker, Ed Baker's mother. I know it's been a while since we've spoken, but..." The voice on the machine wavered. "Ed has away." They could hear her tears in her message. "I'm so sorry," Mrs. Baker sniffled into the phone. "The wake and funeral are this weekend. And I – we – would greatly appreciate it if you could... could be there, and maybe give an eulogy." The message continued on, but Carol was crying too much to actually hear it.

Alex turned, her face was drawn. She was speechless. She approached Carol and they hugged. As Carol held onto Alex, she began to cry even harder.

"This is Ed, your best friend from high school?" Alex whispered.

"Mmmm hmmm," Carol wept.

Alex silently stood holding her woman, part of her wanting to hold Carol endlessly, the other part wanting to get everything in order for Carol. "I'm so sorry, baby," she whispered.

Carol had finally cried herself to sleep. It was late, but Alex was going to make all the necessary calls for her. She didn't want Carol to feel burdened in addition to suffering such a significant loss.

"Hi, Will?"

"Yes?"

"It's Alex, Carol's partner."

75

"Oh hi, what's up? Is something wrong? You're calling pretty late."

"Will, Carol's best friend from high school just passed away unexpectedly. The funeral is this weekend. Would you and Robyn mind taking care of Sugar while we're gone?"

"Who?"

"Sugar: our new dog."

"Oh, that's right, I forgot. Carol told me you just got a dog. Yeah, sure, that won't be a problem."

"Thank you, Will. Thank you so much."

"No problem, Alex. Tell Carol she has my deepest sympathies."

"I will, thanks." She hung up.

On to the next call. It rang several times. No answer. Alex left a voice mail. "Hi, Greg, this is Alexandria, Carol's partner. A very close friend of Carol's passed away unexpectedly. The wake and funeral are this weekend. I'd like her to have some time off. If you don't mind, I think it's in her best interest if she's off work till Tuesday, or maybe even Wednesday. She's taking this really hard and she needs time to recover from all this. I know it's a lot, but it would hurt her more to keep working and she wouldn't be of any use to you. I think this time would really do her some good. If you have any questions or problems, please don't call her. She's so distraught. Just call me instead. Thank you."

Lastly, Alex had to make the most difficult call of the night. "Hello, Mrs. Baker?"

"Yes?" The voice on the other end was weak and shaky.

"My name is Alexandria Whetherby. I'm Carol Mather's... partner. We received your message and I am so deeply, deeply sorry."

Mrs. Baker was crying.

"I've made all the arrangements for Carol to be there this weekend. We haven't spoken about it, but I'm sure she'll do the eulogy as well. I just wanted you to know that she'll be there and to see if there is anything I can do to help."

It took a moment for Mrs. Baker to slow her sobs enough so that she could speak. "No, no. Thank you. And please feel free to come with her. If you're important to Carol, you're more than welcome to come as well."

"Thank you, Mrs. Baker. I look forward to meeting you. Carol has always spoken very highly of you and your family. Again, please accept my deepest sympathies. If you need anything at any time, don't hesitate to call me."

"Thank you." The sobs started up again, and then there was silence.

"Ed was vivacious," Carol started. She was not used to speaking in front of so many people, nor did she want to be speaking about this. "He was fun, he was lively. I don't remember Ed ever not laughing. He was so bright. He always made people smile.

"Ed was more than a friend to me. He was the brother I never had. He was my confidant. We were inseparable. Our friendship was so close and so deep. I trusted him with my life.

"Although we lost touch in college, he was always close in my heart. He brought so much joy in my life it would be impossible to not love him, even from a distance.

"We are all suffering a great loss." Carol's lips began trembling. "Ed was a great man. He is leaving a giant hole in all of our lives. It's not right – it's not fair that we've lost him at such a young age," Carol was crying and shaking by this point. "But, in actuality, even if he lived to one hundred twenty four, it still would not have been enough time."

"He gave us the gift of knowing him and loving him. It wasn't enough time, but at least we're lucky enough to have known him at all. Imagine how empty, how deprived of light and laughter our lives would have been had we never met Ed."

"Ed." Carol continued as the tears still raced down her face. "I love you. I'll never forget you."

After a few tearful moments of silence, Carol stepped down from the podium. As she did so, Mrs. Baker stood up and they fell into an embrace.

Imperfect

Alex, Carol, and the Bakers sat at the Baker's dinner table in silence. There was no food, no drink, no conversation... only sadness.

After an infinite silence, Carol finally spoke. "What happened? I don't remember Ed ever being sick."

Mr. Baker sat in silence as was typical for the extremely introverted man. The pain in his eyes, however, spoke loudly enough for him.

Mrs. Baker hesitated, but finally answered. "We're actually not sure. Ed just said that he was very sick. He wouldn't tell us what was wrong."

"So, he just got sick and...?" Carol's voice became unsteady and trailed off.

"No," Mrs. Baker began to weep. "He didn't see any doctors; he didn't get any help. He – he chose not to fight whatever it was and he just gave up. He decided to end it."

Carol and Alex gasped at the same time. The words shocked Carol. She couldn't believe that her best friend would kill himself and not explain the reason to his parents. The thought of Ed committing suicide was extremely painful. Carol reached over, grabbed Mrs. Baker's hands, and they cried.

Carol and Alex drove home in pure silence. The weekend had been long, painful, and extremely emotional. Now, they were returning home and had to pretend that life was normal again.

Chapter Ten

"So, how are you holding up, Carol?" Will asked. A month had passed since Ed's death. Although Carol saw Will every day at work, she never spoke of her loss. This was the first time in a month that Carol felt up to hosting Will and Robyn again as they had previously done every Tuesday night.

"I don't know," Carol sighed. "It's very surreal. I just can't believe it – it still doesn't make any sense."

"I know this is hard. But sometimes life doesn't make any sense, sweetie." He replied.

"Thank you again for taking care of Sugar." Alex interjected, hoping it might temporarily alleviate her woman's pain.

"No problem." Robyn answered kindly. "She's such a great dog. We love her. We're always happy to help."

"Thanks," Carol mumbled. Although time had passed, she was clearly still very depressed.

Will also wanted to get Carol out of this rut. "Hey, Carol, didn't you say you had a question about that new Windows application?"

"Yeah," she muttered.

"Want to go look at it?"

"Sure." They left the dinner table and went into Carol's office to fiddle around with her computer.

"Boy, she's taking it hard," Robyn whispered to Alex.

"I know. Ed was her only real friend in high school and his family took her in after her father died. I think there was a stronger tie there than any of us could imagine. She's closer to them than she ever was with her own mother. It's just a lot for her to take in."

"Poor girl. She hasn't had an easy go of it."

"No, she hasn't. I wish there was something I could do to ease things for her."

"I know, Alex. It's never easy. Just know that both Will and I are always here if either of you ever need."

"Thanks, Robyn." The two women hugged. Their silence brought Alex some comfort. At least Alex knew she wasn't alone in her love and concern for Carol.

Dave, John, Alex and Carol slowly wandered through the aisles of a gay bookstore in town.

"See, isn't this place great?" Dave asked Carol.

"It is nice. I just hate the fact that we have to have separate bookstores. Know what I mean? It's as if we're hiding from the rest of society," she retorted.

"I don't disagree, but at least we're safe to be out in the open here. Besides the fact that some of the books in here are great works of literature."

"You mean books like, The Art of Cunnilingus?" Carol asked holding the book up for Dave to see.

John rounded the corner laughing. "Ssshhh. Not so loud. That is funny, honey. You have to admit she has a point."

"Well, that may be true, but there are some fine works of literature in here as well," Dave argued his point.

"I don't doubt it," Carol said. "I just wish we didn't have to be defined by our sexuality."

John placed a hand on Carol's shoulder. "I know, Carol. But let's at least enjoy what the gay community has to offer."

"Hey, you guys, do you want to grab some coffee? There's a great coffee shop right around the corner." Alex asked the group as she returned from one of the aisles.

"That sounds like a great idea, baby," Carol responded.

The four walked out into the spring air. Time was ticking away. Slowly, Carol was recovering from Ed's death. The flowers were in full bloom and the trees were filled out with lush green leaves. The signs of new life were easing the pain in Carol's heart.

They sat at a small table right in the window. A young woman came up to take their order.

"I'll have a Chai tea," Dave ordered.

"Decaf mocha cappuccino," John requested next.

"I'll have a regular mocha," Alex said.

"I'll just have regular house coffee, light and sweet, please," Carol ordered. "I feel so bland next to all of you," she said to the group.

"No worries. We love you 'bland,'" Dave joked.

"I've been coming to this place for years," Alexandria said. "All the coffees and teas are to die for. Even the bland ones, babe." She nudged Carol.

"Well, I would like to thank you guys for a nice day out." Carol said. "It's great to be with people who understand what it's like to be gay in Missouri. You guys are fun company and I really appreciate your understanding."

"We know. We appreciate yours as well. It's nice having you ladies around. You get it. That means a lot. And hey, if nothing else, it's just pleasant to get away from all the crap from work." John agreed.

Ironically, Carol's cell phone rang at that moment. She looked at it. It was a client. "Speaking of work," Carol said before she answered. "Hello?"

"Hi Carol. This is Patricia with Kent Manufacturing."

"Oh, hi Patricia."

"We need your help. Things here aren't good. One of the company's servers is fried and there was significant data saved on the server."

"Oh, you're right. That isn't good. Not good at all." Carol replied.

"Carol, would you be able to fix the problem and restore our data?" asked Patricia.

"I can fix it. "After I get you guys running again, I'll just check all your data back-ups and everything. I'll make sure that not only are you guys up and running again, but that you're fully Y2K ready as well. Let me just finish up here. I'll be out there in about thirty minutes, ok?"

"That's great. Thank you."

Carol hung up. The group had been watching Carol. They hated to see her lose her weekends to work.

"I'm sorry, guys. I'm going to need to go. I have to fix this company's system. They're messed up pretty badly."

"It's ok," John replied.

"I'm just sorry for you," Dave said.

Alex just sighed. She wasn't angry with Carol, but her disappointment at losing Carol during a fun day out was unmistakable.

"I'm sorry, baby." Carol said to Alex.

"I know, sweetheart. I know you'd like to have one weekend you're not rushing around. It's ok. I'll see you back at home."

The waitress returned with their beverages.

"Can I get mine to go? I'm sorry," said Carol.

"Sure, no problem." The young girl said and walked back to the counter.

Carol turned back to Alex. "Ok, sweetie. I love you."

"I love you too."

Carol ran to the counter, grabbed her coffee and went off to work.

Another summer had come and gone in an instant. It was already September.

The cooler weather had come to St. Louis. Leaves were changing into bright reds, oranges, and yellows. Alex's twenty seventh birthday was also approaching quickly.

Carol wracked her brain to figure out the best birthday present she could give to her lover. Alex's law firm was working on an extensive case, so it was a rare opportunity that Carol had to be home alone. She invited Will, Robyn, Dave, and John to the apartment to help get some ideas.

"What about something nice? Maybe something like a laptop?" Will suggested.

"I actually had that in mind. Especially with the case she's working on, a laptop would be great for her. But, I want to do something more."

"Is she into electronics like you are?" Robyn asked.

"No. That's why I want to do more. A laptop is nice and practical, but I want this birthday to be special. Very special."

John and Dave looked at each other and smiled.

"Carol, you consider this group to be your closest friends, right?" John asked.

"Yeah. Why?"

"Why not throw a surprise party for her? Most people expect that kind of stuff for big numbers like thirty or forty or fifty. I think it would be fun to have a surprise twenty seventh!" Dave said.

"That's a really good idea," Robyn agreed.

"I like it too." Will smiled.

"Ok, that'll be cool. I'll have Cucina cater it. That was where we went on our first date. I bet she'd love the sentiment."

"Ok, when and how are we going to plan this?" Will asked.

"Well, she's going to be working on this case for at least another week. Her birthday is Tuesday night. Obviously a week night just isn't going to work."

"How about Sunday?" John suggested.

"Then," Robyn said. "You can give her the laptop on Tuesday. That would work out nicely."

"Ok. I like that. That sounds like a really great idea. Thanks guys." Carol smiled and turned to Robyn. "Can you take her out to distract her for a while? This way we can get all set up here?"

"Sure!"

"Great! Can you guys get here by five?" Carol asked Will, Dave and John.

"That won't be a problem," Dave responded.

"Perfect. Robyn, come back here at 6 o'clock. I'll have the food here by then and we can all surprise her."

"Sounds like a great plan." Robyn said excitedly.

Carol quickly set the food up buffet style. Will, John and Dave helped. They only had a few more minutes before Alex and Robyn were due back. Carol peered out the window and saw Robyn's car pulling in.

"Quick, guys, hide!"

The three men hid behind the couch. Carol stood in front of the dinner table hoping to hide the magnificent food that sat waiting. Carol felt nervous. She desperately hoped that Alex would like this surprise party.

The knob on the front door began to turn. Everyone held their breath. Alex entered first with Robyn right behind her. As they entered, the boys popped up and everyone shouted, "Surprise!"

Alex stepped back and nearly fell into Robyn. "Whoa! What is this?"

"We're celebrating your birthday early," Will said.

Carol stepped away from the table. "Look, honey. I got us dinner from Cucina, just like our first date."

"Oh my God, this is awesome. Thank you all so much!" Alexandria went around and hugged everyone. Last, she gave Carol a big, sweet, appreciative kiss.

They all gathered around the table, and helped themselves to the wonderful Italian food.

"Happy birthday!" They all toasted her before they ate.

"Thank you guys," Alex said. "This is the best birthday ever!"

It was after nine at night when Alex finally came home. She was clearly worn, tired, and very stressed.

"Hey sweetie. You ok?" Carol asked as she handed Alex a glass of water.

"Yeah," Alex huffed. "Just beat."

"Oh I'm sorry, baby." Carol paused to think for a moment. It was obvious that Alex was exhausted. Carol wanted her to sleep, but she still wanted to celebrate her birthday as well. After a few moments of contemplation, Carol came to her decision. "Well, it is your birthday and I wanted to get you something nice."

"Thank you, sweetie, but I just don't have the energy to do anything." Alex flopped onto the couch in sheer weariness.

"Oh, no, sweetheart. There's nothing you need to do. I just want to give you this." he picked up and held out the new laptop for Alex.

"What's this?"

"It's your birthday present. It's a new laptop. I thought it might help to make your life easier, especially with this case."

"Wow! A new laptop. Baby, you shouldn't have."

"Yes, I should have. You need it. You deserve it. Happy birthday!" Carol walked over to Alex and handed her the small computer.

"Thank you."

"You're welcome, sweetheart. You want to look at it now?"

"I just don't think I have any energy left. Can we just go to bed and you can teach me how to use it in the morning?"

"Sure, let's get you off to bed. I love you," Carol said lovingly as she guided an exhausted Alex to the bedroom.

Chapter Eleven

1999 was speeding along, and the growing concern for computers and computer systems to work in the new millennium was intense.

Carol was working diligently to ensure that all of Dawson Networking's clients' systems would be functioning normally in the year 2000.

On a cold, crisp autumn day, Carol tiredly dragged herself into the office yet again.

"Carol, can I see you in my office?" Greg asked as she tiredly hung up her coat.

"Sure."

She followed him into the secluded room and he gently closed the door behind her.

"What's up, Greg?" Carol yawned.

"Carol, I have to tell you. I know you're working your ass off, but you're doing a phenomenal job. I can't even tell you the number of good calls I'm getting about you. Clients are specifically requesting you to be their tech. You work hard, you work fast, and you go above and beyond your job. I know you're exhausted, but I have a ton of calls for you to test systems, up-grade systems, and more.

"But, before I let you go there's something I'd like to say to you. Carol, you never cease to amaze and impress me. Your work is superior.

"Carol, I'm giving you a raise. It's going to mean more work for you since in you're in such high demand, but I have faith in you."

"Greg, I don't know what to say. Thank you. I'm flattered. But, this is my fifth raise in the two years I've been here. Are you sure?"

"Carol, you are second only to Will. And you're only second to him because he's been here so much longer than you.

"You are dynamite, kid! Keep up the great work."

"Thanks, Greg. I really appreciate it."

"Ok, Carol. Now for the bad news. Here's the list of companies that have put in requests for you to test and up-grade their systems." He handed her two sheets of paper with what seemed an infinite list of company names.

"Whoa! That's a lot. I'll do as many as I can each day, Greg. All I can promise is my best."

"Your best is excellent. That's all I need."

Carol glanced at her watch while knee deep in computer parts and wires. It was already past 7:30 in the evening. It was going to be another late night. Carol decided to call Alex to let her know. "Hey sweetie."

"Hey, baby. Where are you?"

"Still working unfortunately. These guys at Berman Law Firm are all screwed up. Not only do I have to make sure they're Y2K compatible, I have to replace their mail server. I'm going to be here a while, sweetheart."

There was a strong tone of disappointment in Alex's voice. "Oh. That's too bad."

"I know. I'm sorry, Alex. I wasn't planning on working late again. I'll get home as soon as I can, but I have no idea when that will be."

"I'll leave you some food to heat up in the fridge. Ok, babe?"

"That would be awesome. Thank you, sweetheart. I'm sorry. I love you."

"I love you too."

Carol reluctantly hung up. She felt so guilt ridden that she wasn't spending more time with Alexandria.

As fall turned into winter, Carol found herself coming home later and later. She now typically came home around eleven at night. It gave her just enough time to crawl into bed, gently kiss Alex as she slept, and try to get some rest.

Night after night, week after week, Carol and Alex went without seeing each other. Carol's work schedule was more than demanding. Alex hated the separation. She tried to be understanding, but her level of frustration grew exponentially every day.

Alex couldn't take the separation or aggravation any more. One night she forced herself to stay up and she waited for Carol to come home. With only twenty minutes left until midnight, Carol finally walked through the apartment door.

"Oh, hi. What are you doing up so late?" Carol was surprised to find Alex awake.

"Waiting for you," Alex snapped.

"Oh honey, I'm sorry. I know it's late. You didn't need to do that for me."

"It's not for you... and yes I did."

"Alex, what's wrong?"

"What's wrong? Are you kidding me? You're never fucking home. I haven't seen you in God knows how long and you're asking me what's wrong!"

"Sweetie, I'm sorry. I can't control this whole Y2K thing. You know I don't want to be living like this. But Greg gave me that raise with more responsibility and all these companies are asking for me. Not for Will. Not for Paul. For me. It's a ton of hard work, but it's going to be worth it in the end."

"Oh really? Is it? Is it going to be worth coming home to an empty house? You seem to be more concerned about your damn job than you are about me."

"Oh, Alex, come on. Don't say that. You know it's not true."

"You work every fucking weekend. You're coming home at freaking midnight. I never see you. I never spend any time with you. When we do talk, it's all about this company's computer or that job. All you care about is your damn clientele!"

"Sweetheart, that's not true. I love you. You're the reason I'm working this hard. I'm doing this so that we can have a good life together. I know it sucks and I'm sorry. But this is the nature of the job. You knew this. It's not like I just started this job. I've been doing this for over two years."

"You're doing this for me? Oh yeah. Ignoring me, not spending any time with me or Sugar. I have to do everything by myself, and I'm all alone. I can totally see how that's for me to have a better life."

"Damn it, Alexandria! Stop it! I know that you're all alone and that you're doing everything by yourself. I can't even remember the last time we went on a walk with Sugar. I'd fucking love to spend time with you and to help around the house. But I can't. Not right now at least. The new year is coming fast. I have got to get this shit done. I'm sorry I'm so fucking good at my job."

"It's all about the job. That's the only thing that matters any more."

"No, it's not. But I can only do so much. I can only be in one place at one time. With some of the cases you work on I'd expect you to be far more understanding."

"Understanding? I've never left you alone like this. Fuck you, Carol."

"Alex!"

Alex stormed off into the bedroom and slammed the door shut.

"God damn it," Carol said under her breath. She flopped on the couch and tried to get some rest before another busy day.

It was already mid-December and Carol's work load finally started to lighten, but she was still working long hours. Although still disappointed in her lack of time with her lover, Alex had come to terms with Carol's work schedule. Both women focused on communicating more and appreciating the time they did have together.

Through their various phone calls and brief interactions, the two had had begun to reconnect over the idea of moving. Alex had been in the apartment for years. Carol agreed that with the dog their family had outgrown the apartment. Both women agreed they would love to have a yard of their own. And the idea of having a two car garage was more than tempting.

Although they never came to a solid decision, Alex had expressed an interest in a specific house for sale on Sparrow Lane that she drove passed daily.

Silently, Alexandria was more concerned about Carol's health, though. She was afraid to tell Carol.

Carol had been fighting a cold for over a week and wasn't showing any signs of getting better. Alex didn't want to push things further with Carol being so tired and stressed. So Alex kept the conversations light and often rambled about the house on Sparrow Lane.

Although the women weren't spending much time together, Alex found that she was also getting sick. She must have caught Carol's cold during the brief time they did have.

They both fought the cold for weeks on end while they worked. It was a nasty virus that never seemed to go away. Although they were both concerned, neither vocalized their health concerns for themselves or each other. Instead they continued to work and fight the illness.

It was Christmas once again. Byron and Candace came over to the girls' apartment as was the new family tradition.

The family greeted each other warmly though Byron and Candace kept their distance since Carol and Alex were still battling that same cold.

Even though she was sick, Alexandria was still her usual, excited self for the Christmas holiday. Presents were exchanged almost immediately as Byron and Candace came in to the apartment.

Byron opened his present from Alexandria first. There was a box in the box, he opened the second box. There was a third box. Then a fourth and even a fifth. Finally when he opened the fifth box, there was a gift card for his favorite coffee shop. "Thanks, A."

"Byron," Alex said through all her congestion. "There's enough on there to get you coffee for about a year."

"Sweet. Thanks, Sis."

Candace was next. She opened her small box also to find a gift card. It was to a furniture and home decor store.

"C, I know it's a little early, but I thought we could go shopping for your dorm room with that." Alex sneezed.

"Oh, that'll be great. Thanks, Alexandria."

Carol blew her nose before she was able to open her present from Alex. After throwing her tissue away, she slowly opened the long, narrow box. Inside was a stunning, sparkling diamond and sapphire bracelet. It was breathtaking. "Oh honey," Carol sniffled. "Thank you so much. It's gorgeous. I absolutely love it."

The sick pair hugged and gave each other a quick kiss.

"My turn," Carol said. She handed a card to Byron, a card to Candace and then a small box to Alex. "Ok, so the order is Byron, Candace, and then Alex. There is a point to this," Carol chuckled and then began coughing. "Oh," she gagged. "And read it out loud."

Byron opened his envelope. "All it says is, 'you are.'"

Candace opened her card. "'Invited to.' What does that mean?"

"Just wait," Carol said. "Go on, honey. Open up you present."

Alex opened the box. There was something wrapped in paper. She began to open the paper. There was a set of keys, and something written on the paper underneath the keys. Alex tentatively picked up the keys, and began to cry.

"Read it out loud, sweetie." Carol requested. This was too important. Byron and Candace needed to hear this.

"Our new home." Between her cold and crying, Alex's eyes were overflowing.

"What?" Byron and Candace asked in unison.

"Well," Carol explained. "While I was working on all the Y2K crap, we started talking about moving. Every time Alex walked Sugar, she ran into the landlord and his three rowdy kids in the backyard. We have no privacy here. She's been in this apartment for years. It's been great, but she told me about this house she saw for sale on Sparrow Lane that she just adored.

"I actually got off work early one day, so I called up the realtor. I looked at the house. It was beautiful and it was in great shape. So, I made an offer." Carol then turned to Alex and said, "congratulations, Alexandria. You are now the proud owner of 581 Sparrow Lane."

Alex looked at Carol, she was still crying. "How did you do this?"

"I paid for it, but I put the house in your name. It's yours. I told you all my Y2K work would be worth it."

Alex walked over to Carol and simply held her. "Oh my God! Honey, I am so sorry for everything. This is just amazing. Thank you so much, Carol. I love you so much."

Carol lightly moved Alex back a bit so she could stare into her deep brown eyes. "I love you too, baby. Everything I do is for you, ok?"

Alex nodded, and they again embraced.

New Year's Eve was a cold, cloudy, snowy day. It was a terrible day to move. Even so Carol, Alex, Will, Robyn, Byron, Candace, Dave, and John found themselves moving the girls into their new home on Sparrow Lane. Carol and Alexandria were out in the snow and biting cold and they were only just beginning to show signs of getting over that endless virus they had been combating. Still somewhat sick, the girls were out in the cold, moving furniture and heavy boxes.

"You girls couldn't have picked a worse day to move." Dave snipped as he carried a box out to his truck.

Alex was only a few steps behind him, also carrying a box. "I know. I am so sorry, Dave. You know I wouldn't have planned it this way."

Carol had just unloaded the box with the dishes into the Camry when she heard Alex's remark. "I'm sorry, guys. I know the timing couldn't be worse. I feel horrible, I do. But, at least we'll all have a great New Year."

"You're just lucky that none of your friends have a life," Will huffed as he and Byron carried the couch out to Byron's SUV.

"This has to be the worst New Year's ever," Candace sulked and shivered as she held onto Sugar.

"Oh come on, C." Alex encouraged her sister. "I know it's cold, but it's fun to be with all the people you care about."

Candace rolled her eyes and looked away from Alex.

"Ok, Carol and Alexandria, you two need go through the apartment one last time," Robyn said bringing out yet another box. "This was the last box I could find."

"Thank God!" Dave said.

The rest of the gang warmed up the cars and squeezed into their various vehicles while Carol and Alex walked through their apartment for the last time.

The apartment was a blank slate. What was once their home was now just an empty apartment. Alex slowly opened each cupboard and drawer in the kitchen one last time. Seeing the empty kitchen, the empty cupboards and drawers was an emotional moment for Alex. She fought back the tears.

After searching the empty bedroom and bathroom, Carol came out and saw Alex staring at the emptiness that surrounded her. "Hey, sweetie. What's wrong?"

"It's silly."

"No, it's not. What's up?"

"I've been in this place for so long. This was the first place I was able to get on my own after Byron helped me with my sobriety.

This has been my home for years. It's just hard to see everything so empty. It's hard to walk away. This place has always meant so much to me."

"Oh, honey. I'm sorry. I know it's hard to close this chapter, but think about where we're going to. You're a home owner now. You've overcome so much in your life. This is a huge milestone in your life, baby. It's your life and our house. We're an official family now," Carol said with her arm around her partner. "This is a good thing. Trust me."

"I know. I just don't want to forget this place."

"Oh you won't. We won't. There are lots of happy memories here, memories that we'll be taking with us."

Slowly, the couple walked back out into the snow and back to where the group waited. Alex got into her Camry, Carol into the GTO, and the convoy left for the girls' new home.

The group unloaded all of the vehicles as quickly as they could. It was getting colder by the minute and the snow was coming down heavily.

With so many people working so quickly, the cars unloaded easily and everyone was able to warm up rapidly in the house. Carol got water boiling as well, so that everyone could enjoy hot chocolate as well.

Byron, Candace and Robyn wedged themselves onto the couch and the rest of the group sat on the floor and on various boxes in a circle.

"Well, this was quite the adventure." Dave commented.

"It was. Thank you all so much," Carol said.

"Indeed," Alex said taking a sip of her hot chocolate. "We owe you guys big time."

"Well, I say we get that TV hooked up so we can all watch the New Year's stuff," Byron said.

Will stretched as he stood up. "I'll get it."

"I'm going to start unpacking more stuff, so that we have dishes and furniture, and you guys can all be comfortable for New Year's." Carol said.

"I'm hungry," Candace called out.

"Hmmmm. I'm not sure we can cook up a dinner. Not quickly, anyway. Do you guys want pizza? It is the typical move-in dinner." Alexandria offered to the group.

"Sure, that sounds good," John said. Everyone else agreed.

"Ok, I'll call it in while Carol unpacks and you guys get the TV set up," Alex said.

Robyn and Candace began to unpack more dishes, books, and some small objects.

Carol brought out two rocking chairs and their cushions. Then she set up the dining room table and chairs.

Byron and John carried out a futon that sat in the girls' office at the apartment. This new living room was nice and large. There was plenty of room for all the furniture, and all the company.

After a short while, there was a knock on the door. There was a cold young man with three large pizzas. Alex quickly paid him in order to get him out of the freezing weather.

It didn't take long for most of the necessities to be unpacked. Soon after the group settled in and enjoyed their nice hot pizza.

Will turned on the TV and the group began to watch all the New Year festivities.

Before they knew it the count-down to midnight began. Everyone paired up and they watched the TV with slight apprehension. Although both Carol and Will were sure that Y2K was really not a problem, everyone else wanted to wait and see what would really happen.

"Five...four...three...two...one. Happy New Year!" Everyone shouted and cheered. Each couple, John and Dave, Robyn and Will, and Carol and Alex gave each other a special New Year's kiss. Byron hugged his little sister Candace. After a few moments, the crowd cheered even more.

"Hey, look, the lights are still on!" Dave remarked.

"I told you it wasn't such a big deal," Carol said dryly.

The group was relieved that both moving the girls and the Y2K fear were over.

The crowd stayed for a while celebrating the new year, new millennium, and the girls' new home. They ate, laughed, and enjoyed themselves despite their hard work earlier in the day.

Chapter Twelve

"We should have thought about painting before we moved all the furniture in." Alex said to Carol as they looked at paint swatches for their new home in a giant home improvement store.

"I know, but we couldn't exactly ask the gang to help us with a painting party as well."

"I just don't see how we're going to be able to do this."

"Sweetheart, it'll be fine. It may take us a while, but we'll get it all done."

The couple had agreed on a neutral taupe for the living room, a deep romantic burgundy for their new bedroom, and an egg-shell white for the kitchen. Alexandria picked sage green for her office, which was the second bedroom of the house. Carol decided on a warm, rich buttery yellow shade for the den which she would use for her office.

The sales clerk loaded up their shopping cart with gallon after gallon of paint, trays, drop clothes, rollers, and detailing brushes. By the time they checked out, the cart was so heavy, both women had to push it to the car.

"Are you sure we can do this?" Alex asked as she huffed along out of breath.

"Yeah," Carol grunted. "It won't be easy, but we'll make it work."

Somehow the pair was able to load up the Camry with all of their painting supplies, and they drove back home to embark on a painting escapade.

Every night when the women came home from work they painted. They painted on the weekends. Every spare minute they had was dedicated to transforming their new house into their home. It took several weeks, but eventually the house was warm, inviting, and familiar. Each room was fully furnished and the women were quite proud of their new abode.

One lazy Saturday afternoon, Carol took the last unpacked box and went into the garage. Hearing the door to the garage close, Alex got up and followed her partner.

"What are you doing?"

"I'm decorating the garage," Carol said enthusiastically.

"Say what?"

"Yeah. Over the years, my dad and I had collected a ton of old license plates, classic car ads, and pinup girl pictures. Since my father's GTO is housed in this garage, the least I can do is break these out too."

"How come I never saw any of this before?" Alex asked.

"Remember that box that just sat on my side of the closet in the apartment?"

"Yeah."

"That was all this stuff. I knew I'd get a garage eventually." Carol laughed at herself. From a young age she dreamed of this moment and it finally true.

"Girl, you are insane."

"Perhaps, but you love me anyway." Carol teased.

"Yes I do." Alex pecked Carol on the cheek and left her to decorate her garage.

Carol opened the box and was thrilled looking at all the familiar license plates and pictures. She knew her father would be proud. Without hesitation, Carol gleefully began hammering nails into the garage walls and hanging up her beloved antiques.

A few hours later, she stepped back to take it all in. It was the most beautiful garage she had ever seen. There was a touch of sadness since Carol's father was unable to enjoy it. She knew that somehow, someway, he was relishing the pictures, license plates, and other automotive memorabilia. For a moment, Carol thought she could hear her father's voice telling her he was proud of her.

The next Sunday, Carol and Alex enjoyed a nice warm cup of coffee and a reprieve from their decorating when Carol's phone rang. She quickly got up and answered.

"Hello?"

"Hi, is this Carol Mathers from Dawson Networking?"

"Yes it is."

"My name is Rich. I'm calling from General Media."

"Oh yeah. Hi Rich. What can I do for you?"

"Carol, there is something seriously wrong going on here. Our mail server is really messed up. Several of our computers aren't working, and we've had several clients call us and say that they got e-mails from us and now their computers aren't working."

"Really? That doesn't sound good."

"They thought it was some kind of thank you e-mail, because it said 'I love you.' Have you heard of this?"

"Not that I can think of off the top of my head, but let me grab all my stuff and I'll head right over. This is probably going to be a large job, Rich."

"That's fine. I don't care. Just get us up and running again, please!"

"Ok. I'll be there as soon as I can."

Alexandria watched Carol during the entire conversation. "That didn't sound good, baby."

"It's not. General Media sounds like they got infected with a really nasty virus or something. I'm probably going to be out there for a while. I'm sorry, sweetie."

"It's ok. I just hope it's not too terrible."

"Me too." Carol then grabbed her tools and equipment and went out into the crisp, early May air to check out the situation at General Media.

Chapter Thirteen

Since the "I love you" virus first showed up on May fourth, Carol was working non-stop once again. She would arrive at the office by six in the morning and only be finishing her field service calls by eleven at night.

One extremely late night, Carol arrived home just after one o'clock in the morning.

Completely exhausted, she quietly slipped into bed still in her work clothes. She lay next to Alex, who looked splendid while she rested. As soon as Carol's head hit her pillow, her cell phone rang again. Carol grumbled under her breath.

With a heavy sigh, she climbed out of bed, grabbed her phone and went into the master bathroom, not to wake Alexandria.

Carol spoke as quietly as possible. "Hello?"

"Is this Carol Mathers from Dawson?"

"Yes it is."

"I'm sorry to call you so late. My name is Lloyd. I'm an IT tech at Bruce and Associates law office." He paused.

"I've been trying desperately to save our network. We got that stupid 'I love you' virus, and it's just way over my head. You were highly recommended to us by Rich at General Media."

"Our system is completely shot. Can you help us?" He sounded desperate.

"Yeah, sure."

"How quickly can you get here? We're on the corner of Fifth and Pine."

"Give me about twenty to twenty five minutes. I have to tell you, there will be an over-night charge on top of my hourly rate."

"That's fine. I just can't have everybody come in tomorrow and find that we're completely screwed. I'll see you in a bit."

"Ok, bye." Carol yawned as she hung up. She grabbed clean clothes from her closet and quickly freshened up.

"Sorry, baby. I love you," she whispered to Alex as she left.

Alex appeared to be resting, but she was simply laying in the bed, facing away from Carol. She felt angry, frustrated, disappointed, hurt, and aggravated.

It was just after ten in the morning when Carol flopped into her car. She sighed. She was exhausted.

She swallowed. Her glands were swollen. She was getting sick. She understood why. She had been pushing too hard with work over these past several weeks. Once again, Carol had gotten little sleep, eaten poorly, and been under tremendous stress. She decided to call the office.

"Hey Greg?"

"Yeah, Carol."

"Hey. I just got off a job I started at around 1:30 this morning for Bruce and Associates. We'll need to do the bill for it, but I am just shot. And I think I'm getting sick – I think I've got a cold coming on."

"Take the day off," Greg said. "It's not a problem. You've been working the hardest – even more than Will and Paul. I know we're slammed, but I also know that you need the rest. Just call me tomorrow and let me know how you're doing."

"Ok, that sounds good. I'll call you first thing in the morning to let you know about tomorrow."

"Ok, kid. Go get some rest."

Carol felt badly about leaving Alex last night. She decided to call her.

Alex didn't answer, so Carol left a message. "Hey sweetheart, it's me. I'm really sorry about last night. I'm finally done though. Greg gave me the day off today and I may take off tomorrow too. I feel like I have a bad cold coming on. So I'm going to go home, have some tea, and go to bed. Give me a call when you're on your lunch break, ok? I love you."

Carol rolled over to look at the clock. 3:10 pm. She checked her phone, Alex never called. Carol thought that was very odd. Alex always called her on her lunch hour. Perhaps Alex had a busy day working a big case. Although it was unusual, Carol didn't give too much thought to the lack of a call from Alexandria.

Feeling worse than she had this morning, she wiggled back under the covers again and went back to sleep.

Alexandria stood in the doorway of the bedroom with her arms crossed. Carol slowly sat up.

"Hey," Carol yawned.

"Hi."

"What time is it?"

"6:30 at night." Alex's tone was cold and short.

"Oh wow. I'm sorry. I didn't mean to sleep so long. Want me to make dinner to make it up to you?"

"If you want. Dinner won't be enough though."

"Honey, come on." Carol coughed.

"Come on what?" Alex snapped back.

"I'm sorry. I'm doing the best I can."

"What? To avoid me? To not be home?"

"Oh no, not this again. I am not having this argument again. Especially not after you saw how much my hard work pays off."

"I am working my ass off here. I know this sucks. It's not my idea of a good time either, but I have to."

"You know I'm doing this for you – for the family."

"I don't need anyone to do anything for me. I can do things quite well by myself, thank you. And my family doesn't need your help."

"What the hell, Alex? I bought this fucking house for you. I want to help contribute to your mom's care and to Candace's college too. Damn!" Carol took a deep breath and quieted her tone. "Look, I love you and I want you to be happy. I want us both to have all we ever dreamed of. You know that your family means the world to me. I want to help them. Your family is my family. You're all I have."

"Well, you know what I want? I want a partner. I want a woman who will spend time with me. I want a woman who wants to be with me."

"I do want to be with you, Alex. I don't like working like this, but think of how much the money will help us."

"I don't give a shit about money, Carol!"

"Well fuck me, Alex! I just can't win, can I? I'm trying to do right by you, and nothing is good enough."

Alex glared at Carol.

Carol heavily sighed. "Alright, look. This 'I love you' virus is bad. It's really bad. So many companies are seriously fucked up because of it. Just like last winter, I'm being called out more than Will or Paul. I can ask Greg about changing some of the work calls to them so that we can spend more time together. Deal?" Carol coughed heavily.

"You need to get some rest," Alex replied, then walked away.

Carol pulled the blankets over her head and tried to go back to sleep.

The next morning, Carol woke up and her cold had escalated from swollen lymph nodes to a full blown head and chest cold.

"Greg," Carol's nasally congested voice started the message. "It's Carol. This cold hit me hard – really hard. I'd like to take today off too. I am not well enough to be working near people or machines. I'm really sorry about this. I'm hoping to be back tomorrow."

Carol coughed, sneezed and sniffled her way into the kitchen. Alex had fallen asleep on the couch with the TV inaudibly playing in the background. As quietly as she could, Carol made herself a cup of tea. The tea kettle whistle woke Alexandria.

"Sorry," Carol coughed.

"You're really sick, huh?"

Carol nodded as she took a sip of the very hot tea.

"You going to work?"

"No." Carol answered, then sneezed.

"What time is it?" Alex yawned.

"It's quarter after six."

"I guess I should start getting ready." Alex stretched, and slowly got off the couch. Alex walked right past Carol and went into the shower. Carol sighed knowing that Alex was still mad. As much as Carol adored her woman, Alex was amazing at holding a grudge.

Rushing her normal morning routine, Alex was walking out the door by seven. "Feel better," she said to Carol.

Hurt and confused, Carol went back to bed to try to sleep off her cold.

"Honey," Carol was gently nudged by Alex. Alexandria sat next to her with flowers and a big beautiful grin.

"Hey," Carol wearily replied.

"I'm sorry about yesterday." Alex handed the flowers to Carol. "I know you're working really hard and that you're not trying to avoid me. I just felt ignored again. Luckily for you, Dave put me in my place."

Carol started to laugh which turned into a hard, phlegm-filled cough.

"I'm going to make some chicken soup for you, ok?"

"Yeah, that sounds good. Thank you, sweetheart."

Alex turned to walk away.

"Hey, sweetheart, what time is it?"

"Almost six, why?"

"Six in the evening? Shit! I literally slept all day."

A short while later, Alex returned with a large bowl of warm, home made chicken soup. Carol sat up so she could eat in bed.

"You slept all day? Did you get up at all? Shower? Watch TV? Anything?"

"No. That's just it. I slept like a rock until you woke me. I've never slept like that in my life."

"Well you're really sick, baby. Your body needs it."

Slowly Carol finished the delicious soup and slipped back down under the covers. "Babe, I think I'm going to go back to sleep."

"Ok, honey. I hope you feel better in the morning."

Carol fell asleep quickly. Alex missed her companionship, but it was far too early for her to try to go to bed. Alex watched TV to pass the evening away.

Three hours later, Alexandria joined Carol in the warm bed. She snuggled close to her. Despite Carol's illness, Alex wanted to sleep tightly intertwined with her.

Carol was drinking tea, orange juice and taking vitamins and cold medications daily. Yet, four weeks had passed and her cold was getting progressively worse. She still battled a heavy chest cough, and her sinuses were greatly infected.

With her work ethic intact, Carol did her best to ignore the sickness and she continued to work long, intense hours.

Alex watched her woman's health decline. Her concern grew by the minute.

One night, Carol came home a few minutes after eight o'clock. "Hey." She hoarsely called out to Alex.

Alex stood up and walked over to Carol. "Hi honey. Want me to heat up some leftovers?"

"Sure," Carol sneezed.

"Sweetie, I'm worried about you. You've been sick for like a month now. This is just like last winter. It's not normal to have colds for so long. You have got to see a doctor."

"I'm just sick from stress, working too much, not eating right, and not getting enough sleep. I'll be fine. I just need this whole 'I love you' virus shit to be over and I'll be better in no time."

"Carol, please. I set up an appointment for you to see my doctor tomorrow morning at ten."

"But, I have to work."

"I already called Greg and he thought it was a great idea. He's worried about you too."

Carol sighed. "Ok. I guess I'm going then since you all plotted against me."

Alex laughed. "We didn't plot against you. We're just really worried, and we want you to get better."

"I said I'll go. It's all good."

Alex could easily see that Carol was not pleased. Alex knew that Carol would go even though she was reluctant to do so. "Thank you," Alex said appreciatively.

Carol looked around the exam room. It was pretty typical. The walls were painted a very light, pastel pink. There were generic flower paintings hanging on the walls. Medical posters also hung on the walls and the back of the exam room door. The usual supplies and sink sat on a small grey counter with cabinets underneath it. Carol feigned interest in a poster about the cardiovascular system as she waited.

The room was bland and unimpressive. If Alex felt this doctor was good though, Carol decided she would put her faith in this doctor and staff as well. Alex had high standards, so Carol knew that this would be a good doctor. She still felt foolish, however, sitting on the examination bed.

A gentle rap on the door alerted Carol to the doctor's entrance.

In walked a tall, lean and lanky woman. She had thick, curly brown hair pulled back and it cascaded behind her long white lab coat. Her facial features were sharp, but not unattractive. Her green eyes were bright and friendly. She was striking, and she oozed intelligence. Her presence could not be missed.

"Hi, I'm Dr. Luciano," she introduced herself.

"Hi, I'm Carol." Carol sheepishly shook the beautiful doctor's hand.

"I see you were referred by Alexandria Whetherby. She's been a patient of mine for years."

Carol smiled. "She's my partner."

"She's a great lady."

"Yeah."

"So, what brings you here?" The doctor asked as she checked Carol's blood pressure.

"Well, Alex made me come in. I've had a cold for a few weeks. But I'm working really crazy hours and I'm not sleeping much, so it's just taking me a while to get better."

The doctor listened to Carol's chest, lungs and breathing sounds. "Ok. Is it typical for you to have colds or other illnesses that last for a while?"

Carol paused to think. "Yeah, I guess. Alex and I both had a really nasty cold over the winter and it took us about 6 weeks to get over it. I never really thought much of it though."

"Do you have any chronic conditions? Any autoimmune diseases? Anything like that?"

"No. Well, actually, I was a sick kid. But I've been fine as an adult."

"What do you mean you were a sick kid?"

"I was a preemie. I was born seven or eight weeks early. I was really anemic as a result. It was something I never really outgrew. So I ended up having a blood transfusion when I was six, but I've been fine ever since."

"How's your anemia now?"

"Ok, as far as I know. I try to eat lots of iron-rich foods and I'm on the pill to lessen my periods so I won't become more anemic from that. So, really everything's fine."

"When was the last time you had your blood checked?"

"Oh. I'm not sure. It's been a while," Carol finally admitted.

"Ok. Let's do some base-line blood work. We'll check you for anemia, check your immune system, your liver and kidney function, stuff like that. And I want to run an AIDS test as well."

"An AIDS test?" Carol was shocked. She was just there for a cold, not for an AIDS test.

"It's really more of a precaution, Carol. Your body seems to have a hard time fighting things off, so I just want to rule it out."

"Ok," Carol replied skeptically.

"I'll have the nurse come in and draw blood. In the meanwhile, I'm going to prescribe you some antibiotics to clear this up. I can hear that your chest is pretty congested and we really need to fix that ASAP. If it doesn't get any better, we're going to need to take chest x-rays and possibly put you on some heavy-duty medications and treatments."

"I'll call you when we get the blood results in."

"Ok."

"Nice to meet you, Carol." The doctor stood up and shook Carol's hand.

"Thanks. Nice to meet you too."

One week after her doctor's visit, Carol checked her voice mail on her way home from work.

"Hi, this is a message for Ms. Mathers. This is Tracy with Dr. Luciano's office. The doctor needs you to come back in for a follow up. Please call us to schedule an appointment at your earliest convenience. Thank you."

Chapter Fourteen

Carol waited anxiously for Dr. Luciano to enter the room. The wait seemed endless. As time ticked on, Carol became more nervous about this "re-check" visit. She wondered why the doctor hadn't just gone over the results over the phone. Was it possible that something really was wrong?

Carol's thoughts were interrupted by a knock on the door. Dr. Luciano entered the exam room.

"Hi Carol," she kindly addressed her patient.

"Hi, Dr. Luciano. What's going on?"

"Carol, we need to talk."

"What is it?"

"The reason you've been so sick for so long is not because of stress or fatigue."

"Doctor, what are you saying?"

"Remember I told you that I wanted to run an AIDS test as a precaution?"

"Yeah?" Carol's nervous anxiety sky rocketed.

"Carol, I'm sorry, but your AIDS test came back positive."

Carol stared at the doctor. "But – but – that's impossible. Did you re-run the test? Maybe it was just a mistake. Maybe the lab got my test confused with someone else's."

"I'm sorry, Carol. Our lab always re-runs a sample if there's a positive result. They want to ensure that a mistake has not been made. This is a confirmed positive."

"No. No! That can't be. There's no way. I never did anything. No drugs, no shared needles, no sex with weird, questionable people..."

"You told me that you had a blood transfusion as a young child, right?"

"Well yeah, but they check for that kind of thing."

Imperfect

"They didn't regularly test blood for transfusions 1985, Carol. So little was known about HIV and AIDS at that time. We were only just starting to hear about the virus, so testing donors for HIV/AIDS was simply not a standard procedure 1985. You said your transfusion was before then, around 1981. It simply was not commonplace to screen all blood donors back then. Your donor's blood wasn't checked. I'm really sorry."

Carol tried to fight back the tears, but the shock and fear were simply too overwhelming for her.

"I have a referral for a very good infectious disease specialist for you to see," Dr. Luciano continued. "And we need to test Alexandria as well. Since you two have been together for a while, we have to make sure that she hasn't contracted it."

Carol sniffled as she looked up at the doctor. The possibility of Alex having AIDS was more frightening to Carol than the fact that she had it herself. Her brown eyes were riddled with fear.

Carol sat in the GTO in the doctor's parking lot. She pulled down the visor to look at the faded photograph again. She was hoping it would bring her some peace since her mind was racing. "I wish you were here, Dad." Carol softly whispered to the picture. "I need you. I don't know what to do or say. I feel so alone. I miss you."

Carol took a deep breath to try to clear her mind and arrange her thoughts. First, she knew she had to call Alex immediately. She tried her cell first, but Alex didn't answer. Carol then dialed her office number.

"Ludlow and Kepwick, Attorneys at Law. This is Nancy. How may I help you?"

"Hey Nancy, this is Carol. Is Alexandria around?"

"She's in a meeting. Can I leave a message for her?"

"Nancy, this is an emergency. Would you mind getting her for me, please?"

"Ok, if you insist. Please hold, Carol." Classical music played in Carol's ear as she waited for Alex to pick up the other line.

"Hello?" Alex sounded rushed.

"Baby, I need you to come home."

"Carol, we're working on a really intense and involved case. I can't just go home."

"It's an emergency. I need you to come home as quickly as possible."

There was a heavy sigh on the other end. "Ok. I'll be there as soon as I can." Alex then hung up.

Carol went through the list of contacts in her cell phone. She stared at a number that had always been stored in her phone, but she never called. Nervously, Carol hit the send button.

"Hello – ummm, Mom?" Carol tripped on the words.

"I knew I shouldn't have answered when I didn't recognize the number." The voice on the other end answered coldly.

"Mom, please. I need to talk to you."

"What is it?" LouAnne impatiently asked.

"Mom, I... I have AIDS. I got it from that blood transfusion from when I was a kid."

There was a hardly a pause before LouAnne spoke. "Good. Serves you right!"

"What? Mom, please, don't. I'm trying to tell you something serious here. I'm trying to rebuild our relationship. I'm dying, don't you think..."

"That's what you deserve. You deserve it for living that horrible life style and for killing your father. God is punishing you for all the evil deeds you've done in your life."

"For years, I resented giving you that damn transfusion and all your medical issues. I thought I was being penalized by having a sickly little brat like you."

"Thankfully, now you're paying for all the strife you've ever caused me."

"I am done with this conversation and with you."

Carol began to cry, but she remained quiet. She didn't want her mother to hear her crying.

"Rot in hell!" LouAnne screamed and hung up the phone.

Once her phone became silent, Carol let her sorrow consume her. She cried for the broken relationship between her and LouAnne. She cried for all of the traumas she had endured in her life. She cried for her own mortality and she cried for the future that lay ahead for her and Alex.

Carol's tears never stopped flowing. She struggled to see the road through her tears as she drove home.

111

Alex cooked dinner, but neither woman ate. The food was made well but neither of them had an appetite. They simply pushed the food around on their plates. The house was silent, save for the clanking of their forks against the plates. Sugar seemed to pick up on their stress and depression. She lay quietly on the couch and sighed.

Carol couldn't even look at Alex. She wondered what she should do or say. "I'm sorry," her quiet but quaking voice ultimately ended the silence.

Alexandria sighed. "It's not your fault, Carol. You needed that transfusion. It was before we all knew about it." It. She couldn't even bring herself to say the word: AIDS.

"But now we have to get you tested too. I never meant for this to happen."

"I know." Alex said. She was amazingly stoic at a time of utter chaos and confusion.

"I'm so sorry, honey." Carol broke down crying.

Alex was at a loss for words. She pondered what could she possibly say that would comfort her partner and quell her own fears at the same time. "We're going to get through this together."

Carol lay in the dark staring at the ceiling. Alex was lying next to her. Thoughts were racing through Carol's head. AIDS. AIDS? AIDS! How could this have happened? It seemed prophetic when Carol told Alex early in their relationship that everything she touched died or simply fell apart.

Carol suddenly shot up in bed. "No, no, no!" She screamed in her head. Carol grabbed her hair by the roots and pulled her head down.

Alex sat up without saying a word and gently rubbed Carol's back.

"Ed." Carol's weak voice broke the silence of the night. Tears began racing down her face.

"Ed? What do you mean, Ed?"

All Carol could do was cry and repeat herself, "Ed."

Alex continued to rub Carol's back as she waited quietly.

"Ed – Ed died because of me," Carol finally spat out the words.

"What? No he didn't, Carol. I know you're scared and upset, but let's not blame ourselves for things where we have no control."

"No, you don't understand." Carol needed a minute to catch her breath between sobs. "Remember Mrs. Baker said he was very sick, but he wouldn't tell her what was wrong? Remember she said he killed himself because of whatever his illness was?"

"Yeah," Alex answered.

"I gave him AIDS!" Carol screamed.

Alex sat quietly for a moment trying to make sense of what Carol just said. "How is that possible? You said he was your best friend, but that you two didn't do anything."

"He tried to rape me," Carol's voice quivered.

"What? You never told me that. When did that happen?"

"He tried to rape me right after my dad died. I must have given it to him then."

Alex moved so that she and Carol were face to face. Alexandria took both of Carol's tiny hands into her own. "What happened, sweetie?"

"The day after Dad's funeral was the Baker's anniversary.

"I was so depressed I slept all day. Ed woke me up after his parents left.

"He offered me something to eat. I wasn't hungry. But he insisted that I eat because I had hardly eaten at all since Dad died. He told me I should let him do something nice for his best friend. How could I say no? I finally agreed and he heated up a frozen pizza." Carol started crying again.

Alex gently caressed Carol's hands to try to comfort her.

"When I agreed to have something to drink, he came back with two glasses of wine. I protested, but Ed said that his parents had a ton of wine. He said they'd never even know it was missing. He told me I should drink it because of all I had been through, that it would help relax me." Carol paused to take a deep breath. "Ed always protected me. He never steered me wrong before, so I figured it would be ok."

"We chugged those glasses of wine. Right away I felt light-headed, weak, and almost unable to control my body."

"In my drunken stupidity I told Ed that he was right, I needed that. Then I hugged him. He held onto me for a really long time. I

113

just thought he was being nice and I appreciated the comfort and compassion he was showing me."

"Then, he suddenly grabbed me by the shoulders, pushed me back and kissed me."

Alex listened, appalled. Carol always spoke of Ed in glowing words. This story was shocking and horrifying.

"I was so scared and confused. I didn't really do anything. I didn't fight back. I guess he took that as a sign that it was ok. So then he started groping me."

"I pushed him off of me and asked him to stop. He knew I was gay. He was the first person I ever came out to. I reminded him that I didn't like guys. He told me that was only because I hadn't been with a real man."

"And then he shoved me down onto the couch. He got on top of me and began unbuttoning my shirt." Carol stopped and looked up only to see tears beginning to roll down Alex's face. "I begged him to stop, but he wouldn't. I was able to pull my legs in towards me and slip them underneath him. I kicked him in the chest. I hit him so hard, he nearly fell off the couch. He slapped me hard, so hard that I could taste blood in my mouth."

"As I was rubbing my jaw, he pulled down his pants. With one hand, he grabbed me by the shoulder and pulled me onto the floor onto my knees."

Carol stopped to catch her breath. She never told anyone about this before. The pain was still extremely strong and vivid, even after all the years that had gone by.

Finally, she mustered up the courage to continue. "He – he grabbed me by the hair. He pulled my face right into his crotch. He ordered me to give him a blow job."

"I was scared to death. I let him put his dick in my mouth. I'm not sure what came over me, but I just bit down."

"He called me a bitch and punched me in the eye. I fell backwards. I hit my head on the hardwood floor really hard. I stayed there for a while, scared and hurting. Ed must have run upstairs to his room because by the time I sat up, he was gone."

"I was panic stricken. I didn't want his parents to know what happened. So, I ignored my throbbing head and face. I cleaned up all the dishes and put them away. I dumped out the rest of the wine, cleaned the sink and even hid the wine bottle in the garbage can. I didn't want them to have any inkling that anything had happened. Then I tried to go back to sleep on the couch."

"The next day when Mrs. Baker asked me about my black eye, I told her that Ed had woken me, and I fell and hit my face on the corner of the coffee table because I was so out of it. She bought it and it was never spoken of again."

"And you think you got Ed sick from that?" Alex gently asked.

"Well, I tasted blood when he smacked me and I bit his penis really hard right after that, so..."

"Shit," Alexandria mumbled. She realized that Carol's fears were, indeed, well founded.

Carol began sobbing again. She couldn't stop the tears. Pulling the duvet over her head, Carol cried herself to sleep in her self-made cocoon. Alex lay back down and prayed for this nightmare to be over.

Chapter Fifteen

Alex nervously picked at her hands while she waited for Dr. Luciano. This was the worst doctor's appointment she could ever imagine. She continually shook her head, still trying to understand the gravity and reality of the situation.

"Hi, Alexandria," Dr. Luciano's said softly as she entered the exam room.

Alex looked at her with a frightened expression. "Hi, Dr. L."

"Obviously, you know why you're here. I do have some questions that I need to ask, ok?"

"Ok," Alex answered nervously.

"Alex, how long have you been with Ms. Mathers?"

"Since 1997, Doc."

"Ok, you two live together?"

"Yes. We have for a couple of years now."

"And I'm assuming that you two have had sexual relations."

"Yes, doctor. We have."

"Ok. I'm also assuming that if one of you got injured, the other would help take care of any cuts, wounds, abrasions and what not."

"Yes, Dr. L."

"Alex, do you think it's safe to say that there might have been a risk of blood to blood exposure between you and Ms. Mathers?"

Alex hesitated. She knew it was true, but saying the words was more than frightening. "Uhhhh...yeah," Alex finally mumbled.

"I think there's enough of a risk here that we need to test you as well."

"Dr. Luciano, what happens if it's positive?"

"Well, Alexandria, I gave Carol the name and phone number to a wonderful infectious disease doctor here in town. He'll take good care of both of you. He follows all the latest studies. He's up on all the latest information. We've made a lot of great progress in treating this virus in the past twenty years. He's very compassionate and understanding. He'll treat you well."

"Look, Alexandria, I know this extremely frightening. I completely understand, but don't feel as if you or Carol are going to die tomorrow. With today's treatments and everything, you can still have a great quality of life. There's much more hope nowadays."

One small tear had started to make its way down Alex's cheek. "Ok."

"I'll get Debbie, the nurse, in here and we'll call you as soon as your test comes back, ok?"

Alex took a deep breath. "Ok, Doc."

Alex could hear her cell going off in her purse. Thankfully a meeting had just ended and she was back working at her desk. She reached down into her bag and grabbed it. It was Dr. Luciano's office calling. Alex answered the phone as quickly as she could.

"Hello?"

"Hello, may I speak to Ms. Whetherby?"

"Speaking."

"Ms. Whetherby, this is Tracy from Dr. Luciano's office. We got your blood results. The doctor would like to have you come in so she can go over everything with you."

"How soon can you get me in?"

"I have an opening at two this afternoon."

"I'll take it."

"Ok. We'll see you then. Thank you, Ms. Whetherby."

"It's good to see you again, Alexandria."

Alex put on a brave facade. She needed to face this demon head on. With amazing strength she said, "Dr. Luciano, just tell it to me straight. I don't want to tiptoe around the issue."

"It's positive, Alexandria. I'm sorry. We normally don't see a positive for AIDS rather than HIV happen so quickly, but we've learned that people can be re-infected with the virus repeatedly. It's an ever-evolving virus, so you can be infected with the virus repeatedly as it changes. So, my guess is that you've been infected a few times. I'm sorry, I really am."

Alex swallowed her tears, trying to remain strong and stoic. "I guess we need to see that other doctor then, huh?"

"Yes. I'll give you the name and number again, just in case Carol misplaced it."

"Thank you, doctor."

Dr. Luciano wrote down a name and phone number for Alex. "I'm really very sorry, Alexandria." She left the exam room.

Alex was only a few steps behind Dr. Luciano. She left the room and walked rapidly to the lobby where Carol waited for her. Alex walked right past Carol and out to the car.

Carol hurried to catch up with her. "Well?" She asked as she opened the car door for Alex.

Alex was completely silent. Carol stood over her for a moment with the car door still open. Alex refused to say a word. Carol walked around, got into the car and drove them back home. The silence during the ride was deafening.

As soon as the two women arrived home, Alex stormed off to the bedroom and slammed the door shut.

Carol went into the living room, sat on the couch and cried. Sugar rested her head on Carol's lap, to try to comfort her.

Hours passed by and Carol continued to weep. She had broken her promise to never hurt Alex.

"Why, God?" Carol screamed to the ceiling. "Why did you do this? Are you happy? Are you fucking happy?"

"How could you do this to me? How could you do this to her? What the hell has Alex ever done to you? She doesn't deserve this. I fucking hate you for this!"

Carol cried nonstop. Her guilt from infecting her partner was overwhelming. Sugar was curled up close to Carol on the couch trying to ease Carol's pain and anguish.

After crying for several hours, the bedroom door opened.

With red, swollen, teary eyes, Carol stood up and turned to look at Alex.

"Baby, come to bed." Alex said lovingly.

Carol slowly walked towards Alex and the bedroom. Both women went in. Alex closed the door behind them. Carol watched Alex climb back into the bed.

"Come on, get in."

Slowly, Carol crawled under the sheets, but she kept her distance from Alex.

"It's ok, sweetheart. Come here. I want you to be close to me."

Both women slowly made their way to the middle of the bed. Carol began crying hysterically again. Alex pulled her in close and held her.

"Sssshhhh. Sweetheart, it's ok. I love you."

"I love you," Carol whimpered.

"I know you didn't know. You never meant to hurt me. This is a battle that we will need to fight together, ok?"

"Mmmm hmmmm," Carol mumbled. Her voice sounded weak. She didn't want to fight anything anymore, but since Alex did, Carol decided she would battle this with the woman she loved.

"And remember, not even death can stop true love."

The two women held each other for the remainder of the night. They were silent again, but this silence brought them each peace.

Carol put on a suit she had recently bought. It was a black pants suit with silver pin stripes. She wore a white silk blouse underneath the jacket.

"Mmmmmm," Alex said looking at Carol. "Damn, you look good."

Carol couldn't help but laugh as she grabbed her briefcase. "Thanks, sweetie." She turned around to see Alex reading the paper. Alex had taken the day off just to give herself a break from all the stress and chaos. She wore a grey tank top and boxer shorts. Carol loved it when Alex wore clothes that showed off her sensuous curves. "You're looking pretty hot yourself."

Alexandria jumped up, ran over to Carol and grabbed her. She pulled her in closely, placing her hands on Carol's slender hips. "You keep looking this good and we'll never leave the bedroom." She teased.

"If you keep wearing stuff like that, I'd have to agree." Alex leaned in and pressed her warm lips on Carol's. They shared a long and very passionate kiss. Their love had not waned even in the face of severe illness.

After a few tender moments, Alex gently pulled back. Her tone and demeanor changed quickly. "So, today's the day you tell Greg?" She quietly asked Carol.

"Yeah. I have to. He has to understand the need for time for doctor appointments, recovering from sicknesses, and so on. I hate to announce something so personal, but I trust Greg."

"I know. This isn't going to be easy. Let me know how it goes, ok?"

"You know I will, sweetheart."

"Now, get your sexy ass out of here before I rip that suit right off your body."

Carol laughed outloud, "Ok, honey. I'll talk to you later. I love you."

"Love you too."

As Carol walked into the office, she looked around nervously for Greg, but couldn't find him. Will passed by.

"Hey, Will."

"Morning, Carol. What's up?"

"Have you seen Greg?"

"He's in his office."

"Great, thanks." Carol walked quickly over to Greg's office.

"Hey Greg, do you have a minute?"

"Yeah, Carol. What's going on?"

Carol walked in and gently closed the door. "Greg, I need to talk to you. It's rather personal."

"Ok?"

"Greg...when I was a kid, I was really sick. I was so sick that I actually had a blood transfusion when I was six."

Greg quietly listened, confused about the purpose of the story.

"Well, I just found out that I got AIDS as a result of that transfusion. That's why it takes me so long to get over colds and stuff."

Greg was dumbfounded. He never expected that Carol's colds were the signs of something so terrible. Finally he said, "oh dear God, I am so sorry, Carol."

"Thanks, Greg. I appreciate it. The worst part, though, is that Alex has it too.

"Greg, I'm going to need some flexibility with my schedule so we can go to doctor appointments, or have enough time to recoup if I get sick again. I'm sorry to do this to you and I hope you understand my reasoning why."

"I do, Carol. Don't worry about it." Greg reassured her. "Actually, I've been thinking about retirement a lot lately. I'm not getting any younger. I was debating whether or not to hand the company over to you or Will. Will has the experience, but you have the youth and people skills. I really couldn't decide which of you to pick."

"In a way, I think this conversation is a sign. Owning the company is a lot of work, but it would give you that freedom that you need. If you have a doctor's appointment, you can have the guys do all the work for that day. It might really be advantageous for you, Carol."

"Greg, thank you. I appreciate that, but I don't have the kind of money that this company is worth to buy you out."

"Carol, you know how some people just hand over the reigns of their companies to their kids? I don't have any kids. I don't have anyone that I can just hand this off to."

"My retirement is plentiful. Let me call my lawyer and we will just transfer ownership of the company to you."

"Greg, I'm shocked. Are you sure?"

"Absolutely."

"Thank you so much."

"No problem, kid. Do you want to tell Will and Paul what's going on?"

Carol paused to think. They needed to know about the change in ownership as well as Carol's new ever-changing schedule. She hated the idea of telling them – especially Paul – the exact reason why. Reluctantly she agreed, "Yeah, we should." Carol opened the door and called Will and Paul into Greg's office. As the two men walked in, Carol stood behind Greg's desk and Greg put his arm around her.

"Guys, Carol and I need to talk to you."

"The time for me to retire has come. The company is strong and still very profitable. I don't want to shut this operation down, but, after talking with Carol, I am going to turn the company over to her and leave you in her very capable hands."

Both Will and Paul sat silently. Paul's face clearly expressed shock and discontent.

"Carol, do you want to explain what's going on?"

"Yeah, Greg. I want you guys to fully understand this situation. First I want to be perfectly clear, this is extremely personal and I ask that we all handle this with the utmost of dignity and respect. What is said in here never leaves these four walls. Is that understood?"

Will and Paul both nodded yes.

"Ok, guys. This isn't easy for me to say. You've both seen how I've been fighting colds for weeks on end. I recently found out that I have AIDS. It's something I got from a blood transfusion I had received as a child. Alex now has it as well."

"In this position I have the flexibility that I need for doctor appointments and time off in case I get sick again, and so on."

"Nothing's going to change, really. It's still going to be the three of us. I just need you guys to understand if I don't come in or I come in late or leave early or what have you, it's because of our medical needs, ok?"

"Ok." Will replied understandingly.

Paul sat quietly.

"You ok, Paul?" Carol asked.

"Oh yeah. I just need a moment to speak with Greg."

"Ok, we'll leave it at that for now. Thanks, guys."

Carol and Will walked out of Greg's office.

"You ok?" Will asked Carol softly.

"Yeah, I guess. I mean, it's a lot for both of us to take in, but we have a good doctor. There are lots of new treatments and advancements. It's scary, I'll admit it. But we just have to fight it."

"Well, if there's one thing I know about you and Alexandria, you're both fighters. If you ladies need anything, don't ever hesitate to call Robyn and me, ok?"

"Ok, Will. Thanks."

As the two hugged, the door to Greg's office re-opened. Both Carol and Will looked back towards the office. Paul started walking out towards the front door.

"Paul, you ok, man?" Will asked.

"Oh... yeah. I just need to go home for the day."

Will and Carol looked at each other.

"Paul, I thought we were doing that system up-grade for Yokum?" Carol said.

"Yeah, well... uhhhh... you and Will can do it."

"But I have to do an exchange server for Jake's," Will protested.

Paul stood in silence, unable to give his co-worker an answer. After a few awkward moments, Paul turned and walked out of the building.

Greg stuck his head out the office door. "Will, I'll call Jake's. I think you and Carol can knock out that up-grade pretty quick and then you can go do the exchange server. That sound fair?"

"Yeah, I guess. We'll see you later, Greg."

Will and Carol walked out to Will's car in the parking lot.

"I wonder what that was all about," Carol remarked.

"His inability to deal with the fact that he has a female boss now."

"You really think so?"

"Oh yeah. Plus, knowing the ignoramus he is, he's freaked out about you being sick."

"Shit! I was afraid of that. Do you think that's going to cause problems?"

"Nah. Just let him live in his world of stupidity and ignorance. It'll be fine. It shouldn't affect his work or the company in any way. It's terrible that he's so ignorant, but that's his problem, not yours."

The two drove off together to their field service calls for the day and picking up Paul's slack. They both knew it would be another long day, but they were used to a hectic schedule.

Carol came home to find Alex sitting on the couch in a white tank top and khaki shorts watching a baseball game.

"Hey baby."

"Hey, you're still in that sexy suit," Alex said as she stood up.

"Amazing, huh? And here I was going to take it off at work and just throw it away." Carol teased. "And you, my dear, are in that tank top. You're quite the temptress!"

Alex giggled. "So, how did everything go at work?"

"You wouldn't believe it."

"What?"

"Greg is handing the company over to me."

"What?"

"Yeah. I'm now the owner of Dawson Networking."

"I told Greg what was going on, and that I'd need flexibility. He told me that while it's hard work to own a company, he said I could make my own hours and do what ever I needed for medical care."

"You're kidding?"

"No, I'm not. I can't believe it. It's mine, it's actually mine. It was amazing."

"Wow. Congratulations, sweetheart. I'm so proud of you."

"Thanks, baby."

"Now, we have even more of a reason to celebrate. More than just your sexy suit."

They both laughed as they hugged. Alex was so proud of Carol. Carol was relieved to be in Alex's arms. It was an amazing moment for each of them.

"I never would have imagined this," Carol said as they continued to embrace. "Maybe this suit brings me good luck, Carol laughed.

"I knew that suit was good." Alex chuckled. "It looks amazing on you, baby."

"Thanks, sweetheart."

"But I think it would look even better on the floor next to the bed," Alex quipped.

Carol burst out laughing. Alex was always able to make Carol laugh.

"Oh come on, let me give you a congratulatory massage," Alex pleaded. She wanted to pamper her woman. This was a special day and Carol deserved to be treated well.

"Oh you are such atemptress. I know what that really means," Carol teased.

Alex gently grabbed Carol's hand and led her into the bedroom.

Carol sat on the bed, Alex came up behind her and began gently massaging Carol's shoulders. Her hands rubbed and kneaded Carol's muscles, relaxing her instantly.

After a few minutes of massage, Alex's hands began to wander and sensuously followed Carol's delicate curves through the suit.

Carol stood up and turned around. Slowly, warmly, passionately, the two women kissed. Carol pulled Alex in closer to her. Feeling her heat, feeling the softness of her skin was absolute bliss for Carol.

Alex began unbuttoning the sexy suit and it easilydropped to the floor. Carol lifted the grey tank top over Alex's head. Alex let the boxers slide off right where she was on the bed.

Imperfect

The two women touched, tasted, and explored each other's body. With affection and gentleness, they explored new heights of ecstasy and love.

They continued to celebrate the good news, and each other, in pure pleasure. They thrilled each other constantly and shared beautiful moments of love and intimacy.

Chapter Sixteen

It was a warm, sunny late Saturday morning. The humidity was up, but the heat hadn't really hit yet so it was still a comfortable temperature for Carol and Alex to walk Sugar through the neighborhood.

They took in the grandeur of all the lush, full, green trees; houses with bright flowers lining their walkways and the golden sun smiling down on them. It was a magnificent day.

"It is so nice not working on a Saturday for a change," Carol said to Alex. "I am digging this whole 'boss' thing."

The two women laughed feeling completely light-hearted and happy. A neighbor passed them from the other side of the street. He waved to the ladies.

"Hi," Alexandria waved back.

The two walked in quiet bliss and Sugar happily panted.

"Hey, look at that," Alex pointed to an entry way covered in ivy. It was classic and exquisite. The two women stopped to admire the pretty house.

"That's really nice. I like that."

"Do you think we could do that with the house?"

"I'm sure we could, but I thought ivy took a while to grow like that." Carol responded.

"I don't know. I don't have a green thumb, but that sure looks nice. I'd love to have our front entrance look like that," Alex said hopefully.

"Why don't we start with hanging plants on each side? You know, the type that cascade down. Those are really nice and it would at least be a start until we figure out whether or not we can do the ivy."

"That's not a bad idea, Carol. I like that. We should do that."

"Want to go to the nursery tomorrow?" Carol asked.

"Yeah, let's."

The two women squeezed each other's hands and then continued on their walk. They were serenaded by birds as they reached the end of the street.

"Time to turn back, sweetie." Carol said to Sugar, petting her soft head. The couple and their dog turned around and walked back up Sparrow Lane towards their own home.

"Byron and Candace are coming over tomorrow night?" Carol asked Alex.

"Yeah. You ready to tell them?" Alex slowed her pace and turned to see the nervousness in Carol's face.

"As ready as you are. This is not going to be easy."

"I know. But we have to." Though Alex was firm in telling her siblings about the situation, there was a hesitancy in her voice.

"Oh, I know we have to. And I wouldn't want to lie or hide anything from your brother and sister. I just wish it was good news we were telling them. Not this."

"I know, sweetheart. We'll get through it. We're a family. We'll all get through this together."

A woman walked past them, narrowly squeezing by on the side walk.

"Hi," Carol and Alex greeted her.

"Hi." She smiled back and continued walking away from the pair.

Carol, Alex and Sugar all continued to enjoy the warmth of the summer. Before they knew it, they arrived back home.

"What's this?" Alex asked as she slowly peeled off a piece of paper taped on to their front door.

"I don't know." Carol opened the door.

Sugar ran in to drink from the water bowl. Carol closed the door just as Alex was opening the paper. Alex gasped.

"What does it say, sweetie?" Unable to speak, Alex handed the paper over to Carol. Carol couldn't believe her eyes. It was a note made of letters cut from magazines and newspapers. It read, "Get out of our neighborhood, dykes!"

"What the hell?" Alex mumbled under her breath.

"We've been living here for six months. I don't get it. We don't bother any one here. We're quiet, we're friendly, and we keep to ourselves. Why would someone do this?"

"I don't know, but I don't like this. We're going to have to be careful, Carol. I'm going to talk to Lisa tomorrow to see if there's anything we can do."

"I think we should get sensor lights and an alarm system, too, Alex. We have to be careful."

Alex sighed heavily. "This is so sad. We're good people. We live good, normal, quiet lives. Why the hell can't people just leave us alone?"

"I don't know, sweetheart. But you talk to Lisa tomorrow and we'll start being more careful. We'll do whatever it is we need to do to protect ourselves."

"Look at this, B." Alexandria said as she handed Byron the paper that had been taped to the door the day before.

"Wow. That's harsh. Have you had any problems with any of your neighbors? Any indications that someone wasn't happy when you two moved in?"

"No, Byron. That's just it. No one has said a word to Alex or me. Everything's fine. We've been here for six months and this is the first time we've had any problems." Carol explained.

"Anyone new move in since you've been here?"

Carol and Alex looked at each other.

"No. Not that we can think of." Alex answered.

"Look, Byron, I want us to get those motion detector lights and I think we should get an alarm system as well. Would you be able to help us with that?" Carol asked.

"I can do those lights no problem and I know a guy who does alarm systems. I'll give him a call tomorrow and see how soon he can get here."

"That would be great. Thanks, B. It's so nice having a brother who's a contractor," Alex said.

Carol brought out the dinner plates for everyone. The family began to enjoy the pot roast and mixed vegetables.

Alex looked at Carol with the obvious question in her eyes. Carol took in a deep breath and hesitantly nodded.

"Ok. B, C, Carol and I need to talk to you."

"What's up, Alexandria?" Candace asked.

With a sad and heavy sigh Alex continued. "This isn't easy. I'm not even sure how to say this."

"Let me explain the background," Carol said. "You see, I was a really sick kid. I was born prematurely and was severely anemic as a result. It was something I never really got over. So, I ended up getting a blood transfusion when I was six."

"Ok?" Byron asked confusedly.

"Byron, it was before they began regularly screening blood donors." Carol said as strongly as she could.

"What are you saying, Carol?" There was suddenly a fierce tone to Byron's voice.

"B," Alexandria jumped in. "Carol's transfusion made her sick – it made us both sick."

"Sick?" Candace asked, confused by what her sister was trying to say.

"Alex, sweetheart, let's just give it to them straight. Byron, Candace, the blood I received was tainted. I developed AIDS from it – we both have AIDS."

"What?" Byron barked.

"B, I'm sorry. It's true. Carol's transfusion got her sick. Somewhere along the way, I got it as well." Alex tried to comfort her brother.

"A, you have AIDS?" Candace asked. "How is that possible?"

"We've been living together for years. I've been exposed to it several times."

"You have AIDS? You have fucking AIDS? This is un-fucking-believable!" Byron shouted.

"Byron, I'm sorry. This is the last thing that either one of us would ever want to have to tell you. It's horrible, we know. Trust me, this hurts us as much as it hurts you." Carol said.

"You have no right to talk. You promised me you'd never hurt my sister and yet now you're killing her. You fucking bitch!" Byron slammed his hand down on the table.

"Byron, please, I never meant to hurt Alex. I love her so much. It was worse for me to find out that she has it than it was when I found out I was sick. My intention was never, ever to hurt her. She's my everything. The last thing I ever wanted was to hurt Alex or get her sick. It's horrific, I know. If there was any way I could take this back, I would. And she knows that. She and I have decided to fight this together: as a couple.

"There have been a ton of discoveries, new treatments and information, and so on. There's lots of hope for us to still live normal lives."

Candace was hysterically crying. Alex, sitting next to her, hugged her sister and tried to comfort her quietly.

"You're a liar. You promised me that you'd never hurt Alexandria." Byron shouted again.

"B, please." Alex said.

"What? How the hell can you defend her?"

"B, she had no clue she was sick. She only just found out. When her test came back positive, they tested me because of my exposure risk. We only both just found out. Carol had no bad intentions here."

"Byron, I swear. I didn't know. If I had known, I would never have put Alexandria at risk. I love her.

"Look, this is the worst news any of us ever could have gotten. But, we're a family. We need to stick together as a family. We can all get through this together." Carol pleaded her case.

Byron got up and walked away from the table. Looking away from everyone else he said, "A, after all you've been through. After finally getting your life straight, this is the shit you want to subject yourself to?"

Alex got up and walked behind her brother. She gently placed a hand on his large, broad shoulder. "B, yes, I've been through a lot. I made a lot of bad decisions in my life. But being here and staying with Carol isn't one of them. I have this house because of her. I have so much happiness and joy because of her."

"And you have fucking AIDS because of her," Byron coldly interrupted his sister.

"In sickness and in health, B. We're in this for the long haul. I know this is hard. I'm not expecting you to jump up and down with joy. We both just want you to know the situation and we want your understanding."

Carol got up and walked over to Candace and just hugged her. "I'm sorry, sweetie. I love you and your sister. I'm sorry this hurt you." She whispered in the young girl's ear.

Byron turned around and saw Alex crying. Unable to speak, he embraced his twin.

"I'm sorry," Alex whispered.

"I'm sorry, A. I just want the best for you. I'm scared for you. I love you."

"B, we're scared. But we to stay together as a family and fight this thing in unity, ok?"

"Ok, sis. But I'm not happy about it."

"How are you two holding up," Dave asked.

"As well as can be imagined, I guess," Alex said.

Upon hearing the news that their friends were very sick, Dave and John decided to have them over for dinner.

"It's a lot to take in," Carol agreed.

"I can imagine." John replied.

The foursome sat in an uncomfortable silence for a moment. Dave and John were at a loss for words considering the severity of the situation.

"So, your family didn't take it well, Alexandria?" Dave finally broke the quietness.

"Dave, what would you expect? It's not good news." Alex said as she shrugged her shoulders.

"I know, but was it really that bad?" He asked as his voice continued to climb to a higher pitch.

"They've been happier." Carol said as she tried to make light of the situation.

"Byron took it the hardest. He's angry with Carol. He feels as though she intentionally put me at risk."

"But you didn't even know, did you Carol?" John asked.

"No, that's just it. We found out at the same time."

"It sounds like he just needs some time to absorb what's going on. It's overwhelming. Imagine what he's going through. He has to accept that his twin sister is dying. That's not easy." John said. His words rang true for both Alex and Carol.

"You're right," Alex agreed.

"We know of a really good support group here in town if you ladies are interested." Dave offered what little help he could give to them.

"Thanks," Alex replied. "Give us the information and we'll look into it."

"If there is anything that either of us can do for you, just say the word," John said.

"Thanks. We'll remember that," Carol smiled. "We appreciate that. It means a lot to us. Thank you."

"So, what did Lisa say?" Byron asked from the top of a ladder as he installed the motion detector lights for Alex.

"Well, there's not much we can do. We can file a police report if we want to. But since we have no idea who did it and they didn't cause any property damage, we're kind of screwed. The police report would just go on file. That's not going to do much at all." Alex answered.

"That really sucks, Sis. I'm sorry. I wish there was something you could you do. You don't deserve to be treated like that."

"I just don't get it, B. It's not like we're loud or annoying or nosy. We don't bother anyone. And no one has said anything to our faces."

"Not to your face. For all you know, Carol's hiding something."

"Dammit, B, stop this shit. Carol doesn't hide anything from me"

"She hid that she has AIDS from you."

"Byron Whetherby, so help me God, I will knock you right off that ladder. Stop it. Carol didn't know. She told me the day she found out. I was tested right after that."

"Do you have any idea how hard this is on her? First her father dies and her mom blames her for that. Now she's dying and her mother tells her she deserves it. B, Carol feels guilty about so much. She is beating herself up night and day over giving this to me. It's killing her that I'm sick too. She never meant to harm me."

"How do you know, A?"

"How do I know? How can you ask that? I've been with her for how many years? B, she is the most gentle, caring soul I know. Trust me on this. She wouldn't hurt a fly."

"But she hurt my sister."

"Unintentionally. Please, you have got to let this go. I know you're angry. It's not her fault. For whatever reason, this is our life. We just have to accept it."

"I don't think I'm ready to accept it."

Alex took a deep breath to calm herself. "I can understand that. It takes time, it really does. But I am begging you, please forgive Carol. She's a damn good woman, B. She really is."

"We'll see." There was a lot of doubt in Byron's voice.

Cautiously, Byron stepped down from the ladder. He walked around the ladder and into the vicinity of the lights. The bright flood lights light up the entire entrance way to the house. "Well, your new lights are working, Sis." He said matter-of-factly.

Time passed quickly for Alex and Carol. Yet another Thanksgiving had arrived. Despite Byron's pain and anger, they were both welcomed for the family's annual tradition.

After the table was splendidly set with an seeming endless bounty of food, the four began their prayers.

"Dear Lord," Byron started. "Thank you for another wonderful Thanksgiving. Thank you for giving us yet another opportunity to come together as a family. Thank you for all of this food and the blessings. Thank you for bringing Candace safely back to us from college for this most special of holidays."

"Lord," Alexandria spoke. "I thank you for all the blessings you have bestowed upon this family. Thank you for bringing us all together once again. Thank you for giving Byron a heart of love and understanding and welcoming both Carol and me back into the house. Thank you for Candace being able to return home and for her pursuing her dreams at college. Thank you for Carol who continues to bring light into my world. Thank you for all the advancements and treatments available for AIDS. I trust in you to keep us healthy and well taken care of. Thank you for everything."

Carol prayed next. "God, thank you for this wonderful family. I understand that as family, they have faced many trials and tribulations. I thank you for my welcome into this house and into this family. Thank you for Byron, who continues to be the glue that keeps us together and the rock on which we all stand. Thank you for Candace who is so bright and intelligent. Thank you for Alex, who I will love until the end of time. Thank you for all of our doctors and treatments. Thank you for giving us such wonderful lives."

Candace concluded the prayers for the group. "Lord, I thank you for my family. My amazing brother, Byron. My strong sister, Alexandria. And my sweet sister-in-law, Carol. Thank you for giving me the opportunity to go to college and for me to find my calling as a social worker. May you use me to help people who have fought battles like my sister and Carol have fought. Thank you so much for the opportunity."

In unison, all four said, "Amen."

Alex turned to her sister. "Social work, C? You never told us you wanted to do social work."

"Yeah. I declared my major already. I did a lot of thinking after you and Carol told us about your sickness. Something inside me told me it was happening for some reason. One Sunday at the school chapel, I got this feeling like you were going through this so that I could help other people. I kind of felt like I should make something good out of something bad."

"That is amazing, Candace." Carol said. "I am so impressed. You're an amazing young woman. I'm really proud of you."

"Me, too." Alex declared.

"That's my sister." Byron said beaming with pride.

For a moment, the stiffness and tension between Byron and Carol seemed to have passed. The family continued to enjoy the feast and warm, friendly conversation without a dark cloud hanging over everyone's heads.

Following the family tradition, the group packed up the food and drove over to the nursing facility to visit Mary.

As they entered the facility, Erin was there to greet them as usual. They all smiled and wished her a happy Thanksgiving. As they walked by, Erin handed a small, neatly folded piece of paper to Byron. She blushed a bit when he smiled and thanked her for it.

"Hi everyone," the nurse greeted them as they entered Mary's room. "Your mom just took her medications. She's not feeling very well today."

"You ok, mom?" Alex asked.

"I'm ok, she's making a big deal out of nothing." Mary insisted.

"Her appetite's been a little weak for the past few days," the nurse replied.

"Ok, I'll make you a small plate then." Byron said.

As usual, Candace instantly got to work making plates for other patients and handing them out.

Mary turned her head towards Carol. "Well, well, Miss Carol. You're here again. You come every year. You are so sweet." Mary grasped Carol's hand with her own small, frail hand.

"Thank you, Ms. Whetherby." Carol gently replied. "I just love seeing you every year. You have a beautiful family."

"Thank you," Mary choked on some mashed potatoes. The nurse quickly gave her some water to drink. "Thank you." Mary said weakly. "That's really all I can eat for now."

The kids looked at their mother's plate. She had eaten little of the wonderfully made dinner.

"I'll save the rest in case you get hungry later." The nurse said and then left the room.

"Oooh, I am getting tired," Mary said.

"Ok, Mom. We'll let you rest. It's good to see you again. I love you." Byron said quietly.

"I love you too, Byron."

"Bye, Mommy. Happy thanksgiving." Candace said brightly as she kissed her mother on the cheek.

"Goodbye, my beautiful Candace."

"Bye Mom. Get some rest."

"Bye, Alexandria. I love you."

"I love you too." Alex replied adoringly.

"Good bye, Ms. Whetherby. It was wonderful to see you as always."

"You too Carol. You're a good friend to my Alexandria. Thank you for visiting again."

Carol hugged the small, elderly woman. She felt thinner and weaker in Carol's arms than she had in the past. Carol showed her love by gently rubbing Mary's back as they embraced.

Chapter Seventeen

Carol slowly pulled into the driveway. The roads and driveway were slick from the January ice. As she pulled up, she saw something on the door. She assumed it was a package notice from the postal service.

Carol pulled the GTO into the garage and entered the comfort of the warm house. Sugar greeted her at the door.

"Hey baby," Carol pleasantly said to the dog as she entered. She couldn't pass Sugar with out petting her for a few minutes. Carol's affection for their sweet dog grew by the day.

Carol walked through the house to the kitchen to open the front door and see what the little note said. As she opened the door, Carol was hit with a blast of bitter coldness. There was a small, tightly folded piece of paper taped to the door. Carol's heart skipped a beat. She prayed it wasn't what she assumed. She quickly removed the paper and closed the door.

With great apprehension, Carol unfolded the paper. It was another hate note with the letters cut out from magazines and newspapers again. This letter, though, was even angrier than the first. "It's a new year, get a new fucking house! You're not wanted here, dyke bitches!"

Carol couldn't believe what her eyes were reading. Who could have such hatred for the couple? They had been nothing but cordial and considerate to everyone they met in the neighborhood. Carol started to feel nauseas. The sudden feeling became too overwhelming for her. Carol left the note on the counter and ran into the bathroom to vomit.

As Carol was washing up, she heard Alex come in.

"Hey Sug-sug." Alex greeted their dog. "Honey? Where are you?"

"In the bathroom, babe." Carol did her best to call back. Alex walked in as Carol was drying her face with the towel.

"Honey, you ok?"

Unable to answer, Carol just looked back at Alexandria.

"What's wrong, Carol?" Alex asked with concern.

Carol sighed. "We got another note."

"What?"

"Like that first note taped to do the door. I found another one when I came home. It's nastier. I got so upset, I puked." Carol explained.

"Shit. Are you ok?"

"Yeah, sweetie. I'm fine. Just shaken up."

"That's understandable. Did you save the note?"

"Yeah, it's on the counter in the kitchen."

"Ok, I'm going to bring that one and the original into work tomorrow. Maybe Lisa will know of something else we can do."

"You want to file a police report?" Carol asked.

"I don't know. You think it would do us any good?"

"Probably not, Alex. What are they going to do? It's not like there's an obvious 'bad guy' they can go after."

"Maybe we should just get out of here," Alex said unhappily.

"No! There's no way in hell, Alex. You wanted this house. You deserve to own it just as much as any one else. I refuse to let these bigots win."

Another special Valentine's Day arrived. Carol took off early to cook a special dinner for Alex. Carol rarely cooked, so she thought her girlfriend would appreciate the gesture.

The alarm system had been installed just two weeks prior and both women were still adjusting to the new system. They pretty much mastered it. They had it on during the day, but felt safe enough when they were at home not to arm the alarm.

Carol placed the honey baked ham in the middle of the dining table. A small dish filled with peas and corn sat next to the large platter holding the ham. A bottle of sparkling cider sat in an ice bucket, and two candles glowed romantically.

Alex's timing was impeccable. She walked in just as Carol finished making the table look perfect.

"Wow, Carol. This is beautiful!"

"Happy Valentine's day, sweetheart."

Alexandria threw her arms around Carol. This was such a wonderful sight to come home to. "Thank you so much, baby."

Carol smiled back at her partner. "Sit, enjoy."

The two women sat down and to enjoy Carol's surprisingly well made dinner.

"I can't believe we've been together four years."

"I know. Where has the time gone? I can't believe it's 2001 already. I love you as much today as the first time I saw you in City Girls," said Carol.

"Awe, thank you. I love you too, baby." Alex's voice was still so sweet and smooth. It was music to Carol's ears.

The two continued to enjoy the well-prepared meal. Sugar rested quietly on the couch. Everything was peaceful and romantic. It was the perfect evening.

Suddenly, there was a large crash and glass breaking all around them. Both women ducked and raised their arms over their heads to protect themselves. Sugar ran and hid in the kitchen. Once everything was quiet again, they slowly uncurled to see what had happened.

As they looked around, both women saw that a large rock had been thrown through one of the windows in the living room. The window had shattered and there was glass all over the living room. The biting, cold February air came flooding in through the opening. Carol and Alex looked at each other, each with their heart still racing.

"You ok?" Alex asked, she was out of breath.

"Yeah. You?" Carol was also breathing heavily. "We need to call the cops, Alex. Why don't you call them? I want to go clean up the glass. I don't want Sugar or us to get hurt."

"Ok." Alex ran and grabbed her cell phone and dialed 911. She spoke into the phone, "Hello? Yes. My name is Alexandria Whetherby. I live at 581 Sparrow Lane. We were just having dinner and someone threw a rock through one of our windows."

"Is anyone hurt there, miss?" The dispatcher was a woman with a very kind and soothing voice.

"No. Neither of us is hurt. We're ok."

The operator asked Alex if they had seen who threw the rock.

"No, we didn't see anyone. We ducked because glass was flying everywhere. But we also received two hate letters recently. We still have those for the officers to look at."

Imperfect

"Have you touched the rock, or moved anything from the scene?"

"No. My partner is sweeping up the glass, though."

"Save the glass. The investigating officers may need to look at it."

"Save the glass? Ok." Alex put her hand over the mouth piece of the phone. "Save the glass, honey. The police need to look at it."

"Save the glass? Uhhh... ok."

Alex went back to the conversation with the 911 dispatcher. "Ok, I'm sorry about that. Is there anything else we should or should not do until the police get here?"

"No. Just bring out those hate letters and let the police do their job."

"Ok, thank you."

Carol continued to sweep up all the tiny shards of glass. "Can you get me a plastic bag to dump all this in, Alex?"

"Yeah." Alex ran to a cabinet, and grabbed an empty shopping bag. "Here, honey."

"Thanks. Are the cops en route?"

"Yeah. They'll be here soon."

Carol stayed close to the floor and swept up an infinite number of glass pieces.

Finally, the police knocked on the door, Alex ran to open it. Two tall, white, plain looking men in police uniforms stood in front of her. Neither man seemed the slightest bit warm or sympathetic.

"Come on in, officers. I'm Alexandra Whetherby." Alex let them into the house. "It's all right over here." Alex led them to where Carol still knelt with the dust pan and broom. "This is Carol Mathers."

Carol shyly looked up at the two men. "Hello, officers. I'm just cleaning up the glass so no one gets hurt. The... rock is right behind me if you want to look."

The uniformed men walked past her and picked up the rock.

"This is pretty sizable," one mumbled to the other.

"Yeah, they meant business."

The first turned back around to Alex. "You were both eating dinner?"

"Yes, sir." Alex responded.

"And you own this house, Miss Whetherby?"

140

"Yes."

"This is a predominantly white neighborhood."

"So?"

"Well, it's just not always in a person's best interest to live where they're not with their own kind."

Alex glared at the cop. How dare he make such a racist comment.

"Miss Mathers resides here also?"

"She's my partner. We're a couple."

The police officer sneered. "I see. Neither of you saw anything?"

"No, sir. We were just enjoying a quiet Valentine's dinner, and the rock came crashing in. We ducked, we had no idea what was going on. We both had our eyes closed for several minutes."

The two officers looked at each other.

"You said you have hate letters?" The second officer asked.

"Yes, officer. Right here," Alex handed over the two papers.

The officers looked over the two notes and the rock. Carol finished sweeping up all of the shards of glass. She stood up and walked over to the officers.

"Well, I think it's safe to say that these notes are from the same person who threw the rock into your window." The second officer stated the obvious.

"The dispatcher told us that you might want to look at the glass." Carol humbly offered the plastic bag filled with the glass pieces. "Maybe it will help."

"No," the first officer completely dismissed Carol.

"Well ladies, we'll file an incident report. But there's really nothing more we can do."

"What?" Alex walked right up to the officers. She was furious.

"We'll fill out a full report, including your statements. But since you didn't see anyone, there's nothing more we can do."

"Wait a minute," Alex snapped back. "You didn't really take full statements from either one of us. Why don't you check the glass or rock for finger prints? What about asking the neighbors if any of them saw anything?"

"In this weather," the second officer started. "No one would go without gloves. It's way too cold. So, it's really not worth the effort. We're not going to come up with anything. And since it's so dark out, I doubt anyone saw anything. You've told us enough for statements... our job here is done."

"But you didn't do much of anything. Look, I work for two of the best lawyers in town..."

"That's great for you. Sorry we couldn't be any more help, ladies. You have a good evening." The first police officer answered back. The two police men then left.

"They didn't leave us a card to call them – nothing! This is insane. This is not normal protocol." Alex's anger was rising by the moment.

"Bring everything into work tomorrow, sweetheart. Maybe Lisa can help – I hope."

"This is ridiculous." Alex's fury was so great that she didn't hear a word Carol said.

"I totally agree with everything you said, Alex. We were treated very unfairly. We're an inter-racial lesbian couple in the Midwest. We're not exactly everyone's idea of the perfect family in this town. I hate to say it, but we really shouldn't be surprised by this prejudice. It's not right; I'm not trying to justify anything that happened here tonight. The reality is, though, people like us just aren't well liked."

"This is such bullshit." Alex began to cry. Carol walked over to her and just held her.

This was a Valentine's night they'd never forget, but not for the right reasons.

"Hey, B." Alex said into her phone.

"It's a good thing you called, Sis."

"Is it now? And why might that be?"

"Mom's not doing well, A."

"What? What happened?"

"Remember at Thanksgiving how her appetite was crappy?"

"Yeah."

"She's been eating less and less. They're transferring her to the hospital today. They're going to put in a feeding tube."

"Are you kidding me? Shit! When it rains it pours." Her voice indicated just how overwhelmed she was by all that was occurring in her life.

"Why? What's going on, Sis?"

"Carol and I had received another hate letter a few weeks ago. Then last night someone threw a rock through our window. The cops came and they didn't do anything. They totally dismissed us like we weren't people; like this wasn't a legitimate case.

"I was calling to let you know what happened. And to see if you could put in a new window and get the alarm guy to hook it up as well."

"Shit, A. What the hell is going on over there?"

"I don't know, B. And now you're telling me about mom..."

"Yeah. I mean, she'll be ok for a little while. Candace is flying in for the weekend. We were going to offer for you and Carol to join us to visit mom at the hospital over the weekend."

"We're there. There's no two ways about it.

"How quickly can you get here to fix the window?"

"Let me come over now. I know it's early, but I have to put up dry wall starting at ten. This way, I can get all the measurements and put in the order for the window. I have a friend who's a glazier. He might be able to put a rush on the order.

"Regardless, we'll have that window installed and alarmed by the time the weekend rolls around. We can't screw around with this.

"I'm really worried about you and Carol. Have you considered moving?"

"Yeah, I mentioned it. But Carol was insistent that we stay because I had wanted the house so much. Plus, she feels that we have every right to live wherever we want."

"She's right about that, but I'm just worried about your safety."

"As are we. I guess we'll have to keep the alarm on all the time now. It'll just be set to 'away' while we're home so we don't set off the sensors."

"A, that's no way to live."

"It will work for now. We'll figure something out."

"Ok, just be careful. Now, just give me a few and I'll come over and look at your window. We'll get you all hooked up."

"Thanks, B. I really appreciate it."

Candace, Byron, Carol and Alex stood around Mary's bed as she lay sleeping. She had an IV line dripping fluids into her small veins. The feeding tube came out of her abdomen, but was covered by the hospital blankets. An EKG consistently beeped. The room was dark, but a small pool of light came through the window. Mary appeared peaceful, but the sight was horrific for her children.

Alex quietly cried. Byron pulled her close to him. Candace just stared, trying to soak in every detail of the vision before her. Carol sighed, wondering if this was what her father looked like in the hospital before he passed away. The four children remained silent, tears escaping everyone's eyes. Hours passed as quickly as seconds while Mary continued to rest.

The small pool of light finally faded away. A nurse walked in and told the kids that visiting hours were over. Slowly, quietly, and tearfully the children left their mother resting.

"You know I never went to school, right?"

Carol looked at Will confused. "What?"

"Yeah, seriously. I never went to college. I never studied computers the way you did or anything. Experience is really the best teacher.

"I got into computers at a young age. I was the right age at the right time. Computers and technology were just starting to boom. I could play with them and I watched computers go from room-sized monstrosities to the laptops and cell phones and things we have today."

Carol turned her gaze back to the server they were working on. "Wow. You've really seen it all change. I just remember being a kid when a Commodore 64 was the coolest shit." Carol laughed at the simplicity of the Commodore 64 machine.

Will laughed. "Oh yeah, I remember those. Remember how we had to put in all the command prompts?"

"Oh yeah." The two laughed happily.

"I was there, man. I was a part of that whole revolution. The Osborne I, the Apple I, Apple II, the Lisa. Real progress.

"Greg hired me because like him, I had so many years of experience."

"That is so cool," Carol said as she replaced a board with a new one. "I'm really glad he did. You're a good friend and the best damn tech I've ever seen."

"Thanks, Carol. That means a lot to me. Speaking of good techs, my personal mail exchange server suddenly crapped out this morning. I have it in my trunk. Would you mind taking a look at it?"

"Yeah, sure. Have you checked all your connections to make sure it wasn't one of your cables? You know how cable problems can mimic equipment failure."

"Oh Yeah. But no, I didn't test for it. I don't have a neat little tester like you have. That's why I'm asking. I'm hoping it's just a cable, but you know how these machines are."

"Yeah, no kidding. But sure, that won't be a problem. Just remind me and I'll take it home with me tonight."

"Thanks."

Later that night, Carol hooked her cable tester to Will's mail server. One of the cables wasn't reading right.

"Hmmmmm," Carol said to herself. She got up and got one of her own cables. She attached her cable to the machine and replaced Will's original cable. One tester was attached to the front of the server, one to an end of Carol's cable. Carol patiently waited. Suddenly both testers lit up in unison. Each tester had four lights which were numbered one through four. Thankfully each light lit up 1-2-3-4. Perfect. Will only needed a new cable.

Carol picked up her phone to call Will. "Hey Will, it's Carol."

"Hi. So, what does it look like?"

"Just a cable, my friend. My cable is new, so you can keep it. I'll bring it all in for you tomorrow."

"Great, thanks." Will continued to ramble on, but Alex appeared in the doorway of Carol's office. She looked distraught.

"Will, I hate to cut you off, but I've got to go." Carol said and then hung up.

Carol drove in silence. Mary, who was once so vibrant and happy despite her condition, was gone. Carol knew the pain that weighed heavily on Alex's heart. She thought it was best to just let Alex sort through all of her emotions as they drove to the church for the memorial service.

There was the small, older church. They pulled in to the almost full parking lot. The memorial service wasn't set to start for another forty five minutes.

Alexandria went around the car, took Carol by the hand and led her into the church.

The stained glass windows let the sun shine brightly into the small sanctuary. There was frayed and faded red carpeting in the aisle. The pews were old wooden structures that had clearly seen better days. It was a small Gospel church. There was a feeling of warmth and familiarity, but Carol stood out like a sore thumb due to her fair skin.

Carol and Alex walked up to the front pew. Carol sat next to Erin, from the nursing facility.

"Hi, Erin." Alexandria greeted her with a large hug.

"Hi Alex. I am so sorry for your loss."

"Thank you. It was sweet of you to come..."

"Byron let me know about your mother and I thought I should pay my respects. She was a very special woman."

"Yes, she was. It's good to see you."

"Good to see you too."

Alex turned to Carol. "I have to go in the back, sweetie. I'll see you later."

"Ok, babe. I love you," Carol said gently squeezing Alex's hand.

Alex turned and headed to the back.

Carol turned to Erin. Erin's shiny jet black hair was down and gently swaying just below her shoulders instead of pulled into the ponytail that Carol was used to seeing. Instead of her usual scrubs, Erin was wearing a black dress that sat nicely on her tiny frame. Her Asian pale skin contrasted sharply against her black hair. There was a to Erin that Carol had not noticed before.

She was also a welcome sight to Carol. They were the only non- African descent in the building.

"It was really nice of you to come." Carol said. "I'm sure it means a lot to Byron."

"It seemed to, when we spoke. I'm happy to be here for him. Mary had been with us at the facility for so long. Sometimes patients become like family to us too. We see them every day. It's hard for us to say good bye as well."

"I'm sure. This affects all of us. Alexandria is putting up a good front, but I know how hard this is." Carol whispered back.

The church's pastor walked up to the pulpit. "We are all here to celebrate the amazing life of Mary Whetherby.

"Mary was a splendid soul. She was a strong woman. She was dedicated to her children. She was loved and loving. She welcomed us all into her home. Mary was totally selfless and generous.

146

"I find it fitting that she is named Mary. Named after Mary, the mother of God. The same name as Mary of Magdalene, a woman who had seven demons cast out. Two women who struggled significantly, but followed the Lord with all their hearts. Our Mary was no different. Her circumstances caused her to go on the street, but her heart was pure and fully devoted to God. She knew that her sins were forgiven. She was truly a beloved child of God."

There were random shouts of "Amen" and "Hallelujah" from the congregation. Carol tried not to be conspicuous as she looked around. She thought it was very strange that the parishioners would interrupt the pastor.

"Mary had three amazing children: Alexandria, Byron, and Candace. They are here and they want to share their love and memories of their mother. First let us all honor the life of Mary Whetherby with a prayer."

"Dear Heavenly Father, we thank you for the opportunity to celebrate the life of Mary Whetherby today. Thank you so much for blessing each and every one of us with her presence in our lives.

"Lord, we will miss her. Now we send her into your open arms. Embrace her. Love her. You are the great healer. Take away her pain and her sins. May she join with the angels and sing your praises. Make sure she has a good spot in heaven. She deserves it."

"Lord, I ask for your blessings upon Alexandria, Byron and Candace as they come and share their mother's life and love with us. You know the pain they carry in their hearts. Take that pain away. Let us all remember the good times, the positive things; let us celebrate the life of Mary, not mourn it."

"Thank you for all your blessings you have bestowed upon this family and this church. In your name we pray. Amen."

Everyone in the congregation shouted, "Amen!"

Candace went up to the pulpit. "My mother," she heavily sighed. "My mother was an amazing woman. My mother was strong. My mother was caring. My mother was joyous. My mother was an angel. My mother will always be in my heart."

"My mother was not given an easy life, but she always remained positive. She had a poor childhood and no formal education. She was left by her husband because she carried his children. She walked the streets for us. My mother would have done anything for us, her children. And she did. My mother was the most selfless, giving person I have ever met."

"Despite all of her hardships, my mother emphasized the importance of education to all three of us. My mother taught us

147

about unconditional love. She showed us how to be disciplined. She taught us about God's love and the love of family. My mother was called a prostitute, yes, but she was also a hero. My mother gave us so much of herself. She wanted the best for her children, and she gave each of us the best. She gave us her life and her love. We are so blessed to call her mother, friend and role model."

An older woman in the congregation shouted, "Amen!"

Carol turned to Erin and whispered, "I feel so out of place. I've never been to a church like this before."

"Neither have I. I was raised Buddhist."

Candace continued. "My mother did what she needed to do to provide for the family. Like Reverend Luther said, my mother's heart was fully devoted to the Lord. My mom knew that God understood. Our God is not a God of anger or hatred. He is a God of forgiveness. He forgave my mother and she now resides in heaven with him."

There were more shouts of hallelujah, praise God and Amen from the congregation.

"Death is sad. We all mourn the fact that my mother is gone. She enriched our lives so much. We will all undoubtedly miss her, but today I celebrate. Her pain is gone. Her disfigurement is gone. My mom is whole, healed and complete in heaven. Today is not a day to cry. It is a day to rejoice. My mother's pain and suffering is finally gone. The Lord is good and he has welcomed my mother with open arms. Hallelujah!" Candace finished.

"Thank you so much for sharing that with us, Candace. We are all blessed by your words and your presence today," the Reverend said. "Now as we all know, Mary loved the classic Gospel hymns. Byron and Alexandria have decided to share Mary's favorite hymn with us today. This song will always be sung in honor of their beloved mother."

Alex and Byron came out in Gospel gowns, followed by a large Gospel choir, also in full garb.

The organist started the introduction to a familiar song. Byron and Alex began singing the song in perfect harmony. Carol had never heard Alex sing with such soul or depth before. Her voice was smooth, rich, and powerful. Byron's vocalizations were strong and deep. Together, they sang amazingly.

"Amazing Grace, how sweet the sound that saved a wretch like me..."

Alex and Byron harmonized perfectly throughout the long Gospel song. It was a glorious tribute to their mother.

After they finished, the congregation clapped, cheered, and continued to shout hallelujah, praise the Lord and Amen"

The preacher returned to the pulpit. "Thank you, Alexandria and Byron.

"I hope we all heard this song – really heard this song. May we remember its true meaning and its meaning to Mary. May it lift us up in this time of mourning. May we remember Mary every day of our lives. And may we remember that she lives on in our hearts for all eternity."

The congregation all said, "Amen."

On the ride home, Carol had to ask about the service they just attended. "Hey Alex, can I ask you something?"

"Yeah, sweetheart. What is it?"

"Well I... I'm not even sure how to say this. I guess I'm just a bit confused about your mom's memorial service."

"Why?"

"Because it was so different."

"Do you mean because it was because it's different from your up-bringing?"

"Yeah. It just seems weird to me that it was so celebratory and happy. Your mom just died. I would have expected it to be more solemn and depressing."

"It's a celebration for us because all of my mom's pain and suffering is over."

"When my dad died, it was the worst physical, mental and emotional anguish I ever experienced."

"Carol, I think there's a big difference between your father's death and my mother's." Alex paused. "Your father died unexpectedly. He left the house under bad circumstances. There was a lot of hurt already surrounding the situation. Your father meant the world to you and you were still a kid."

"Not to say my mom didn't mean the world to me, but this was a blessing for her." Alex continued her explanation. "My mom was given a second chance at life. Unlike your dad, she survived her accident. She had a lot of pain and problems though. It wasn't a great life, but it was a life none the less. This also wasn't a surprise for us. We're happy to see her out of pain. All of mom's suffering is over."

"So you believe all the things you guys said and sang?" Carol asked.

"Absolutely." Alex shrugged. "This was the church I was raised in. It's all I know, all I believe."

"But Alex, we don't go to church. I've never heard you sing songs like that before."

"I know. I believe what I believe and I just kind of keep it to myself. To me religion should be personal. Besides, I don't need to hear condemnation from the church because I'm a lesbian. I would just rather live my own life."

Carol was still perplexed. "Yet you still kind of believe all this. I don't understand that. Look at what you and I have both been through, all of the bullshit, the pain and the hate. How can you believe in this wonderful, forgiving God they talk about?"

"How could God allow your dad to walk out on your mom and make her go through that? How could God let you get into drugs and alcoholism? How could God just randomly kill my dad? Hell, how could God give us AIDS?" Carol's voice was filled with emotion.

"I believe that God doesn't control us. We choose to do what we do." She took a deep breath in. "My dad chose to walk out. That's not God's fault. God didn't let me get into drugs or alcoholism. That was my choice."

"As far as your dad and AIDS, I don't know honey. I just don't have an answer for that." Alex looked at Carol lovingly. "Regardless, life and all the things that happen to us are what we make of them, good or bad. We just have to choose to make positive things happen from the negativity that occurs in our lives."

"I don't know, Alex."

"What don't you know?"

"That there really is a God out there. That there's a God who cares. If God is so wonderful, why have we both been through so much pain, so much hurt, so much loss and so much hatred and prejudice? I just can't see how God would let that happen."

Chapter Eighteen

The first Thanksgiving without their beloved matriarch arrived. Each family member approached this holiday with apprehension.

Carol and Alex picked Candace up from the airport the day before and decided to have a girls bonding time. They all talked, cooked and even did shopping in the short amount of time they had together. The three young women enjoyed themselves, but the holiday still had an undertone of sadness.

All three piled into Alex's Camry and drove to Byron's house on Thanksgiving day.

The November cold nipped at the girls through their heavy coats and clothing as they walked towards Byron's house. After a few bitterly cold moments, Byron opened the door. The siblings all greeted each other with loving hugs. They didn't speak of their loss, but the sadness was visible in everyone's eyes.

As the girls all entered the house, they could see that someone was seated in the living room.

Each woman approached the room curiously and the mysterious person stood up and turned around.

"Erin! What are you doing here?" asked Alexandria.

"Hi. It's good to see you all. I'm here because... well, Byron invited me."

In perfect choreography, Carol, Alex and Candace turned around and looked at Byron.

"Erin and I have started dating. She is off from work today so I thought it would be nice for her to join us."

"You're dating?" The three women harmonized as they asked the question.

"Yeah. Well, it's only been a few months." Byron explained.

"I should explain," Erin interjected. "Last Thanksgiving, when you came to visit your mother, I gave Byron my number. I always thought he was kind of cute. So really, I went after him."

The girls all chuckled.

"It's fine, Erin." Alex said. "I just wish we had known. It's good to have you here. Welcome to our family." Alex hugged Erin.

"It's good to see you again. Welcome," Candace hugged Erin next.

"I'm thrilled you're here. Welcome to the family." Carol said as she, too, hugged Erin. "Hey, Byron, can I speak to you in the kitchen?"

"Sure," he said perplexed. They walked into the kitchen. "What's up?"

"An Asian girl?" Carol jokingly asked.

"Yeah. Look at her, she's very pretty."

"Yeah, she is. So, does that mean it's not so bad that your sister is with a white girl?"

"You know, Carol. I've had the time to watch you over the years. I saw how my mother took to you. Candace loves you too."

"I'll admit, it took me some time. I get it now. I'm sorry if I ever offended you."

"No, Byron. Not in the least. I just wanted to rib you a bit." Carol nudged Byron and laughed.

"Thanks, Carol. I appreciate it. So, what do you think?"

"Well, we know she's a very caring person. We both agree she's pretty. So, I think you're off to a good start."

"Thanks, Carol. I appreciate it."

Carol and Byron walked back into the living room to find Erin, Candace and Alex talking and laughing.

Carol leaned into Byron and whispered. "I take it back. I think you're off to a great start."

On their way home from Thanksgiving that night, Carol, Alex and Candace talked about Erin and how well she seemed to fit in with the family. Despite their mother's absence, Thanksgiving dinner had gone tremendously well. The conversation flowed. Erin was very respectful of their traditions and she brought new life to the family. The girls were also thrilled that their brother was finally dating. He never dated much. He had been alone most of his life. All three were relieved that he was with someone. They all hoped that Erin would be good for Byron.

As Alex's car pulled into the driveway, Candace pointed out that something was stuck to the front door.

"Oh no, not again." Carol got out of the car and ran to the door. Another note was taped to the door. Nervously, Carol unfolded it. "Get the hell out of town! How stupid are you that you haven't left yet?! LEAVE HERE NOW!" With a heavy heart, Carol folded up the paper and stuck it in her pocket.

Carol met Alex and Candace inside.

"Was it?" Alex asked nervously.

"Yeah," Carol said in a depressed and defeated tone.

"What's going on?" Candace asked.

"We've been getting hate letters for a while. It started once we were in the house about six months." Alexandria explained.

"Have you done anything about it?"

"Sort of," Carol answered. "The same person who leaves us these nasty notes threw a rock through our window on Valentine's day. We called the cops, but they didn't do anything."

"I spoke to my bosses," Alex added. "They said we could try to file a complaint about how poorly the two responding officers acted, but they told me that cops typically stand behind other cops so more than likely it wouldn't be worth the effort or the stress."

"That's insane. I can't believe they won't help you."

"We agree, Candace. But, as I reminded Alex, we're an interracial lesbian couple. We're not exactly the ideal family, not by Midwestern standards anyway."

"That is so messed up. When are people going to let others just live and let live?"

"I know it sucks, C." Alex said. "But even with St. Louis being a big city, this is still the 'heart land.' Most people are still very traditional in their thinking."

"That's fine. People are allowed to believe what they want. But why do they have to hate you two when you did nothing wrong?"

"You're absolutely right, Candace. Unfortunately, people are just afraid of things they don't know or don't understand," Carol said. "It's not fair. It's certainly not right, but it is what it is. We can't force them to like us. Sometimes people have a hard time as seeing others who are different as people too."

"Well, I'd like to start our group by introducing two new members. This is Carol and Alexandria." Juanita, the group leader, was a middle-aged Hispanic woman. She was heavy set with thick, curly black hair. Her skin was a dark olive tone. She was very warm and pleasant.

"Hi," Alex and Carol both said sheepishly. They were the only lesbian couple.

There were three gay male couples and one solitary man who used to be a heroine addict.

"Please tell us a bit about yourselves, ladies." Juanita said, gesturing that they speak to the entire group who stared back at them with large, unblinking eyes.

"Well, we've been together for almost five years now. I'm a paralegal and Carol owns an IT company.

"We found out that we have AIDS in 2000. Carol had a blood transfusion when she was a kid, before they screened blood donors for AIDS. So, that's how she got it. And I got it from her."

Carol looked down at the floor.

Carol and Alex heard all of the men shudder and mumble various apologies.

"How are you both handling the news?" One handsome gay man asked.

"We're just going day-to-day. We work. We're trying to retain a sense of normalcy."

"How about you?" The same man asked Carol who still stared at the floor.

"I don't know. Ok, I guess. I mean, I wish it was just me. It eats away at me that Alex has it too. I didn't want to make her sick."

"None of us wanted to get our partners sick," another young gay man spoke up. "But, this virus is scary. It can infect the people we try to protect the most. The most important thing is that you, as a couple, fight the disease together." His boyfriend took his hand and squeezed it.

"Oh we are," Alex said. "I know it really hurts Carol, but I'm not going anywhere. This is our fight."

"It sounds like you have a good handle on the situation," Juanita stated before moving on with the meeting. "Since we just celebrated a new year, we're going to state our new years resolutions. Let's start with Ken."

Ken was the one solitary man, the one who had acquired AIDS as a result of a drug habit. "I'm going to continue to work at the rehab center and remind the patients of their risk of getting HIV/AIDS from shooting up." His voice was gruff and harsh, but his sincerity couldn't be questioned.

"That's great, Ken. I am so proud of you for continuing to do good things and creating good from your struggles and problems." The group leader said. "Tom?"

Tom was one of a pair of men, but he had remained silent until now. His hair was straggly and light brown in color. He looked like he hadn't shaved in a while. "I send money to AIDS research every other month and I'm going to look at our finances to see if I can increase that to every month."

"Wow. That could make a huge impact ion the treatment and possibly even the cure of AIDS. Great resolution!" Juanita encouraged him. "Zachary?"

Zachary was a short man and very clean cut. He was an odd match for Tom from a visual standpoint. "Since I'm on disability and available during the day, I'm going to speak at as many schools and events as I'm physically able to. It's not much, but at least I'm doing something."

"Zachary, education and awareness are extremely important for this disease. There are so many myths and misconceptions about AIDS. Don't downplay what you're doing. It's extremely important." Juanita was clearly supporting everyone's efforts in the groups. "Steven, what about you?"

Steven was the first man who spoke to Carol and Alex. He was tall and very handsome. He had sandy blonde hair. His eyes were a light, crisp blue. He was muscular and well groomed. "Like Tom, I'd like to increase the amount I send to support AIDS research. Things are still unstable at work so I can't be sure that I definitely can; but I am absolutely going to try."

"All you can do is your best, Steven. And your best may do more than you could even imagine." Juanita seemed to believe what she told everyone. "Henry?"

Henry was as handsome as his partner Steven. He was tall and muscular as well. His hair was a rich, chocolate brown. He had a thick mustache. His eyes emanated warmth and kindness. "I am working on getting a local theatre company to perform RENT. I loved the show and I think it would really touch a lot of people. I'm finding out that a lot of work is involved, but it will be worth it in the end."

"That is such a creative idea, Henry. I love it." Juanita was clearly excited and enthused by Henry's creativity. "Now, Nathan, what about you?"

Nathan was the second man who had spoken to Alex and Carol. He was a mousy, nerdy little man. He wore thick, round glasses, and wore a suit that seemed far too large for his small frame. "Well, since I've been able to convince so many co-workers to donate to the cause, I've decided that I am going to approach my boss and see if the company would be interested in donating or supporting it in some way. He likes me and has been very accommodating to my condition. Plus it's a tax write-off for the company, so I think there's great potential there."

As usual, Juanita was encouraging. "That is a phenomenal idea, Nathan. How great to get so many people, and even an entire company, involved. Good for you. Aaron, you're next."

Aaron was Nathan's partner. Aaron was taller than Nathan, but still on the short side. His chestnut hair and green eyes were striking. He was far less formal than his guy. "I've signed up for a clinical study about AIDS treatments. I don't know what will come of it, but I thought it might just help."

"Aaron, clinical studies will always help us to understand the disease and how to better treat it. I think that's a really great idea." Juanita was sincere.

"Ok, Carol and Alexandria. I know this is your first time here," Juanita started. "But have either of you made any consideration towards contributing to the HIV/AIDS community?"

Carol and Alex looked at each other.

"Ummmm... well not really." Carol hesitantly admitted. "We've avoided going to the infectious disease doctor; we haven't done our wills. I think we're still a bit in denial. To jump right in would mean we really have to admit that we have AIDS."

"But you've known for two years?" Ken asked.

"Not quite," Carol corrected him. "It'll be two years in June. There's been so much going on."

"We've been getting hate letters taped to our door, and Alex's mother recently passed away. There's just been so much going on in our lives."

"It's ok," Juanita comforted Carol. "It sounds like you've both been under a lot of stress. But you do need to follow up on all your medical needs. Maybe that should be your New Year's resolution. Taking care of yourselves is the first step in helping the community on the whole."

"I think we can do that," Alex said.

"Hi there. My name is Alexandria Whetherby. My partner and I were both referred by Dr. Luciano. We need to set up an appointment with Dr. Jacobs."

"Ok." The receptionist responded cheerfully. "Are there any particular days that are best for you?"

"Our schedules are flexible. Is it possible for us to see the doctor together?"

"Oh sure, that's not a problem. Let's see here... it looks like I have an opening on Wednesday the twenty first at 1 pm. Does that work for you?"

"For both of us?"

"Yeah. I just looked for a time when he had two openings back to back. That was the first one I found."

"Thank you. That's perfect. We'll see you then."

"Ok, sounds good. Have a great day, Ms. Whetherby."

Alex walked back into the main office from the break room. As she made her way back to her desk, Lisa walked past her.

"Lisa!" Alex called out.

Lisa turned around. "Yeah, Alexandria?"

"Carol and I were able to get an appointment with the infectious disease doctor on the twenty first at one. Would you mind if I leave early that day?"

"What day of the week is that?"

"Wednesday."

"Oh, sure. No problem. Frederick and I both told you we'd be willing to work with you. This is very important."

"Thank you so much for understanding, Lisa."

"No problem, Alex." Lisa turned and walked away.

Alex sat at her desk and began reading through the case file on her desk. A few pages into the file, Dave walked up.

"So, you finally went to that support group, huh?" Dave asked Alex in his typical high-pitched, effeminate voice.

"Yeah."

"So, how did it go?"

"It was good, I guess. I think we'll go back. How did you hear about this group again?"

"John used to work with Zachary. When Zach and his partner came up positive, they found the group. I guess they wanted us to know in case we needed it."

"But you guys are fine, aren't you?"

"Oh yeah. I think it just gave them a sense that they weren't alone if they gave us the info. Zachary and John still talk every so often, too."

"Oh, that's good. Well, thank John for us."

"I sure will. I hope the group helps you and Carol."

"I'm sure it will, Dave. Thanks."

Dave tenderly placed his hand over Alex's. They smiled at each other. The friendship, love and compassion in Dave's eyes was undeniable. After a moment, he walked away and Alex reluctantly went back to reading her case file.

Carol and Alex sat next to each other and holding hands in nervous anticipation. The reality had finally hit them. They were about to see an infectious disease doctor because they both had AIDS. It was a hard reality to swallow. They sat in silence, trying to comprehend this truth.

In walked a tall, but somewhat pudgy, man. He was very fair skinned and had bright red hair. His eyes were a rich green that rivaled the hills of Ireland. "Hello, ladies. I'm Dr. Jacobs, but you can call me Dr. J." He introduced himself.

"Hi, Alexandria Whetherby." Alex said, extending her hand to shake his.

"Carol Mathers." Carol followed suit.

"It's not every day I have two patients in the same room. Tell me, what can I do for you?" His voice had a light, crisp tone.

"Well, you see, doctor, Carol and I... I'm not sure how to say this."

The doctor smiled encouragingly.

"Carol was a sickly child and she received a blood transfusion before they began screening blood donors. The blood was tainted, I guess. She... got... AIDS as a result of her transfusion. And I have AIDS now, too."

Carol looked away, still feeling guilty and ashamed for what she had done to Alex.

"Ok. How long have you two been together?"

"Several years. Since 1997 to be exact." Alex spoke as Carol continued to sit in silence.

"Ok. Were you diagnosed as HIV positive or with full blown AIDS?"

"AIDS, sir."

"When were you diagnosed?"

"A year and a half ago, by Dr. Luciano."

"Dr. Luciano, she's a great doctor." He made a notation in a file folder he carried. "But, a year and a half, ladies? I have to scold you a little for that one. Waiting is not a good option when it comes to treating and living with this virus."

"I know we should have come in sooner. The timing was horrid. My mother was dying. Carol took over her own business. We've been busy."

"I'm sure you have, Alexandria. I can understand that. The important thing for you two is to take good care of yourselves. Your health is of the utmost importance. We need to get you both on a good treatment regimen."

"We live in a good time. There's constantly emerging data about the virus. We're constantly finding more and better drugs that help our patients to have a good quality of life. So, you ladies are quite lucky in that regard." He managed to sound positive. "We do also have several clinical studies going on for potential medications as well. Would either of you be interested in participating in one of our studies?"

"No," Alex said firmly.

Carol finally looked at the doctor. "No, thank you." She said meekly.

"Ok. That's fair enough. Now, here's what I want to do. I want to start you ladies on some medications. These will help your body to heal faster, to boost your immune system, and to actually slow down the process of the virus. I'd also like to see you ladies fairly regularly. I think we should do check ups every six months."

"Every six months?" Carol asked.

"Yes and I'll tell you why. Number one, you waited so long to get in here. A lot of time has passed and I need to get good base line blood work on both of you. You both need treatment now."

"Also, since our knowledge and treatment of the disease changes and improves so much so quickly, if we find something better than the meds you're currently taking, I will more than likely want to change things. Obviously, there are always several factors to consider when it comes to the various medications, but I want my patients to receive the best treatment possible."

"Lastly, I like to do regular blood checks on all of my patients. Not only do I get a base line this time, but down the road I can see how your system is reacting to the various medications. I like to check all major organ functions. Call me overly cautious, but I think it benefits you greatly in the long run."

Carol and Alex looked at each other. They didn't expect their treatment to be so intensive, but they knew that it had to be done. They wanted to survive. They both refused to let this disease get the best of them.

"Whatever you say, doctor," Alex said.

"We want to fight this thing, so we're both on board one hundred per cent." Carol added.

Chapter Nineteen

"We finally went to the infectious disease doctor last week," Alex told the group. Everyone was there, except for Carol. She was working late again.

"How did it go?" Ken asked.

"It went ok. The doctor is just very intense and there are a lot more meds and blood tests than we originally thought."

"Who's your doctor?" Steven asked.

"Dr. J, I mean, Dr. Jacobs."

"Oh we see Dr. J also." Aaron said.

"Us too," Zachary said.

"I guess we all do." Ken added. "He's one of the best in the city. You got a good doctor. Do what he tells you. He'll take good care of you."

The flew open and Carol walked in. "Hey everyone. Sorry I'm late." She quickly moved to an empty chair.

"Carol," Juanita said. "Alex was just telling us about your visit with Dr. J."

"Oh, yeah," Carol said quietly.

"We're talking about taking the time to smell the roses. Taking care of ourselves and enjoying our lives." Juanita explained.

"That's rather ironic since I work so much." Carol said just loud enough to be heard.

"What do you do, Carol?" Nathan asked.

"I own Dawson Networking. I'm an IT tech, we service companies all over the city. We fix home computers, set up networks, do data back up and we restore systems that have been infected with viruses. You name it, we do it as far as computers are concerned."

"Carol, is that really how you want to spend all of your time?" Juanita asked.

"No. I have a great partner. We have a nice house and a beautiful dog. I have my father's '67 GTO. I'd love to be able to do more. But when you own your own business, it's kind of hard. I have two technicians that work under me, but I still have to do the majority of the work."

"What do you think you can do to lessen your work load?" Henry asked.

"I don't know, Henry. That's kind of a tough question. Again, it's not a matter of wanting to work this hard, but it comes with the territory."

"Back in 1999," Alex interjected. "Carol was hardly even home she was working so hard trying to make sure that all of her clients' computers were Y2K compatible. Then, in May 2000, that 'I love you' virus thing came out and she was home even less. She got really sick both times. That's how we found out she has AIDS."

"Do you want to literally work yourself to death?" Juanita asked.

"No, I don't. I really don't. But that's the nature of the business I chose. Once I took over the company, the workload increased significantly.

"I try to give my two techs as much work as possible, but there's still all the business crap like taxes that I have to deal with. No one can do that for me. What am I supposed to do?"

"Can you take time out for your family? Take time out to do the things you want to do? Actually enjoy your life instead of working all the time?" Ken asked.

"I do what I can." Carol tried to defend herself.

"She does, she really does." Alex backed Carol up. "Like she said, it's not easy. There's a lot of pressure on her. But, she's taking the time to go to the doctors with me. We always spend Sundays together. We take walks around our neighborhood when we can. It's not an easy thing to balance, but she works really hard to try find that balance."

"Ok," Juanita said. "We are just about out of time. Tell me one thing you're each going to do this week to 'stop and smell the roses,'?"

"I'm going to take my camera and go to a park and just take pictures." Ken said.

"I have a wonderful new novel I just bought, so I'm going to make some time every evening to read." Henry spoke next.

Steven then said, "I'm going to take Henry out for a nice dinner on Saturday night so we can spend some good quality time together."

Zachary's turn came next. "I am sleeping in Sunday morning and just giving myself to have the entire day to do whatever I want."

"There's a local Jazz club in town that I've been dying to go to, so I think I'll do that one night this week." Tom said.

"I'm going to watch The Princess Bride with Alex," Carol said. "It's her favorite movie."

"Well, Carol's birthday is this week, so I can't really say, but it'll be nice," Alex said.

Aaron was the next to speak. "I am going to cook a really nice home-made dinner for Nathan."

Finally, Nathan spoke. "I'm going to watch a documentary on the Civil War this weekend."

"It sounds like you all have great plans. Go out, enjoy your lives. I'll see everybody next week," Juanita dismissed the group.

As Alex and Carol were getting their purses, Nathan walked up to Carol.

"Hey, Carol?"

"Hi Nate. What's up?"

"I'm not sure if you're hiring, or even if you just want an extra set of hands, but I'm also an IT tech. I work at First Call."

"Oh yeah, I know them."

"It's not nearly the same caliber as Dawson, but here's my card in case you're ever interested." Nathan handed her a card with his name and phone number.

"Thanks, Nate. I will definitely keep you in mind."

Carol was on her way home from another long day of work when her cell phone rang. It was the bank calling.

"Hello?"

"Hi, may I please speak with Ms. Mathers?"

"This is Carol Mathers."

"Hi, Ms. Mathers. My name is Kathleen. I'm calling from Missouri State Bank. Did you authorize a purchase for... five hundred seventy eight dollars and sixty four cents?"

"No, Kathleen I didn't. What check number is it?"

Imperfect

"It was a debit purchase. At," she paused to look up the information, "Louis Tack and Feed."

"Louis Tack and Feed? You've got to be kidding me. I don't own a horse or a farm. My card is in my wallet, so no one could have stolen it from me."

"Ooops, I see what happened here. Your card number and this person's card number are only different by one number. Sorry about the inconvenience, Ms. Mathers."

Carol hung up without saying another word. She had this account with Missouri State since she started working at Dawson. Over the years, there had been a significant number of mistakes and problems. Carol was really annoyed by their lack of professionalism. She contemplated filing a complaint with the branch manager.

Carol's birthday was here. She prayed that Alex would keep it as a quiet night at home. After the bank fiasco the other day, she didn't want to be bothered by anyone. The constant bank issues put her in an antisocial mood.

Carol walked into the house and found it decorated in all things St. Louis Cardinals. There were baseball banners, baseballs, hats and mitts. It was cleverly put together.

"Happy birthday, sweetheart!" Alexandria said running up to meet Carol.

"Thanks, babe. This is really cute. What's with the baseball theme?"

"Look at this." Alex handed Carol a card.

Carol opened the envelope. It was a greeting card with a snow covered pine tree and a cardinal on the front. Carol opened the card and two tickets fell to the floor. Carol bent over to the pick them up without even reading the card. "What are these?"

"Two tickets to the Cardinals opening home game."

"No way!"

"Yep!"

"Oh honey, thank you so much! This is great," Carol said as she grabbed Alex and hugged her tightly. It was the perfect gift. Carol wouldn't have to deal with people tonight and she'd soon be enjoying watching a live baseball game. That was simply incredible.

"Happy birthday, love." Alex's smile was bright and warm. She tenderly kissed Carol. Despite all of the time that had gone by, Alex's love and devotion were unwavering.

Carol and Alex drove home in the warmth of the late afternoon after a gorgeous spring day watching the Cardinals opening home game of the season. The Cardinals lost, but the women enjoyed their day anyway.

As the GTO rumbled up the driveway, Alex saw another note on the door.

"Oh no, not again. Honey, go ahead and pull into the garage. I'll meet you inside," Alex said as she got out of the car to see what was on the door.

Carol quickly pulled into the garage and ran inside to see what the note said. "What does this one say?"

Alex unfolded the neat creases of the paper. "Go away, you stupid lesbos! This is our neighborhood! Trash like you does not belong here!"

"They just will not give up, will they?" Carol asked.

"It certainly seems not."

"Add it to the collection," Carol said cynically.

Alex went to go place the note in a file where they kept all the notes and the rock. They knew they would need them.

Suddenly, Carol's cell phone began to ring.

"Hello?"

"Hey Carol, it's Will."

"Hi Will, what's up?"

"I'm just calling to let you know you're going to see a req form from me for overtime."

"Ok. Why?"

"Remember how Paul was to do that complete set up for that new spa and salon?"

"Yeah?"

"I got a call from the salon owner saying that Paul didn't complete the job, he seemed rushed, and that they were extremely disappointed with his work."

"Shit. You have got to be kidding me."

"Nope."

"You didn't invoice them a second time, did you?"

"No, Carol. I knew we couldn't charge them for this."

"Good. Ok, finish up the work there and I will speak to Paul first thing tomorrow morning. Thanks for letting me know."

"No problem, Carol."

"Hey Will, are you and Robyn going to be up for coming over tonight?"

"Yeah, sure. I don't think I'll be here too much longer."

"Ok. We'll call in for Chinese. Sound ok?"

"Yeah, sounds great. See you in a bit."

"Ok, Will. Thanks."

Alex waited until Carol hung up the phone. "What happened?"

"Will got a complaint call today saying that Paul didn't complete an assignment I gave him, that his work was sloppy. All kinds of bad stuff."

"I know Paul's an ass, but I thought he was a good worker."

"Typically, he is. That's why this is so strange. I'm going to have to talk to him in the morning and see what he has to say for himself."

"That is so weird," Alex commented.

"Yeah, you're not kidding. I don't get it. He's really been getting sloppy lately. Oh well.

"Anyway, Will and Robyn are still coming over later. I thought we could just do Chinese. I know I'm not really up for much tonight." Carol noted.

"Ok, that sounds good to me, too, baby. I wasn't in much of a mood to cook anyway."

"How about you go set up the table and I'll call the order in. Sound good?" Alex asked.

"You got it, baby." Carol kissed Alex on the cheek and began to set up the house for Will and Robyn's company.

When Carol walked into the office, the first thing she did was look for Paul. "Paul!"

He didn't respond.

"Paul!" Carol called out louder.

Paul turned around.

"C'mon into my office for a second."

Paul hesitantly followed Carol into her office.

166

"Paul, what's going on?"

Paul fidgeted, and seemed anxious and agitated. "Nothing."

"Paul, Will had to return to a site that you were called out to do."

"Which one?"

"The salon that you were supposed to set up. They called here and complained that you didn't complete the job, that you weren't focused, and that your work was sloppy.

"Paul, that's not like you. You're normally very thorough. You always complete your assignments. This is completely out of the ordinary for you."

"Is everything alright?"

Paul looked at the floor. "Yeah."

Carol looked at him inquisitively. "Are you sure?"

"Uh-huh."

Carol watched Paul for a moment. He seemed distracted, disturbed. "How about this, Paul? How about you only do a half-day today? I'll give you a couple of easy assignments and then you can go home and just relax. Sound good?"

"Sure," he said, shuffling his feet all over the floor.

"Ok." Carol said as she went through her list of calls for the day. "How about a home computer repair and a data back up? You think you can do those?"

"Yeah."

Carol gave Paul all the information and watched as Paul rushed out of the office.

"What's wrong with him?" Will asked Carol as she walked out of her office.

"I don't know, but something weird is going on."

Another year was slipping away and Alex's September birthday was quickly approaching. Carol wanted to do something spectacular for her. They had gone to so many restaurants, they had the house and the cars. They didn't need any more luxuries. Carol wanted to do something different. She wanted to share a special day with her at home, just the two of them.

Alex arrived home on her birthday. There was a note for her on the counter. "Dear Alex, happy birthday! I have something very special for you. First, you need to go to where the sun rises every morning."

"Where does the sun rise every morning?" Alex wondered. Then she remembered their large, east-facing window.

She ran over to the window to find another note. "You're getting closer. Now, find the place where beauty always reflects back."

"Damn," Alex thought to herself. Carol wasn't making this easy.

Then she thought about all the times Carol called Alex her 'beauty'. Trying to think of beauty and reflections, Alex wracked her brain. Then it hit her, mirrors reflect. Alex went into the bathroom, and on the mirror was another note. "Touché, my love!" Alex said to herself.

She opened the letter. "You're just about there. Now, come into our special place for your birthday present."

Alex walked into the bedroom. The bed was covered in rose petals. Small candles were glowing all around the room. On the middle of the bed, surrounded by rose petals forming a heart shape, was a small box.

Alex walked to the bed and picked up the box. Carefully, she opened the box. Inside sat a beautiful diamond ring. The stone was large, clear, and radiant. Alex gasped at seeing such a stunning ring. She never imagined she would own such a lavish piece of jewelry.

"Happy birthday, sweetheart!" Carol said, walking up behind Alex.

Alex turned around, her smile was as wide as a river and her eyes glistened with tears of joy. She hugged Carol tightly. "I love it, thank you!"

"You're welcome, sweetheart. I love you more and more every day. Remember that every time you look at the ring." Carol said softly.

"Carol, you are incredible. I am so lucky to have you. You are amazing, you know that? I love you so much!"

Another year was gone in the blink of an eye. Even the traditional Whetherby Thanksgiving had already passed. The holiday season was already in full force.

Candace decided to stay with Carol and Alex for Christmas.

"So, how's school going?" Carol asked on a bright, chilly Christmas morning.

Candace had blossomed into a gorgeous young woman. She strongly resembled Alexandria now. "It's going really well, Carol. I love what we're doing in school. I'm really glad that I decided on the social work major. And VCU has a great social work program. I'm really happy."

"That's great."

"And how is good old Virginia?" Alex asked, sitting down next to her sister.

"It's ok. For the most part, it's nice. Richmond is a weird city, though. It can be pretty rough in areas. And then there's Monument Avenue."

"Monument Avenue?" Alex repeated.

"Yeah. It's this pretty, historic, cobble stone road with all these beautiful memorials and monuments. The thing is, they're all paying homage to confederate soldiers and generals. If you didn't know American History, you'd think the south won the war."

All three women laughed loudly at the irony of Monument Avenue.

"But you're happy there and school is going well?"

"Absolutely, A."

"Good. I'm glad to see my little sister is doing so well."

"Yeah, I am."

"Speaking of doing well, what do you think about Byron and Erin?"

"They're cute," Carol said.

"They're an odd pair, but they seem really happy." Alex chimed in.

"Yeah, they do. It's nice to see Byron dating."

"No kidding. After all the sacrifices he made for both of us, he deserves to be happy." Alex said.

"So, Candace, anyone special in your life?" Carol teasingly asked.

"No. I don't really want to date. Not right now. School is my main focus."

"Good for you," Carol said with pride. "I'm proud that you are so focused and aren't letting anything get in the way of your dreams."

"Ok, ladies." Alex said as she rose from her chair. "I think we need to cut the chit-chat. Sorry. Byron and Erin will be over in two hours. I think it's time we get this place set up for Christmas." Alex said with her customary holiday exuberance.

Though they would have loved to talk endlessly, Carol and Candace knew they needed to get the house ready. So, the three women began rearranging furniture and decorating the house for the festivities. It was going to be another special holiday for the family. As usual, Alex could not contain her excitement as the decorations made the house bright, cheery and festive.

Chapter Twenty

The new year brought more hate letters. The frequency had increased to an average of one letter per week. Carol and Alex continued to save each letter. They saved them them with the rock in a filing cabinet they had. They knew they had to hold onto these letters and the rock. As painful as it was to house the hate within their own home, instinct told both women that it was necessary.

One blustery March evening, Carol came home to find yet another note on their front door. Like all the others, the letters were clipped from magazines and newspapers. Except for one. It looked as though a clipping had been glued, but it must have fallen off. In its place was a hand-written 't'. Although it was only one letter, there was something familiar about this 't'. It was as if Carol had seen similar writing elsewhere. She couldn't quite place where, how or why she'd recognize one letter, but she filed the letter away with all the others and hoped that an answer would come to her.

Aaron and Nathan had been missing from the group for over a month. No one had heard anything from either man.

Juanita hadn't been able to get in touch with either one for seven weeks after they stopped coming. Then she did.

"I have some terrible news to report." Juanita said looking down. Her usually enthusiastic and happy demeanor was gone. She was clearly upset. "Aaron has passed away. That's why he and Nathan haven't been here in so long."

"Aaron got very ill and was hospitalized. Unfortunately, he only continued to get worse. Although no one from the clinical study will confirm or deny anything, it seems as though the trial medication he was receiving was probably the cause."

Everyone in the group gasped at the horrible news. Their friend was gone. Aaron was special to everyone within the group. He was a wonderful, bright, intelligent, caring man. The group would never be the same without Aaron.

"Nathan is home. He's having a rough time of things and is not ready to come back to group alone." Juanita finished.

The group sat in silence trying to absorb what they had just heard.

Finally Alex spoke up, "May I make a suggestion?"

"Yes, Alexandria. What are you thinking?"

"Well, I would like to do something in Aaron's honor. I think it would be a nice way to memorialize him, as well as do something for Nathan."

"What did you have in mind?" Juanita asked.

"Why don't we, as a group, contribute to AIDS research in Aaron's memory? We don't all have to give the same amount. Everyone should just give what they can and we'll pool it. Then we can send it all in for Nathan and Aaron."

"I think that's a great idea," Ken said. "That is such a wonderful way for us to remember Aaron, and I know that would mean the world to Nathan."

"Is there anyone who doesn't like the idea or has another suggestion?" Juanita asked.

No one said a word. It was the perfect way to honor their dear friend.

"Well, I think we have our answer. I don't want to push anyone, but I'd like to get this done in a timely manner. Let's have everyone's money within two weeks? Is that fair?"

The group agreed.

They all hoped their gesture would honor Aaron and bring Nathan peace. They knew nothing would bring back the kind soul that was Aaron, but they all loved the idea of honoring him. From the depths of their souls, they hoped that somehow Nathan would find tranquility and comfort with this gift.

One warm spring night, Carol was working late at the office. She sat alone in her office going through paperwork. As she sorted through various invoices and requisition forms, she noticed something odd. She took a closer look. No, it couldn't be. She stared at the paper in front of her. There was a 't' on a req form Paul had filled out that looked like the 't' on that hate letter she and Alex received over a month before.

Confused, worried, and angry, Carol took the paper home with her to compare it to the note.

"What are you doing?" Alex yawned as she came out to the kitchen where Carol was studying the notes and the form from Paul. The light shining down the hall had woken her.

"Alex, I think I know who's been sending us the notes."

"What? How? Who?"

"I hate to say it, but I think it's Paul."

"Paul? As in the obnoxious guy who works for you, Paul?"

"Yeah. Take a look at this."

Alex sat next to Carol. Carol slid the note over with the hand-written 't'.

"Look at that," Carol said.

"Ok, so the asshole forgot a letter and wrote it in. So?"

"So, take a look at this req form I found at work today. Look at the 't.'"

With her eyes still a bit fuzzy, Alex strained to read through the form. She noticed that the 't' looked terribly similar to the one in the hate letter. "Ok, I see where you're going. But how do you know it's Paul?"

Carol pointed to the bottom of the form where Paul had signed the form. "That's Paul's signature."

"Oh shit."

"Yeah, no kidding."

"What are you going to do, sweetie?"

"Not much. I mean, I will address it with him privately. If he says anything, he's fired. If he doesn't, he'll at least get a stern warning from me."

"What if that stern warning pisses him off more and we get another rock through a window or something?"

"We'll have more evidence. Maybe the cops would actually do something then. I hate to say it, but it's a risk we have to take."

After a twelve week absence, Nathan finally came back to the group. He was welcomed with tears and bear hugs.

"How are you doing, Nathan?" Juanita asked when group officially started.

"It's a huge adjustment. The house is so empty. My life is just not the same without Aaron."

"Is there anything we can do?" Carol asked.

"No, thank you. It's something that we all have to face at one time or another. I don't know if it would have mattered if I had another day or another decade with him. I don't think you're ever truly prepared for something like this."

"Is there anything you can do to get back at the clinical study people?" Tom asked.

"No. When you go into a study, you sign a consent form stating that the medication has not yet been approved by the FDA, and that there are risks involved. There's nothing I can do."

"Oh God, I am so sorry." Henry said.

"I would like to thank all of you for the donation in Aaron's memory. Getting that letter really meant a lot to me."

"You're more than welcome," Juanita said gently. "It was the least we could do for you and for him."

"I think I speak for all of us here, Nate." Carol said. "You have our numbers. Please don't hesitate to call for anything. We're all here for you."

"Thanks, Carol. I really appreciate it." Nate wiped a tear from his eyes.

The group continued on as it always had, but Aaron's absence was still very noticeable.

Dave, John, Carol and Alex walked Sugar and Dave and John's dog, Max. They strolled through a local park on a hot, sunny, summer Sunday afternoon.

"You really think you know who the letters are from?" Dave asked nervously.

"It's a hunch," Carol said. "I'll find out tomorrow. I'm not thrilled and to be honest, I'd love to be wrong."

"What happens if your hunch is right?" Dave slowed down to hear Carol's answer.

"I don't know, Dave. All I can do is take this one step at a time right now."

"Are you worried about your safety?" John asked.

"Absolutely." Carol answered. "I'm very worried about Alex, Sugar, the house – everything. We don't know if this will end it all or aggravate the situation. But I also don't want to lie down and let some bigot get the best of us. This is our house and I refuse to be harassed like this."

"How about you, Alexandria? How do you feel about all of this?" John asked.

"I'm scared. I'm worried. Especially if it is who we think it is."

"Carol has a good point, though. This is our home. We've lived there for years and haven't bothered a soul. We deserve to live there in peace."

"Keep us posted. You know we worry about you," John said.

"I'll tell Dave everything at work as soon as we know. Let's just hope that that this brings an end to all of this crap." Alex replied.

"I hope so. I'm just worried about the both of you," John said uneasily.

Carol closed her office door and dialed Yvette in accounting.

"Accounting."

"Hi Yvette, it's Carol."

"Hi Carol. What can I do for you?"

"Listen, I just need you to tell me something real quick. I don't need a house number, but can you tell me if Paul lives on Sparrow Lane?"

"Hmmm. Let me see. Lucinda keeps the personnel files so just hang in there with me as I go through her filing system here. Wait, ok. Here's Paul's info. Address... address... Ok, here we go. Yes, Carol, he does live on Sparrow Lane."

"Thanks so much, Yvette. Much appreciated."

Carol went through her list of the day's calls. Paul was on a large call. She expected him to be gone all day. She called him to arrange a meeting first thing the next morning.

Paul's cell went straight to voice mail. "Hi Paul, it's Carol. I know you're on a big call today. Something very important came up today and I need to have a meeting with you first thing tomorrow morning. I'll be in at eight, I expect you in my office by 8:30 sharp. Thanks. I'll see you tomorrow."

Alex and Carol just sat down for dinner when Carol's cell rang.

"Damn it. Sorry, baby." She looked at the caller ID and saw that it was Nathan. "It's Nate, Alex."

"Pick it up!"

"Hello?"

"Carol?" Nathan was crying.

175

"Hi, Nate. What's up?"

"It's just so empty and lonely here. I wish Aaron was here."

"We all do, Nate. I would love nothing more than to have him be there with you."

"I can't stand being in this house all by myself."

"I can understand that. It has to be extremely difficult." Carol paused for a moment and looked at Alex. Alex's eyes were full of concern and understanding. "Nate, would you like to come over here? Alex and I were about to have dinner. You can join us. You can stay as long as you like."

"I don't want to be a problem."

"It's no problem, Nate. Just come on over. You're always welcome here."

"Thank you so much, Carol." Nathan sniffled into the phone.

Within a half hour, Nathan sat with Alex and Carol at their dinner table. The ladies ate. Nathan was too upset to eat.

"Thank you for letting me come over. It's so hard to be in that empty house. I feel empty inside too." Nathan began to cry.

"I can understand," Alex said tenderly. "No one wants to lose a loved one. Like you said, no amount of time would have eased your pain."

"As difficult as it is, you need to find a way to honor him in every day of your life." Carol said. "That's what I did when my father died. It's not easy, but it does bring meaning and solace."

"I know you're both right. I just want him back. God, what I wouldn't do to get him back."

"I know, Nathan." Alex said. "But he'll always live on in your heart. I know that sounds cheesy, but it is true."

"My father lives on in pictures, in my memories, and in the GTO, Nate. They never truly leave us," Carol added.

"How do I make my house not feel so empty?"

"That takes time." Alex said gently.

"Whenever it gets to be too much just call us, Nate. You're always welcome here. We're friends. We're always here for you." Carol said.

"Thank you so much, Alexandria and Carol. I don't know how I'd get through this without you."

"You're not supposed to. That's why we have friends, Nathan. We're never supposed to go through any trial in life alone. That is what friends are for. It's going to be ok. We'll all get through this together," Alex tried to comfort him. She got up, and put her arm around him. Nathan once again broke into tears. Alex gently rubbed his back and prayed that he would find solace in her words.

"What's up, Carol?" Paul asked impatiently as he sat down in her office.

Paul, can you please write the sentence, 'I don't write, I take things to people, and I don't like tea.'?" Carol handed Paul a notepad and pen.

"Carol, why am I doing this?"

"Please just write it down, Paul."

After a few moments, Paul was done writing. Carol took the notepad and looked at it. All of the 't's' matched the 't' on his req form, as well as the 't' in the hate letter.

"Paul, I have something I want to show you," Carol said reaching into her bag. She pulled out all of the hate letters collected over the years, the rock that had been thrown through their window, and the latest note with the hand-written 't'.

"What's all that?"

"We'll get to that. One thing at a time. Can you do me a favor and pick up the rock?"

Paul picked up the large stone with one hand. He seemed strong enough that he could have thrown that through a window.

"Thanks, Paul. I'll take that back now." Carol used both hands to put the rock back in her bag. "Now, I want to show you something very interesting."

Carol took out the req form and slid that with the note pad to Paul. "Paul, do you agree that you filled out this req form? Obviously, you just wrote this. So you'd say that both of these match. They're both your handwriting?"

"Yeah, so?"

"Well, now look at this." Carol slid over the note that read, "Don't ever come back here again! Get out, lesbos!"

"What am I looking at? These are all cut out letters."

"All except for the 't' in 'out.' Now, take a look at that 't' and look at the 't's' on your req form and on this notepad."

"So, they're similar. So what?"

"Paul, I'm going to cut right to the chase here. I know you live on Sparrow Lane, as do Alex and I. I know you don't like gays or

177

women. It also doesn't take a rocket scientist to figure out that this handwriting is all the same. You also held that rock like it weighed nothing. That rock was thrown through one of the windows in our house."

Carol paused and watched Paul. "Do you have anything you want to say to me?"

"No." Paul said in anger, but he looked away.

"Paul, I'm going to be straight up with you. Police reports have been filed. We're not taken this lying down. Right now all the evidence points to you. All I have to do is call the cops again and they will investigate. If this is you, a friend or relative of yours, or someone who in anyway is associated with you, we will find out.

"I strongly suggest you do us all a favor and quit this shit already. Whether it's you or your friends, it's got to end. Trust me on this one. Remember that Alex works for a law firm. This is not something you want to be involved in.

"I'm going to be nice and not say a word. But, if I so much as get one more letter, one dirty look, anything, I will get the police involved in no time. Do you understand?"

"Yes." Paul sighed as he looked at various spots on the floor.

"Ok. Go finish your call from yesterday. Have a good day, Paul."

Paul walked out of Carol's office without saying another word. He closed the door behind him.

Overwhelmed with emotion and pride that she stood up to him, Carol gave herself a few minutes to cry in her office. She didn't know that she could be so strong. She was proud of herself. She defended and protected her family. The hate that they had endured for so long was finally over. Her fears, her concerns, her worries were finally quelled. The feeling of relief was amazingly powerful. The nightmare was officially over.

Carol went on-line to check her bank statement. For some reason, it wasn't matching up to her register, nor to the printed statement she had received in the mail. She looked through each transaction. After several minutes of intense scrutiny, Carol found the error. According to the internet statement, she had been charged twice for the same transaction.

She immediately called the bank.

"Missouri State Bank, this is Kathleen. How may I help you?"

"Hi Kathleen, my name is Carol Mathers. I'm calling regarding my personal checking account. According to your website, I've been charged twice for the same transaction on the sixteenth."

"Oh yes, I see that here."

"Well, if you look at the printed statement and my register, that should only be one transaction, not two. Can you please reverse those charges?"

"Oh, yes. I can do that for you. It may take twenty four to forty eight hours before you see the change on the website, but I will fix that for you right away."

"Thank you, Kathleen. Have a nice day."

Another year was winding down and Thanksgiving was fast approaching. As the Whetherby family made their plans, Candace called Alex for a question regarding the family's famous holiday dinner.

"Alexandria?"

"Hey C, what's going on?"

"I have a question for you and Carol."

"Ok. What's up?"

"I was wondering if you would mind if I brought someone with me for Thanksgiving."

"Are you staying with Byron?"

"Yeah."

"Did you ask him?"

"Oh yeah."

"And what did he say?"

"Byron doesn't mind at all."

"So, Candace, why would Carol or I mind?"

"Well, it's a guy. A guy I've been dating for a while."

"C, that's great. Of course we want to meet him."

"Are you sure?"

"Of course. Why are you so concerned about whether or not we want him there?"

"I don't want to make you uncomfortable, Alexandria."

"Why? How would you do that?"

"Because you and Carol would be the only homosexual couple in the family."

"Oh Candace, don't think like that. We don't care. No worries. We're just excited for you and we definitely want to meet this young man, ok?"

"Ok. Thanks, A."

Thanksgiving had arrived. The family gathered at Byron's house, as usual. Erin, Byron, Carol, and Alex all eagerly awaited meeting Candace's new beau, a young man named Tyrone.

Tyrone was a tall, extremely handsome young man. He shaved his head bald and it was a very flattering look for him. He was tall and very muscular. His eyes were a dark, rich brown. His skin was darker than Candace's. They were a gorgeous couple.

The three couples all sat down to Byron's traditional, wonderful Thanksgiving meal.

As usual, they each said a quick prayer of Thanksgiving. Tyrone fell right in line with the family's tradition. Like Candace, he was eloquent and articulate. He was a highly intelligent and studious person.

"So, how did you two meet?" Erin excitedly asked Tyrone.

"In school. We're both social work majors," Tyrone explained. His voice was deep and seductive, sweet and sincere.

"How long have you been dating?" Byron asked. Despite the younger man's height and muscular build, Byron still towered over Tyrone and he had no problem letting him know how protective he was about his younger sister.

"For about seven months, B." Candace answered. She knew Byron would come down hard on Tyrone and she wanted this Thanksgiving to be a fun and relaxed holiday for everyone.

"Carol," Tyrone said. "Tell me more about what you do."

"I pretty much do everything when it comes to computers. I own my own networking business, but we do everything from home repairs and installs to server build outs, network setups and more.

"It's not glamorous by any means. It's a lot of work, a lot of hours and you have to be able to keep up with all the technological changes."

"My younger brother was thinking of going into computers when he goes to college," Tyrone explained.

"There's always work to be had, but let him know that there will be times he's married to his job."

"It's true," Alex added. "One of the biggest strains on our relationship has been the amount of time she spends working."

"He likes to work. He's one of those brain children whose mind is always going a million miles an hour. He needs to be occupied and mentally challenged. It doesn't take long for him to get bored, he needs constant mental stimulation."

"Then, it might just be the right job for him." Carol said.

"Would you mind if I ever gave him your name and number as a contact for advice or experience?"

"No. Not at all, Tyrone. That's no problem at all."

Tyrone won everyone over rather quickly. His charm, stunning smile, and active interest made a great impression with the family. The Whetherby clan all approved of Candace's new man.

"Tell us more about your family," Alex said.

"There's my younger brother and me, and our parents. There's really not much to tell."

"Where are you from?"

"Well we're army brats, so we're from all over. We moved a lot when Isaac and I were kids. We didn't have a set home, so to speak."

"Was that difficult?" Carol asked.

"It was to some extent. More so with our educations. Moving from school to school, each time the schools were never really sure how or where to place us.

"Education was extremely important to our parents. So, we were taught a lot at home as well. For example, when we lived in Europe, our parents taught us German, Spanish and French. Granted, we stood out as the only black kids in our classes, but we could communicate with our teachers and schoolmates in their native languages."

"That is extremely impressive." Alex said.

"Where do your parents live now?" Byron asked.

"Dad's retired from the military and my mom works in a small book store in Glen Allen, a suburb of Richmond."

"Your parents are still married?" Erin asked.

"Yep. They're still madly in love. They've been excellent role models for my brother and me."

"That's practically unheard of, nowadays." Carol stated.

"I know. We're very lucky to have the family that we do."

"That's great that your family is so close," Alex said. "Family is so important."

"I know it. That's one thing that I really admire about Candace. All of you are so important to her. She talks about each of you constantly. I think it's great. So many families are so disconnected nowadays.

"But not you guys. You always come together as a family. Despite all your differences; all your trials and tribulations. Between that and her good looks, Candace was hard to resist," Tyrone said lightly.

"Well, I'm glad to see that you understand the importance of family." Byron said. "You're right, our family may be small, but we're all we have. So, someone who can appreciate and respect that is always welcome in our home."

"Thank you, Byron." Tyrone said.

"On a totally different subject and more serious note, how's everything been since you spoke to that one employee, Carol?" Byron asked.

"Paul? You mean with the hate letters and everything? Done. It all stopped. I think I instilled some serious fear into him. It had to be him. The fact that everything stopped as soon as I spoke to him just tells me that my gut was right."

"May I ask what was going on?" Tyrone asked.

"Carol and my sister were constantly getting hate letters. Someone even threw a rock through their window one time." Candace explained.

"It was your typical anti-gay stuff. It was threatening, trying to get us to leave the neighborhood and what not." Alex added.

"And it was an employee of yours, Carol?" Tyrone asked.

"I'm pretty sure it was. There was one letter where he had handwritten one letter, a 't.' That 't' actually clued me in because I noticed it matched his handwriting.

"I approached him about it, and warned him that I could and would get the police involved if it didn't stop. But, it stopped right after that."

"Yet, you didn't pursue anything with the police?"

"We tried, Tyrone." Alex spoke up. "The police wanted nothing to do with us. When the rock was thrown through the window, you would have thought we called them because there was a spider in our house. They didn't look at anything, they didn't take any statements. They didn't do a thing."

"Nothing?" Tyrone asked in complete shock.

"Not a damn thing," Alex answered. "We don't know why. Carol thinks it's because we're an interracial lesbian couple."

"That shouldn't have any bearing on anything," Tyrone objected.

"You're right," Carol said. "I could be wrong, but it's what makes sense to me. Regardless, we were both really lucky that we never got hurt and the only thing that was ever damaged was a window. It's over now, so at least we can live in peace."

"Thank goodness." Tyrone said.

Tyrone fit in with everyone perfectly. There was a tremendous feeling of warmth this Thanksgiving. Tyrone seemed to be right person to complete this family.

Chapter Twenty-One

It was yet another new year and Carol was continually finding herself writing 2005, and sometimes even 2004, when it was already 2006. Time had been flying by so quickly.

Candace and Tyrone would be graduating later in the year with their 's degrees. Byron and Erin were still very happy and doing quite well.

"Where have the past two years gone?" Carol wondered. "They were eaten up in doctor appointments, work and group." She said to herself. "It's just amazing how quickly time flies," Carol whispered out loud as she waited for Dr. J to come into the exam room.

Finally, Dr. J's warm, familiar face peered around the door, and brought Carol back to the present moment.

"Hey Carol."

"Hi Dr. J, how's everything going?"

"Well, Carol, I'm a bit worried."

"Worried? Why?"

"Your liver enzymes are high. At this point, all I can assume is that the meds are taking their toll on your liver."

"What about Alex? How are her liver enzymes?"

"Her blood work looks really good."

"How can that be? We're on the same medications, Dr. J."

"I know. But, everybody is physiologically different. Your liver might be more sensitive than hers."

"So, what do we do?"

"I'm actually doing some research into some of the newer medications to see if they might be easier on your liver. In the meanwhile, there's a supplement known as SAM-e, and it works very well for liver issues. I want you to start taking that."

"I also want to check your blood work again in a month. We will re-check your values until you hold steady. I'm also putting in an order for an ultrasound of your liver."

"An ultrasound?" Carol was shocked and scared.

"Carol. I just want to make sure that your liver is the normal size, that we don't see any malformations or mottling as we call it. I want to be sure that your liver itself looks good overall."

"Damn," Carol said under her breath.

"I know it's a lot to take in, Carol. Don't worry. I've seen values much worse than yours. It's my job as your doctor to note these problems and try to nip them in the bud. I think you're going to be fine, but as you know by now I'm an overly cautious doctor."

"And that's why we keep coming back, Dr. J. Just give me all the information I need for the supplement and the ultrasound, and let's just do it."

"How is everyone?" Juanita asked.

"I got a bit of bad news last week." Carol said meekly.

"What's going on?" Juanita inquired.

"My blood work showed that my liver values are high. I'm on a new supplement and I'm supposed to have an ultrasound in two weeks."

"I had that," Steven said. "It's not uncommon. We're on so many medications that it's not unusual for us to have some minor liver issues. Just do what your doc tells you. I know it sounds scary at first, but you'll get through it."

"Carol, so many HIV/AIDS patients get all kinds of complications whether due to our medications or our poor immune systems." Henry explained. "Steven is right. It is scary at first, but you get through it. Once you understand the disease better, the fear goes away."

"I think we can all understand just how scary that news is to hear, Carol." Juanita said. She turned directly to Carol and spoke softly. "Just think about all that you have been through so far. You can get through this too."

Carol rushed into her office. "Will, come in here now, please!" Will ran a few steps to catch up to her. She quickly shut her office door behind him.

"Carol, what's going on?"

"Will, today is my ultrasound. I don't have much time before I have to go. But there's something that I have to do first."

Carol was quickly scribbling something on a piece of paper.

"Will, I want you to promise me that you and Robyn will take care of Sugar if anything happens to us. And, I want you to run the company in case I'm sick or die."

"Carol, don't you think you're being a bit over dramatic?"

"I don't care if I am, Will. I need to get these things taken care of. I don't know what the ultrasound is going to show and I just want to have all my ducks in a row. Here." Carol handed him a piece of paper stating what she just said with her signature and the date.

"Ok, Carol. If you insist."

"Thanks, Will. I've got to run. Have a good day." Carol shouted as she ran out of the office.

Carol lay on the table while the ultrasound technician squeezed the cold, wet jelly onto her abdomen.

"Ok, there's going to be a little pressure." The technician said. She took the wand and gently pressed it over Carol's abdomen. The woman was silent as she looked at the grainy screen.

She continued to silently smear the wand and jelly all over Carol. Carol tried desperately not to breathe too hard, nor to let the chill from the jelly get to her. The slightest move, hiccup, or breath could affect the ultrasound, or so she had been forewarned.

Carol lay as still as she could. The silence and the cold jelly both sent shivers down her spine. Carol hoped that her liver would be ok and that the ultrasound would be done soon.

It seemed like an eternity, but after a chilling while the ultrasound was finally over. The technician wiped the jelly off of Carol.

"Do you see anything?" Carol nervously asked the technician.

"Your doctor will call you with the results." She replied matter-of-factly.

"Oh." Carol was disappointed and worried now that she had to wait for the results.

"Ok. You're all set. Sit up slowly." The technician reached out her hand and slowly pulled Carol up. "Your doctor will call with the results." She technician repeated herself.

"Ok, thank you." Carol replied.

"Carol?"

"Yes?" Carol said into her phone. It was eight o'clock on a Thursday night.

"It's Dr. J."

"Oh hi, Dr. J! How are you?" Carol tried to ignore the nervousness she felt inside.

"Good. How are you feeling?"

"I'm doing well, thanks. What's up?"

"I have some very good news, Carol. I got your ultrasound results in. Your liver looks great. It's normal in size and shape. There's no mottling. Everything looks good. Keep up with the SAM-e and we'll re-check your blood work in a few weeks, ok?"

"Ok, Dr. J. That sounds great. Thank you."

"You're welcome. Have a great night."

"You too."

Relieved, Carol sighed as she hung up her phone.

Alex walked up behind Carol. "So?"

"Everything looks great, babe." Carol turned around to see Alex's face light up with joy. "No problems with my liver. I still have to stay on the supplement and he wants to re-check my blood in a few weeks, but for the most part everything is ok."

"Oh that is such great news! I am so relieved."

"Me too." Alex whispered as the two women held each other tightly. They held each other for a tender eternity. "I don't know what I'd do without you," Alex whispered.

Dave, John, Alex and Carol enjoyed some coffee together one beautiful spring afternoon.

"So how are you feeling, Carol?" John asked.

"Ok. I'm still on the supplement, but my blood work has been improving according to the doctor. So, it's just another pill to add to the collection."

"It's so hard to keep up with all these various medications." Alex chimed in.

"I know this has been tremendously difficult on you both, but we're just thrilled that you're both doing so well." Dave said.

"Thanks," Alex said. "It hasn't been easy, but the medical advances are just astonishing. That alone gives us a lot of hope."

"Thank God." Dave said. "We only want the best for you two."

"Thanks, Dave." Carol smiled and replied.

After a moment, John turned to Carol. "How's the company going?" He asked.

"Busy. Way too busy. Don't get me wrong, I'm glad we have such a great client base and that the business is doing well. But, it is so hard for me to keep up. It's been worse with the liver scare. I've been playing catch-up a lot lately."

"Is everyone on the staff doing their job?" John tentatively asked. He worried that Carol was pushing herself too hard.

"Yeah, for the most part." Carol sighed. "Ever since I confronted Paul about those hate letters though, he's been slipping a bit. It hasn't been anything too big... yet. I just worry that he'll end up doing something that will hurt the company. Otherwise, everything's been going well."

"The thing with Paul is," Alex jumped in, "he's always been a bit of a pompous ass. He was trouble even back when Greg owned the company. So his behavior could just be Paul being Paul."

"That is true." Carol agreed. "We don't know. We never know, really. We'll just have to wait and see, I guess."

"So," Will said as he and Carol carried a server into their client's building.

"So?" Carol huffed as she manipulated the large, heave machine through the door. "What?"

"So, don't you think you over reacted with that whole note signing the dog and company over to me?"

"Yes and no. You have to understand how scary all this is for us, Will. I didn't know what to expect."

"And truth be told, I want things to stay that way. As much as there have been amazing medical advances in the treatments of this damn disease, the end result is still the same. I just want to make sure that every 'i' is dotted and every 't' is crossed. Alex and I spoke about it and it was something we both agreed on."

They put the server on a shelf in a server rack. It was the last one they had hauled in. Now they both pulled out all of their cables and wiring and began to wire up the system.

"Ok. I still have the note. I'll hang on to it."

"Please do, Will. It may seem over dramatic to you, but it brings Alex and me serious peace of mind."

"Ok, you're the boss."

"I'll admit, it was actually really hard for both Robyn and me to look at that though. You're so much younger than us, Carol."

"Age has nothing to do with it. You know that."

"I know, but that doesn't make it any easier. It's just not right, that's all."

"I know, Will. There's nothing we can do but just deal with it. I have no choice but to accept this as my reality. I have to do what I have to do. I can't live in denial forever."

"I know. And it's not to say that Robyn and I aren't happy to do our part. Just know that both you and Alexandria mean a lot to us, and we hate the thought of losing you."

"Thanks, man. I appreciate that. You guys are like family to us and that's why we did that. We trust you with everything. You're amazing people, and we love you. We know that you'll take care of everything with the utmost care." Carol paused to take a deep breath. "Now, let's get this system wired up and running before our wives give us shit about being home late for dinner."

They both laughed. They continued to talk about various unimportant subjects as they hurriedly finished the task at hand.

It was summer and Candace was finally graduating with her M's degree. Tyrone was graduating with the same credits as well.

The couple decided to move to St. Louis to be near Candace's family. They both had good job offers as social workers in the area and an apartment waiting for them after graduation. Their relationship was solid. Tyrone was adored by everyone in Candace's family and vice versa. The couple's decision to move-in together was accepted by all.

Erin, Byron, Carol and Alex flew to Richmond for Candace's big day. The hot Virginia summer sun beat down on the crowd and the humidity was stifling. Even though the weather left a bit to be desired, the ceremony was nice and the family was very proud of Candace and Tyrone.

After graduation, both families took the new grads out to a celebratory dinner. It was the first time the two families met.

Tyrone did the introductions. His parents were very kind and hospitable to the Whetherby family. His younger brother, Isaac, was as sharp and quick witted as Tyrone had said.

The table of nine was boisterous and happy. Both families were so proud of the two graduates and their plans for the future. The atmosphere was light and full of merriment.

"Now, Byron," Tyrone's father started. "I expect that you'll keep an eye on these two." He gestured towards Candace and Tyrone.

"Of course, sir. That's my little sister. I always keep an eye out for her!"

"Good man." He exclaimed.

Isaac struck up a conversation with Carol. "So you're in computers?" He asked.

"Yeah. I own my own networking company." Carol smiled at the bright young boy. He seemed wise beyond his years and Carol was enjoying their conversation.

"That's cool. I like building my own computers and electronics. I've been taking things apart and rebuilding them since I was a kid. I'm even starting to build my own robots now."

"Wow." Carol was quite by the teen's remarkable intelligence. "My networking stuff would seem like small potatoes to you."

"You're obviously very smart. Where do you want to go to college, Isaac?"

"I'm hoping to go to MIT."

"Somehow, I have a feeling you'll get in there." Carol smiled and winked at him. This young boy had a very bright future ahead of him.

"Thanks." Isaac had a large and very proud smile across his face.

The two families continued to talk throughout the evening. Conversation flowed easily and both families meshed well together. Everyone in the group was beaming with pride over the two graduates. This was an important and fantastic celebration. All of the family members wanted this moment to last forever.

Imperfect

Six months flew by in the blink of an eye. Tyrone and Candace were doing well in their new jobs and their new life together.

Byron and Erin hosted the traditional Thanksgiving dinner. As always, it was warm and sweet. The family always cherished their holiday time together.

When Christmas came, the Whetherby family decided that each couple would spend a quiet holiday independently of the others.

Tyrone and Candace were in Virginia to spend the holiday with Tyrone's family.

Erin got called to work at the last minute, so Byron spent a quiet day by himself.

Carol and Alex spent the holiday together in the peace and quiet of their own home. They decided not to get presents for each other. Sugar, however, was quite spoiled by Santa.

Chapter Twenty-Two

It was dark and bitterly cold one January evening as Carol and Alex walked to group. They walked as quickly as they could to keep warm.

The usual members were there and a new woman who sat quietly by herself. Her face was riddled with pock marks and scabs. Her eyes were sunken and she looked very worn. Her face silently spoke of a hard life. Her hair was stringy and disheveled. Her clothes were dirty and torn. Carol and Alex looked at her, she somehow seemed familiar to them.

Juanita started the group as she always did. "Hi everyone. We have a new member with us today. I'd like you all to say hello to Marlene."

The name sounded familiar to her, but it took her a moment. "Marlene," Carol thought to herself. "No, it couldn't possibly be Marlene from school. Could it?"

Everyone greeted the reticent woman.

"Marlene, why don't you tell us a bit about yourself," Juanita softly encouraged her to speak.

"Well, umm... I just moved back to town from Kansas City. I was living there for the past ten years. I was married to a man named Brad."

It was Marlene, Carol's old college roommate. Not wanting to embarrass her friend, Carol quietly listened to Marlene's story.

"Brad was unfaithful. A lot. He had girlfriends, mistresses, and even prostitutes. That's... how I got sick."

"After five years of marriage, he left me for some eighteen year old twit. I don't know if he knew that he was sick at the time or not. I didn't know yet."

"I just kept getting sick repeatedly and never getting any better. That went on for about a year and a half after he left. That's when they told me I was HIV positive."

"I couldn't handle the pain or the stress. It hurt so much. I had given up my life for this man. He cheated, he left me, he gave me a fatal illness."

"I'm not proud of this, but I tried to numb the pain as best I could. It didn't take long to find out about Meth and Heroine. I was shooting up several times a day, smoking ice. I was doing whatever I could to just not feel, to not face my reality."

"I was arrested for drug possession several times and eventually forced into rehab. I've been out of rehab for two weeks now. I'm just trying to get my life straight again."

"That's Marlene from school, remember her?" Carol whispered to Alex.

Carol was still with Alex, ten years later. Both Carol and Alex were well dressed and groomed. Despite their sickness, their life was a good one. Staring back at them was what their life could have been. Marlene had indeed taken a very different path in life.

"I was in a similar boat, Marlene." Ken said. "I got AIDS from using. I know what you're going through. It's not easy, but you can do it. I had some very dark days, but in the end I was able to build a good life for myself. This still isn't how I pictured my life, but I don't think that any of us pictured our lives to turn out this way."

"It's ok, though. We're all doing the best that we can and trying to give back to AIDS research and what have you."

"That's really nice," Marlene said softly. "This is my first time on my own and not high. It's hard and it's scary. I don't know where to go or what to do. I don't have a job, I don't have family. They all disowned me because of my drug use. I have no home, no car. I just feel lost right now."

"That's ok, we all felt lost in the beginning," Juanita said. "What you're going through is emotional and strenuous. You have to be patient with yourself. You have a lot of healing to do in several areas of your life. The main thing is that you are patient and gentle with yourself as you go through this process."

After group, Carol and Alex hesitantly approached Marlene.

"Hey, Marlene," Carol said gently.

The straggly woman looked up at her.

"It's Carol, Carol Mathers, from college."

Marlene stared at Carol for a minute. "No way," she whispered.

"Yeah. I'm glad to see you again."

"I'm so sorry about Brad and everything." Carol said as she hugged her long-lost friend.

"Yeah, thanks."

"How come you're here?"

"I received a blood transfusion as a child."

"I remember you telling me that."

"It was before they began screening donors, I got AIDS from my transfusion."

"Oh shit."

"Yeah."

"And do you remember Alexandria? She and I met the night you took me out to City Girls for my twenty- first birthday."

"Yeah. You were infatuated with her."

The three women chuckled softly.

"We've been together since then. She got AIDS from me."

Alex shook Marlene's hand. "I am so sorry for everything that you're going through. I'm also a recovering addict. I've been sober for thirteen years. Look, your friendship meant a lot to Carol back then. You're more than welcome to come to our house if you ever need. We're both happy to help you in any way. Don't hesitate to ever call either one of us, ok?"

Alex and Carol both handed Marlene their cards.

"Thanks," she replied. "I'd better get going. It was good to see you again. See you next time."

"Bye Marlene." Carol said and hugged her again.

"So, how do my values look, doc?"

Dr. J smiled at Carol. "They're holding. You seem to be handling this regimen well, so I want to stick with it. But I still want to re-test in 3 months. After that scare, I would just feel better checking your blood more often."

"Ok. As long as things look good, I'll do whatever you say."

"You're a good patient, Carol. Keep taking good care of yourself and I'll see you in a few months."

"Ok, Dr. J. Sounds good."

"Bye, Carol," he gently said as he left the exam room.

Carol left Dr. J's and drove towards her office. She called Will from her blackberry. "Hey, Will!"

"Hi Carol, what's up?"

"I just finished up at the doctor's, so I'm heading in. I figured I'd call to see what was going on."

"We had five home repair calls and Paul took them all."

"Shit. I'll talk to him about that again tomorrow. What are you working on?"

"Right now, inventory. It looks as though an order was placed for a snap server, but I can't find it."

"Who placed the order?"

"It was for Murdoch's."

"Who put in the requisition?"

"Supposedly Paul."

"Do you have a date when the order was placed? I don't remember seeing an order for a snap server."

"It looks like it was back in December some time."

"Double shit. Call all of our suppliers and see if we ever placed that order with any of them. If not, find the cheapest one and do an over-night delivery."

"As soon as I get there, I'll help you sort through inventory. I'll also look through all my req forms to see if Paul ever gave me one."

"Ok, Carol. Sounds good. See you in a bit."

"Lisa!" Alex called out before her boss walked into her office.

Lisa turned around. "Yes, Alexandria?"

Alex ran a few steps to catch up to Lisa so she could speak quietly with her. "I was wondering if you or Frederick knew of any good will and estate planning lawyers."

"Yeah, we do. Why? Are you and Carol..."

"Yeah. We have to, Lisa. It's long overdue. You know that."

Lisa gave an understanding nod. "Hold on for one second." She walked into her office, grabbed a card and handed it to Alex. "This is a good friend of mine. Let him know you work for me, I'm sure he'll take good care of you."

"Thanks, Lisa. I appreciate it."

"No problem, Alexandria."

Alex looked at the card in her hand. It felt surreal that she was about to speak to an estate planner. She sighed heavily and walked away as Lisa walked back into her office.

8

Robyn and Will were over for their usual Tuesday dinner with Carol and Alex. The group all enjoyed Alex's home made tomato soup and Garlic bread.

"So what did Paul say when you talked to him about the home calls and the req form?" Will asked Carol.

"He said he was sorry. He said he didn't know that he couldn't just do home repairs all day."

"Bullshit! You made it very clear that those jobs were to be divided between the three of us."

"Thank you," Carol replied. "I'm glad that my message did actually get through to someone. Anyway, he also claimed that he did put in that req form for Murdoch's."

"He did?"

"Yeah, yet neither Yvette in accounting nor I have copies of the form. Since it's a triplicate form, that's kind of hard to explain."

"Yeah, no kidding. Plus none of our suppliers had an order placed by him or by you."

"I know. I'm getting really sick of his attitude and sloppy work. He's just been getting worse and worse. When he's good, he's great. But when he doesn't care, his work is horrible."

"What do you think you're going to do, Carol?" Robyn asked.

Carol sighed. "I don't know. Right now, I can't even worry about it. Alex and I just scheduled an appointment to do our wills. It's all I can think about. Paul's juvenile crap just has to wait. It's hurting the business, but it just can't be my top priority right now."

Robyn turned to Alex in astonishment. "You're doing your wills?!"

"Yeah," Alex softly replied. "We have to. We really should have done it a while ago. We can't hold off any longer."

"Geez. You're both so young for that. Damn." Will paused to take a deep breath. Though this conversation pained him, he understood the necessity. "When are you going?"

"Next Thursday," Alex replied.

Robyn and Will sat in silence looking at the younger couple. The pain and sadness was easily seen in their eyes.

Juanita was very solemn when group started. "I have some bad news to share with all of you."

Imperfect

All the members of the group sat making a sound, apprehensively awaiting the next words to come from Juanita's mouth.

"You remember Marlene who just joined us last time. Well, she died. She apparently went back to drugs and over dosed. It's unclear whether it was a suicide or a mistake."

"Oh my God." Carol whispered and began crying.

"You knew her, didn't you, Carol?" Juanita asked.

"She was my roommate in college."

"I saw you and Alexandria talking to her last week." Ken said. "What did you say to her?"

"We opened our home to her if she needed, we gave her our numbers to call if she wanted to talk. I explained to her that I used to be an addict and I'd be happy to support her through everything." Alex explained while Carol still cried into her hands.

"I mean no disrespect, Alexandria, but do you think it was possible that you actually did more harm than good?" Ken asked.

"How?"

"You own a home. Your relationship has lasted the past ten years when hers didn't. You're clean. You both have good jobs and dress nicely. I don't think you meant anything by it, but you as a recovering addict should understand how that could have hurt her more."

"I suppose you're right, Ken. But what are we supposed to do? Have a change of house clothes in the car so we don't come in our work attire? Not offer her a place to stay if she needs?" Alex was defensive.

"Regardless of any of that, Marlene chose whether or not she was going to let those factors affect her." Juanita interjected. "We don't know what was going on with her. Maybe she just ran into someone who had a hit of Meth and it just became too much for her to stay clean. We can't blame Carol and Alexandria for trying to reach out to an old friend."

"I don't think Ken was trying to blame them," Steven said. "Look at all of us. We share the same diagnosis she had. Most of us are still working. We all maintain some kind of normal lives.

"Ken, you were the closest person she could relate to because you got sick from drugs. And look at you. I'm sure your example could have had as much an emotional impact as Carol's."

"Wait," Carol sniffled. "You made a good point, Steven. We all have fairly normal lives despite our illness. We've all been through a lot, but we kept fighting."

"Very true," Juanita agreed.

Carol continued. "My point is this, how do we handle situations like Marlene's when none of us intended to hurt her? We wanted to inspire and encourage her. We all wanted to help her in some way. Alex and Ken knew what she was going through. They both tried to reach out to her and yet here we are debating whether or not the ability to relate actually pushed Marlene to do what she did."

"We will probably never know what went through her mind those last few moments of her life. How do we embrace and accept someone without hurting them? How do we inspire and encourage them to have a normal life without rubbing pain from the past in their face?"

"That's a great point, Carol. Why don't we discuss that?" Juanita suggested.

"Why?" Carol shouted. "What's the point? Every person's reaction will be different. And it's too late. My friend, a very good woman, I might add, is now dead. What difference does it make now?" Carol stood up and ran from the room.

Losing her father, losing Ed, now having lost Marlene, and knowing that she might lose Alex one day suddenly became too overwhelming.

Carol went outside and stood in the frigid air, crying under a street lamp. She stayed there until group was over.

Carol reluctantly walked into work, she was enjoying the warm air too much. Late spring was here. Once again she found herself thinking about the speed of time as she walked in from the bright sun.

As she walked into the main work area, she noticed that Will was rebuilding a server. After watching him for a moment, she realized he was working with latex gloves on. Confused, she hesitantly approached him.

"Morning, Will."

"Good morning, Carol. How are you?"

"I'm fine, thanks. How about you?"

"Same old, same old."

Carol stood by him for a minute before she picked up the conversation again. "Will, why are you wearing gloves to work on that server?"

Will looked up her in puzzlement. "Because that's what we're doing now. Don't worry. Paul told me. He said that you wanted to hold a meeting, but I had been out on a call the day you decided to have it. He said that you said it was safest for all of us to wear gloves in case we got cut or something."

Carol restrained her anger. "Will, did you ever get a memo about this?"

"No."

"Do you really think I would have held a meeting, especially such an important one, without you?"

"I did think it was odd, but Paul said that your doctor said it was of the utmost importance. That it had to be done A.S.A.P."

"Are you kidding me, Will?" Carol took a deep breath to try to calm herself. "What exactly did Paul tell you?"

"That your doctor said that since we work with small parts and risk getting cut, we should protect ourselves by wearing gloves. We should have done that as soon as you got your diagnosis."

Carol now fought even more desperately to contain her anger. "Will, do you not understand how HIV/AIDS is transferred?"

"Well yeah, but I thought maybe the doctor found out some new information or something."

"No! Will, nothing has changed. Certainly not about how the virus is transferred. Those gloves will do you no good. You can take them off."

"Ok, Carol." Will looked up at her. She could see the regret in his eyes, but her anger was all consuming. Carol furiously walked away.

Alex and Carol nervously sat in the lawyer's office. It was a dimly lit room, full of dark wood book cases that housed an infinite number of leather-bound books. The chairs were dark green leather. It was a posh workplace, but by no means was it a comfortable or welcoming environment.

The man who sat before them, although a friend of Lisa's, did not share her warm personality. He seemed distant and strictly business.

"You both need your estates planned?"

"Yes," Alex spoke up, but her voice cracked.

"I normally don't work with two clients at one time."

"I work for Lisa Ludlow and Frederick Kepwick."

"I understand that," he replied .

"Sir," Carol said. "We've been together for ten years. Our plans are pretty much identical. We just need to go through the formalities of it all. We both know what we want. We've already discussed everything and we're on the same page."

"I've heard that before. I've seen couples together much longer than ten years argue over their estates. There are more family disputes and arguments over wills. I simply do not deal with such petty behavior."

Carol tried to be strong as she spoke. "I can assure you that will not be the case here. We have a very small family and no children. We both need to get our wills in order as soon as possible for our family's sake. Please, we will work quickly with you and there won't be any debates."

He directed his attention to Alex. "And you, Miss Whetherby?"

"This is a necessity. We just want to get this done. There are no points to argue. We just want to do whatever we need and have everything in order."

The lawyer took in a deep breath. "Ok," he said reluctantly. "Let's go over all of these details and get your estates in order."

Carol and Alex looked at each other. They felt like a burden to this man because of his tone. They wanted, and needed, to have their wills finalized. This lawyer was doing them a favor by not charging them because of Alexandria's connection to Lisa, but the women both wished he had been kinder towards them.

Byron, Erin, Candace, Tyrone, Carol and Alex all sat around the table for Christmas dinner. Another year had flown by and they were happy to spend another holiday with each other.

Byron had specifically requested that no one exchanged gifts this year. Though the family thought it was odd, they all honored his wish.

As everyone was ready to begin dinner, Byron stood up with his glass in hand. "I'd like to make a toast," he said.

Everyone listened.

"To my family, though we've been through so much, we've always stayed together. To Erin, for being with me for so many years, and joining our family. To her love, patience and devotion. And to our up-coming wedding!"

Everyone at the table was shocked. No one was expecting this, but everyone was very happy for the couple.

"Your brother proposed to me last night," Erin quietly explained. "We've decided to get married in late June or early July. We'll pick an exact date within the next week or so."

"Seriously? Are you kidding?" Candace exclaimed.

"No, C. This is real. And we'd be honored if you were all a part of the ceremony," Byron said.

"Of course." Everyone shouted without hesitation.

Byron turned to Tyrone. "Tyrone, I'd like you to be the best man."

"It would be my honor." Replied Tyrone.

"And I'd like you three ladies to be my bridesmaids," Erin said.

"Like there was any question!" Candace joked.

The holiday dinner progressed through the evening. The family excitedly discussed wedding plans. Everyone was enjoying the excitement of the up-coming nuptials.

Chapter Twenty-Three

Erin, Candace, Carol and Alex sat around the table going over the details of the impending wedding. Spring was already in full bloom, there wasn't much time left to finalize the tiniest of the wedding details.

Erin stood up to stretch and get herself another cup of coffee. "Do you think you'll ever get married to Tyrone, Candace?" Erin asked as she walked back to the table.

"I don't know," Candace shrugged. "We're happy with things as they are. Life is good. We like what we've got." Candace looked down at the table and paused for a moment. "Actually, we do have news we wanted to share with everyone. We were supposed to wait until everyone was here, though."

"Oh?" Alex asked.

"All of the women are here. Why wait?" Candace brightly joked.

The women all laughed. Then Carol, Alex and Erin leaned in to listen intently to the young, beautiful, articulate Candace.

"Tyrone and I are..."

"Are?" Alex interrupted, unable to wait.

"We're pregnant!" Candace shouted.

Each woman cried out in excitement.

"No way! You're kidding?" Carol said gleefully.

"No. No, it's definite, Carol. I did a home test and then I went to my OB/GYN to confirm." Candace was smiling from ear to ear.

"How far along are you?" Alex asked her sister.

"Only about 6 weeks. I conceived in early May."

"Wow, that is great. Congratulations! So exciting." Erin exclaimed.

"Indeed, congrats, C!" Alex added as she grabbed her younger sister's hand and gently squeezed it.

"Oh my God! I am so exited for you. That is so amazing. Congratulations, sweetie." Carol said and smiled.

The girls all enjoyed the sweet moment. They were silent, but their smiles spoke volumes.

After a few minutes, Erin spoke up. "Now how are we supposed to finish the wedding planning after hearing that?" Erin teased Candace and messed up her hair.

"My sister is pregnant, and my brother is getting married. I just can't believe all of this." Alex told the group.

"Congratulations," Ken said.

"You said you can't believe all of this. What exactly do you mean by that?" Juanita asked.

"Candace is my little sister. She's ten years younger than me and she's about to have a baby.

"And my brother... well, he rarely dated. Then he started dating Erin, they dated for years. We always teased them about marriage, but we never thought it would actually happen."

"Do you feel that you and Carol are somehow being left behind since we still can't get married and due to your health you can't have children?" Henry asked.

"Personally I do," Carol admitted. "Alex and I have been together for eleven years and all of a sudden, it seems like life is passing us by. These are landmark events in life and it's happening to people we love, but it's happening so quickly."

"Are you jealous?" Zachary asked.

"I don't think Carol's saying that we're jealous. I think what she's trying to say is that my brother's marriage is monumental enough, but add my sister's pregnancy, too, and our lives are the same. Same jobs, same home," Alex explained.

"Is there anything wrong with stability, Alexandria?" Juanita asked.

"No. Stability is great. I'm glad our lives have been stable. It would be nice if we could get married, or if we were in a position to adopt or have one of us conceive."

"I agree, stability is great." Carol added. "I know that I would just prefer it, if I could have a preference, that it be one event at a time."

"Don't get me wrong, this is all very exciting. And the family is including both of us in everything. But to see someone ten years younger than Alex starting a family is a lot for both of us to absorb."

"Do you really think it's because she is so much younger than both of you?" Juanita asked.

"For me it is," Alex answered.

"In all honesty, that's the kind of life that we were supposed to have. I always wanted to marry Alex. I would have loved to have kids with her. Those options were taken away from us pretty early on in the relationship. Our life isn't quite complete. It's imperfect... because of me." Carol sighed. Admitting that she felt responsible for the unhappiness and imperfections in their lives was a tremendous burden for her to carry.

Carol and Alex sat with the lawyer in his dark office again. It was a cold, austere room. Both women felt uncomfortable, but the meeting was necessary.

"What brings you ladies back?" He asked.

"Well, there is one thing that we would like to change in each of our wills." Alex explained.

"Ok, what do we need to change?"

"Regarding the house. We both want it to go to Candace, Alexandria's sister, once we're both gone." Carol said as she sat uneasily in her chair.

"Ok. That's easy enough. In order to make sure there aren't any questions or problems, I need her full legal name. Is her full name Candace Whetherby?"

"Yes, Candace Whetherby," Alex answered.

"Ok," the lawyer responded. "You have the house going to each other in case of your individual deaths."

"We want that to stay," Alex said. "Once we're both gone, Candace will need the house. She's going to have a baby, we want to make sure that she and her baby are cared for."

"Do you want the baby's father to be added as well?"

"Tyrone isn't a bad guy, but I need to watch out for my sister and her child. Let's just leave it for Candace."

"Ok. We'll change that and draw up the new papers. Once it's all set and we need your signatures, we'll call you."

"Thank you so much. We appreciate your changing this for us. It's really important, it means a lot to us." Carol said.

It was a gorgeous and warm, early summer day. The sun glowed brightly and welcomed everyone entering the Whetherby family church. Everyone basked in the beauty of the day. It was the perfect day for a wedding. Byron and Erin's big day finally arrived and the setting was ideal.

Carol, Candace and Alex were bridesmaids. They stood at the front of the church in their matching pink dresses. They held their bouquets and smiled as the organ began to play Here Comes the Bride.

Alex looked over and saw her brother tearing up as Erin made her grand entrance in a slinky mermaid style wedding dress. The dress hugged her small body beautifully. She wore a small tiara with rhinestones, but no veil. The sequins and embellishments glistened as she made her way towards Byron. Erin was a stunning bride. She proudly walked down the aisle alone.

The ceremony was simple and short, but beautiful. Byron and Erin had seamlessly integrated both Buddhist and Gospel elements into the ceremony. Candles and incense burned around a statue of Buddha. Light from the stained glass windows highlighted the Buddhist shrine. The two religions complimented each other during the ceremony. Though the Whetherby pastor officiated, he did well integrating Buddhist prayers and offerings into the service. It was a wonderful reflection of them as individuals and as a couple.

Before anyone even realized it, the ceremony was over. The vows and prayers had been read. Byron and Erin were officially married.

Byron and Erin walked onto the dance floor, both were glowing. Nat King Cole's Unforgettable was playing. After a few minutes, the DJ invited all the couples to join the newlyweds. Candace and Tyrone made their way up to the dance floor. Carol and Alex looked at each other. Alex nodded, they too, went up to dance.

Carol and Alex danced in bliss along with their family. Carol looked around to take it all in. It was a beautiful moment that all three couples were sharing.

"That's why darling, it's incredible..." Alex gently sang along with the song into Carol's ear. "That someone, so unforgettable, thinks that I am unforgettable too."

"Well, that was a nice wedding," Carol said as she took off her uncomfortable pink shoes.

"Yeah it was. I'm really happy for Byron." Alex agreed. "It was a nice ceremony and there's no doubt that he and Erin will make it." Alex began to unzip her pink dress.

"What do you think you're doing?" Carol teased.

"Taking off this hideous pink dress that I'll never wear again."

Carol couldn't contain her laughter. "But you look good in it, babe."

"Right," Alex said jokingly.

"Oh come on, Alex, I rarely see you in a dress. The pink compliments your skin so well. I think you look sexy."

"Well I think you look sexy, miss thang!" Alex replied.

"Now you must be crazy. A pale white girl in a big pink dress? How on earth is that attractive?" Carol laughed as she spoke.

"I'll tell you what. You and I were the best looking couple at the wedding."

"Why? Because we matched?" Carol laughed heartily.

"Maybe." Alex seductively teased as she began to caress Carol's shoulders.

"Oh don't start," Carol joked. She grabbed Alex's hand and kissed it.

"Oh, I'll start alright," Alex tenderly nibbled on Carol's neck.

"That's it." Carol exclaimed frivolously. She turned aroundand planted a big kiss on Alex, teasingly at first. Then it slowed down and became warmer, softer, and more passionate. Even after more than a decade together, the two women still felt a spark every time they kissed.

They began to lovingly caress each other's bodies. Both their hands gently felt their way around the other's curves and crevices. Their touches were soft, loving, satisfying, electrifying. They still enjoyed every second with each other.

The two continued in their slow tango of love; feeling each other's heat, breathing into each other. They savored each other.

Imperfect

They teased each other. They thrilled each other. Their hearts raced. Their souls soared and coiled into one.

Time had not taken away their love or passion for each other. Even though it was Byron's wedding day, they shared this night together as if it was their own.

Each year seemed to fly by faster than the previous year. 2008 was no exception. As the year progressed, Carol and Alex watched the economy plummet into a horrible recession. The stock market like the infamous crash in . The value of their house decreased significantly. The news became increasingly depressing each day. Work slowed for both women, but they were lucky enough to be able to keep their jobs when thousands of others didn't.

November came. For the first time, the Whetherby family didn't come together for Thanksgiving.

Erin worked. She had plenty of opportunities for overtime and holiday work. Byron struggled, his contracting work had diminished with the economy. He couldn't afford to host his growing family this year.

Candace and Tyrone spent the day together in their tiny apartment. Candace was getting bigger by the moment. Her pregnancy was going well. She preferred to stay home rather than risk the cold and driving in her condition. She and Tyrone needed to save as much money as they could for the new baby. As much as they would have enjoyed the family's company, it wasn't practical for them to go anywhere, nor could they try to squeeze everyone into their home.

Carol and Alex shared a quiet evening at home over a simple dinner. Like so many others, the couple cut as many expenses as they could. They were thankful that they both still had jobs and a home considering the severity of the economic situation.

One bitterly cold day in December, Carol received a letter from Missouri State bank stating that one of the larger national chains had taken over. Yet another fatality in the dying American economy.

Carol hoped that with the issues she had with the bank in the past that this might actually be more helpful. She was still skeptical, though, considering the horrible state that all banks and the economy were in.

Chapter Twenty-Four

Carol sat in front of her computer, frantically looking back and forth from the monitor to the paper in her hand. This couldn't be possible. She sighed out of confusion and frustration. "Hey babe," She called out to Alex, who was in the living room.

"Yeah, honey?"

"Can we run to the bank before we do everything else?"

"Yeah, why?"

"Because my statement and the on-line balance don't match."

"By how much?" Alex asked as she walked in and stood behind Carol.

"Five thousand dollars."

"Five thousand?"

"Yeah. This is just ridiculous. Missouri State was never great but ever since that other bank took over, everything's been messed up even worse."

"Maybe we should check out First Federal."

"That's not a bad idea," Carol agreed. "But I want my money back first!"

"No shit," Alex replied. "Let's go do that. Then we'll run our other errands after."

Carol and Alex waited several minutes at the bank before they were finally seen by a less than competent teller.

Carol sighed heavily again. "Look, Kathleen, you can see that my register and statements are exactly alike. Then why the hell does the online statement say there's five thousand less in my account?"

"I don't know. My computer is showing the same thing."

Again, Carol huffed. It was all she could do to contain her anger. "Can you please get your manager out here?"

"Certainly."

As Kathleen walked away, Carol turned to Alexandria. "Argh! This is such bullshit. I'm sorry, babe."

"It's ok. We just have to get this fixed."

"Yeah. I hope the manager has a brain."

Suddenly, Carol noticed Alex's eyes grow wide and fear washed over her face. Carol turned around just in time to see a tall, broad shouldered man wearing a ski mask standing right in front of the door.

"Everybody down!" He ordered. He waived a dark hand gun. Even though it looked small in his large hands, it was extremely intimidating.

Slowly, every person in the bank slumped to the floor. The gunman noticed Alex lying behind Carol. The bank was located in a predominantly white neighborhood and Alex was the only person of color in the bank.

The gunman made his way towards Alex. "What's a nice little darkie like you doing here?" The man's muscular arms nearly ripped through his black tee-shirt as he pulled Alex up. Carol watched helplessly as he dragged Alex back to where he was originally standing. Then, he placed the gun to her head.

Carol couldn't lay on the floor while Alex stood helpless with her life in danger. "Wait," Carol weakly called out. Very slowly and cautiously, Carol stood up and held her hands up. "Please, leave her alone. She's with me."

The gunman walked towards Carol while still holding Alex. "Is that so?" The tall man was clearly angry and despised Alex's presence. Carol's attempt to stand up for her woman only aggravated this man more. "Now, why would you do something stupid like that?"

"Look." Carol's voice shook as she stood there, still holding her arms up. "You didn't come here for her, let her go."

"She's just the icing on the cake," he said in a frightening tone. He turned and addressed everyone in the bank. "I want everyone's cash and the tellers to empty out their drawers. NOW!"

Everyone scrambled through their wallets and purses and tossed their money on the floor in the gunman's direction. The tellers emptied their cash drawers. Paper money flew around the lobby like confetti.

During the commotion, one teller was able to nonchalantly press the silent alarm button. No one saw her do that. Everyone in the bank prayed that the police would show up somehow.

The gunman stared at Carol, still standing. She was the only person who didn't empty her purse for the criminal. "Give me your damn money, bitch!"

"Sir, I have no cash on me. I promise." Carol pulled her wallet out from her purse and flashed its empty contents to the man. "Now, will you let her go?"

The man began to laugh heartily. "Don't you think it ironic that you don't have anything to give me in return for her life?"

"You've got everyone else's money. If you just take it now, you can run. Having a hostage would slow you down." Carol tried to reason with the criminal.

The man stopped to think. She actually had a point. After a moment, he pushed Alex down and towards Carol. Alex fell hard and slid forward a bit on the slick tile floor.

No one in the bank had seen the police swarm around the building outside, the gunman included. One SWAT officer thought he had a clear shot of the criminal, but just as he pulled the trigger Alex was thrown forward. The police officer's bullet pierced the glass and landed deep in Alex's arm. The gunshot, glass shattering, and Alex falling to the ground created mass chaos in the bank. People began screaming, adding to the disorder.

Carol leapt forward to cover Alexandria. When she saw the amount of blood pouring out of Alex's arm, she quickly ripped off a shoe, then her sock. Carol took the sock and made a make-shift tourniquet tied to Alex's upper arm in the hopes it would decrease the bleeding.

As Carol tightened the sock on Alex, shots were being fired in every direction. Glass was flying all over the place. Carol laid back down in front of Alex in order to shield her from the bullets and glass. The various screams, the breaking glass, and the loud popping sounds from all the guns created a deafening hell of fear.

After several minutes of , the robber fell to the ground and blood was oozing from several holes in his now lifeless body.

As soon as Carol noticed the quiet, she grabbed Alex and ran out of the bank. Alex stumbled trying to keep up, but she knew that she had to in order to survive. Thankfully an ambulance waited within a few feet.

"She was shot in the arm, she needs help. She has AIDS." Carol shouted at the paramedics. The medics ran up to Alex and placed her on the gurney, then lifted the gurney into the ambulance. Carol rushed up to the ambulance and started to get in.

"No, ma'am." A male medic said. "Family only."

"That's my damn wife!" Carol exclaimed as she pushed her way into the ambulance.

Carol waited in the ER waiting room. Byron and Candace were on their way. Carol hoped and prayed that her partner of nearly twelve years would pull through. The severity of the situation beset Carol. She buried her face in her hands and sobbed.

Carol's crying was interrupted by a tap on the shoulder. Byron and a very pregnant Candace stood in front of her with love and concern in their eyes.

Carol rose and the three embraced.

Byron gently asked, "You ok?"

Carol simply nodded. She had a few minor cuts from the glass, but she had escaped major injury from the day's battle. Carol sat between Byron and Candace and held their hands while they waited for any news.

A dark-haired male doctor stepped out into the waiting room. He spotted Byron and Candace. "Are you the Whetherby family?"

"Yes," Byron answered.

"You can come with me."

Carol stood up along with Candace and Byron.

"I'm sorry, miss. Family only." The doctor said coldly.

"She is family. She's coming too." Byron stated forcefully.

Considering Byron's size, the doctor wasn't going to argue. He led the group into the area where Alex was resting.

"The bullet was lodged pretty deep in the muscle," the doctor explained. "We were able to surgically remove it without any difficulty. Obviously, our biggest concern is her AIDS status. So far she seems stable, but all we can do is watch and see how her body heals."

Alexandria opened her groggy eyes. Carol was sitting in a chair, asleep, holding her hand. It was a precious image for Alex to wake to. She smiled at her sleeping beauty, and went back to sleep.

The first week passed and Alex didn't show improvement. Carol rarely left her side. Byron and Candace visited as much as they could. The family constantly asked for information on Alex's condition. The doctors said they weren't worried. Though she didn't seem to be improving, the doctors said her healing would be slow due to AIDS.

Day after day and night after night turned into a second week that passed. Alex was no better. She slept often. She didn't seem to be responding to the various treatments. Everyone was concerned, yet the medical staff still insisted that this was to be expected. The doctors and nurses explained that a compromised immune system would slow her body's ability to heal from trauma.

By the third week, Carol's concern elevated. A nurse came to take Alex's daily blood sample, something in Carol's gut told her this time the results would be different. Alex still slept most of the time and ate very little. Carol knew that today's blood sample was going to bring bad news.

"Hi Will," Carol spoke softly into her phone. "Yeah, she's sleeping right now."

"So, what's the status?"

"Not much. Her healing is slow, but they say that's typical with AIDS patients. They're pumping her full of fluids and all kinds of medications. I don't even know what half that shit is."

"Do they seem optimistic, Carol?"

"They're not really saying either way. They just keep telling me it's too soon to tell."

"Damn, I'm sorry to hear that. Carol, I hate to ask, but are you going to be up for working tomorrow?"

"I suppose. Why?"

"We've got Dr. Gregory's office to set up tomorrow," Will answered.

"Oh shit, I forgot all about that. Yeah, I'll be there. I don't want Paul to screw that one up."

"How about I pick you up from the hospital? You just stay with Alex tonight."

"Robyn's having fun with Sugar, so she has no problem continuing to take care of her. That'll be one less thing for you to worry about."

"Besides, the hospital is on the way to the office. I can come and get you in the morning no problem. This way you spend more time with Alexandria."

213

"Thanks, Bud." Carol said fighting back the tears.

"No problem. See you in the morning."

Carol struggled to reach her phone while she was entangled in wires and computer parts.

"Hello?"

"Carol, it's Byron."

"Hi Byron. What's going on?"

"I think you should come back to the hospital."

"Why? What's going on?" The panic in Carol's voice was easy to detect.

"Alex is sleeping, but I need to speak to you in person. I really think it's best you get here soon."

"Ok." Carol choked on the words and hung up. Not wanting Will to see her cry, Carol stood up and looked away as she spoke. "Will, I have to go. You'll need to do this one without me. Paul is out on an easy call. Call him if you need help." Carol simply walked away. She knew Will would understand.

Twenty minutes later, Carol was about to walk into Alex's room when she ran into Byron, Erin, Tyrone and Candace in the hallway.

"Byron," Carol sighed a heavy, depressed sigh.

"Hey," he quietly addressed her.

"What's going on?"

"Let's talk over here." Byron said ushering Carol away as Candace began to cry with Erin and Tyrone comforting her. He spoke so softly, he was hardly audible. "Carol, Alex isn't doing well. Her immune system is even weaker. She really sick. The doctor said she has sepsis."

"What?" Carol couldn't believe what she was hearing.

"She's septic. It looks as though her blood absorbed some of the lead from the bullet. Her body hasn't been able to fight it. She's got a systemic infection now. It doesn't look good."

"No!" Carol began to cry.

Byron embraced her. "Just be with her," he whispered. "We all need to be with her and enjoy every second we have."

Carol fell into Byron's warm, supportive arms and wept.

Byron, Candace and Carol surrounded Alex's bed while she slept. Multiple IV lines provided drugs and fluids into her veins. Various wires constantly monitored her heart rate, blood pressure, and how much oxygen her body was able to absorb. Small, clear plastic tubing delivered much needed oxygen directly into Alex's nose. Anxiety, tension and sadness flooded the eerily silent room. The once vibrant angel had been reduced to a still, motionless, heavily wired body.

After several hours of quiet, Carol looked around. Both Byron and Candace had fallen asleep in their chairs.

Carol gently kissed Alex's hand. "Not even death can stop true love." Carol cried silently. She wiped away the tears. "I love you Alex. And, I am so, so sorry." Carol noiselessly cried for hours.

A little past two in the morning, Alex woke up and saw her lover crying. "Hey baby," she weakly whispered.

Carol looked up. She stood up and ran to be next to the hospital bed. She grabbed Alexandria's hand with her left hand and tenderly placed her right hand on the side of Alex's soft, gorgeous face. Alex never lost her beauty, not even from severe illness.

"Hi sweetheart," Carol answered tearfully.

"Don't cry, baby."

"Alex..."

"It's ok, Carol. You gave me the best twelve years of my life. I fell in love with you the minute I saw you at City Girls. You've made me laugh a lot. You took good care of me and my family. You even protected me in the bank. Thank you."

"Don't thank me. I made you sick. I caused this. I'd do anything to undo that."

"Carol, don't you see all the good you did for me? I can never thank you enough for all the joy you've brought to my life.

"Remember teaching me how to drive a stick? Or us screaming our hearts out to Hendrix? Remember that wonderful dinner you cooked for me that Valentine's Day? Remember all the baseball games we'd watch? Or the number of times you sat through The Princess Bride for me? Remember that gay bookstore we went to with John and Dave? Remember throwing me that surprise birthday party?" She had to stop to catch her breath.

"You embraced me and my sobriety. You came with us to the nursing facility every year at Thanksgiving. You bought me a house! I am the luckiest woman in the world to have you as my partner."

Alex sounded exhausted. "You always made me laugh. You brought so much fun, joy and happiness into my life, Carol."

"I'd do it all over again for you. I love you so much, Alex."

"I love you too. I always will." Alex paused as she watched tears stream down Carol's face. "Baby, remember that not even death can stop true love."

Carol leaned forward and tenderly kissed Alexandria on her forehead. "I love you," she sobbed.

"My sister," Byron said between the tears, "was a gift from God. She was an angel. She was radiant, intelligent, strong, and joyous. She was a fighter. She was an inspiration to us all. Today, the world loses one of the greatest people that ever walked the planet: my sister, Alexandria." Byron's tears flowed uncontrollably. He could no longer speak. He fought to breathe. Gradually, he walked away from the podium.

Candace slowly pushed her pregnant body up and traded places with her tearful brother. "What does anyone say at a time like this?"

"Alexandria was such a bright, glorious soul. She touched every life she encountered. Her presence was so strong and yet so gentle. Her presence in any room brought joy and peace to everyone there. She touched so many people. She will be missed."

"My sister was my idol and my inspiration. She taught me to persevere. She showed me that hard work paid off. She taught me about love, about optimism, about how to be truly happy. She told me to never give up on my dreams. My sister was the best role model imaginable."

"She's no longer with us, but she'll always live on in our hearts. Alexandria was too amazing to ever forget. Her love has penetrated all of our hearts. She will always be with us. She'll always watch over us."

"Everything I do from this day forward will be in my sister's honor. I dedicate my life, my work and my every day to Alexandria. I love you, A." Candace stepped down from the podium and the tears poured down her face as well.

Slowly, reluctantly, Carol stood up and made her way to the podium. She took a deep breath before she began to speak. "Alex, Alexandria was a treasure to us all. She was so beautiful, inside and out. She had such a splendid, generous, caring heart. She was so vibrant. Alex was the kind of person we should all aspire to be."

"She was my everything." Carol said as the tears flowed freely. "For twelve years, my life was blessed by Alex's amazing spirit. She gave me so much in that time. She gave me light, laughter, joy, happiness, love, and so much more. Although twelve years is by no means enough, I'm still the luckiest person in the world to have shared that time with her." Carol had to stop. The pain was all consuming. Her tears flowed freely and Carol was unable to contain hers emotions.

"Finally and most importantly," she sniffled, "Alexandria Whetherby taught me that not even death can stop true love. I will always carry that with me."

"I love you so much, Alex!"

Will raced up to help Carol step down. She couldn't contain her tears, she was literally paralyzed with pain.

After the funeral, Will drove Carol home. Carol's hysterical weeping filled the car. Will was at a complete loss for words to console his friend.

Carol's sobbing finally started to slow down as they pulled up to the house.

Will slowly opened the door. Being back home without Alex was too much for Carol, she once again wept uncontrollably. Sugar was still at Will and Robyn's house., the house was void – truly void of any life. The emptiness of her home mimicked the emptiness in Carol's heart.

The pain, the loneliness and the quiet all consumed Carol. She collapsed onto the floor from the heaviness of this burden. Will picked Carol up, carried her into the bedroom and gently placed her on the bed. He sat next to her until Carol finally cried herself to sleep. Unable to bring her any words of comfort, he simply ran his fingers through her hair until the crying had ceased.

Carefully and quietly, Will exited the house, praying that his dear friend would soon find peace.

Three days of loneliness, depression, solitude and silence passed before Carol finally reached out and clutched her phone.

The other end rang and rang. Eventually, voice mail picked up. Carol wasn't terribly surprised. As much as Byron had accepted Carol and her relationship with Alex, he also had his reservations.

After the funeral, he had expressed how hurt he had been that Carol had not kept her promise to never cause harm to Alexandria. The pain from his twin sister's death was completely devastating and he held Carol fully responsible.

"Hey Byron, it's Carol. Look, I know you're hurt and angry. I think you are completely justified in that."

"It's just I had an idea. I'd really like to set up a fund in Alex's name. Maybe we could use it for AIDS research, or college scholarships for young girls at high risk of being on the streets, whatever you want to do. I just want to honor her somehow."

"When you're ready, please call me and let's see what we can do."

Two weeks of pure isolation crept by and the time had come for Carol to take control of business again. Paul had set up an appointment for Carol tomorrow. It was a high-end company and a good potential client. This was an ideal way to get Carol back into reality.

Although she didn't feel ready to carry on after Alex's passing, Carol didn't have a choice. She couldn't wallow in misery forever.

Chapter Twenty-Five

Carol wore a black pants suit with silver pin stripes and a cream colored shirt underneath the jacket. This had always been Alex's favorite suit on Carol. Carol hoped that by wearing it Alex would somehow be with her. She ran her fingers through her soft, brown hair. There was nothing left she could do to enhance her appearance.

As she walked through the house, she noticed the grey, dismal sky and the endless raindrops through the windows. The weather was a perfect reflection of Carol's emotional state.

Carol got into the GTO. She couldn't even think of driving Alex's car even if it was more practical with the high gas prices.

The rain was coming down in torrents. Carol strained to see in between each swipe of the wiper blades. She was focused intently on the road. Her enthusiasm was more than lacking, but she knew that she needed to attend this meeting and land this client. With a heavy breath, Carol refused to let this rain or depression stop her.

The drive was long and treacherous. Carol arrived at the large impressive corporate building with five minutes to spare. She opened her umbrella and carefully stepped out of the car onto the wet, nearly flooded parking lot. Carol grabbed her laptop bag and cautiously sloshed towards the entrance.

Once inside, Carol tried not to shiver as she waited for a man named Robert to meet her.

"Ms. Mathers?" Carol turned around to see a tall, slender man with thick, dark brown hair. His navy blue suit complemented his physique and skin tone well. "Hi, I'm Rob Martin."

"Hi, Rob." Carol replied. She put on a wonderful facade so that no one could notice even the slightest hint of her pain. Carol extended her hand to shake his.

"Let me show you around." Rob said, never touching Carol.

Quietly offended, Carol walked behind the man.

Rob made idle conversation as he showed her the company's main offices and work rooms. Carol paid no attention to his meaningless words. She carefully examined all the hardware and electronics from afar. She noted the age of the equipment, the conditions of the cords and all of it. These details gave Carol a silent warning. These machines were not in good condition. If she were to take them on as a client, she'd have a lot of work to do in order to get them running properly.

Finally, Rob led Carol downstairs. In a completely rude and ungentlemanly manner, Rob opened the door and barely kept it open enough for Carol to follow.

Rob kept stepping downward without paying attention to his guest. Carol quietly huffed out of anger and frustration as she quickly stepped down the stairs to catch up.

Keeping the main powerhouse in a cold basement meant even more work for Carol. She was adding up all the factors in her head.

"So, here's the brains of it all." Rob said pointing to a huge server rack with several machines all humming with lights blinking and lit up as they should.

Carol approached the cage of computers. Methodically, she inspected the condition of the rack. If it was dented, appeared old or beaten, it might not have the strength needed to house these heavy machines. The rack appeared to be sturdy enough. The wiring was in good condition. The servers also seemed to be newer machines that were in good condition. Overall, this set up looked good, better than the work station computers anyway.

Standing up, Carol turned back towards Rob. "You've got some good machines. But we have a problem here, Robert."

"What's that?"

"You can't keep your servers in a basement. Humidity, dampness and temperature all have a huge effect on the equipment. They may run poorly, or you could even be looking at a possible fire hazard. This has to move now." Carol firmly stated.

"Let's go back upstairs. I want to sit down with you. We can discuss moving the servers and any other necessary changes we need to make."

As Carol said "Ok," Rob once again rudely turned his back towards her and went back up the stairs. Carol rolled her eyes in annoyance and followed his lead.

"So," Rob let out a sigh as he sat across from Carol. "We need to move the servers. What else?"

"Well, your workstations all need to be up-graded. Your servers are more than powerful enough to support better computers."

"We have to re-wire everything. The wiring at each of the workstations is in terrible condition. Bad wiring can lead to equipment failure. It can fry the mother boards, or worse." Carol was unwavering in her speech. This man had shown her no regard or respect, so she was going to play hardball.

Rob huffed. "So, what are we looking at for all this?" He didn't sound pleased.

Carol had taken out her laptop and began typing. Using her special business software, Carol was able to come up with an estimate in just a few moments. Like a car dealer, she turned the laptop so Rob could see the figure on her computer screen. She wasn't going to risk anything on miscommunication, or this man's pompous attitude.

Rob winced when he looked at the monitor. "Whoa! That is a lot more than we were looking to spend."

"That's fine," Carol replied flatly. "But, I will tell you that you get what you pay for. Dawson Networking has been one of the top computer and networking companies in St. Louis for so long for a reason. If you want to do it cheaper, go ahead. You won't get the quality that you'd get with Dawson." Carol began to shut down her laptop and put it back in the case.

"But," Rob interrupted her actions. "You come very highly recommended. If our computers aren't working at their best, this company is seriously screwed."

Carol looked up at Rob.

"How quickly can you get this started?"

Carol took out her blackberry and checked the calendar. "I can have Will out here on Monday.

"I noticed you had a room that looked like it was designed as a server build-out. You're using it for storage. Change that. Make sure that room is temperature controlled and is completely ready for the servers by Monday morning. Warn your staff that you'll be down for a few hours, but I'll make sure Will moves all your servers and gets you up and running again by Monday afternoon. We'll take care of the workstations in small increments over time so that doesn't totally take the company down. Ok?"

"Deal."

Again, Carol extended her hand. Rob smiled back feebly. Carol packed up and left. She was offended and wanted to leave this man's presence quickly.

Carol sent a text message to Will to let him know of his assignment for Monday.

As she sat in the car, Carol sighed heavily. She dialed Paul's number.

"Hello?"

"Hey Paul, it's Carol." Carol's tone was sharp and cold.

"How did it go?"

"That's why I'm calling, Paul."

"Why? You didn't land the job?"

"Oh, they're a new client alright. But Rob Martin is extremely rude and inconsiderate. Why was he your contact?"

"He's the closest thing to an IT department that they have. His was the name given to me as the contact on the initial call. What happened?"

"He didn't shake my hand; he didn't hold doors open for me. He was extremely unprofessional."

"Oh, that's probably because he's afraid of getting AIDS from you."

Carol couldn't believe what he said. She was livid. "What?"

"Yeah. I felt that it was important that he knows. You know, just in case."

"Paul! You have absolutely no right to tell anyone my personal information, do you understand that? It is not important for Rob Martin, or anyone else, to know anything regarding my health. AIDS is not passed by just shaking my hand. God damn it, Paul! What the hell is the matter with you?"

"Look Carol, I'm just trying to look out for other people. I will not be held responsible for anyone to get sick on account of you."

"Paul, this man was at no risk. You had no right to do what you did. You are on very thin ice. I could easily terminate you for something like this. If you ever do anything even remotely close to this again, I will fire you without hesitation."

"You are my worst employee. You are nothing but a risk for me and for this company. Paul, I am putting you on thirty days probation. I am done with your bullshit!"

"I don't care, Carol. I did the right thing, the moral thing. If you want to hide the fact that you could potentially kill everyone in your path, that's your problem. Like I said, I refuse to be held responsible for putting anyone's health at risk."

Carol battled to fight back the tears. She could not let know Paul that she was experiencing any emotions other than anger. "That's it, Paul. You are fired! I will have Will ensure that you pack up all your belongings. I don't want you near Dawson Networking ever again." She hung up. The tears finally won. Sniffling, Carol sent Will another text message that Paul was fired and that he needed to escort him out of the office immediately.

Carol sat and cried for a few minutes, unsure of what to do or where to go. She finally decided to just drive home. The cold, the rain, and Rob and Paul's asinine behavior had all just taken too much out of her. Carol had no energy, no enthusiasm, no life left in her. She was less than apathetic. Carol felt hollow as she drove home.

Carol replayed Rob's rudeness in her head repeatedly. Her conversation with Paul was on an endless mental loop. Her mind started swirling in a bottomless pit.

She remembered the day that Will told her that he had been told it was company policy to wear gloves to protect themselves from her. Alex's death was so fresh that it still stung. Her mother's angry and hateful words pierced her soul over and over again. The hate letters that she and Alex had received were carved into her mind.

Carol thought of her father's death, Ed's death, Marlene's death, and Alex's death. It was her fault, each one was her fault. They were all her fault. Carol would never stop blaming herself. She couldn't take it anymore. All she heard in her head were: "imperfect," "failure," "mistake," "ruined," and "it's all your fault." The repetitive pattern sped up. The volume climbed and climbed. It was consuming Carol from the inside out.

"Stop!" She screamed as tears rushed down her face. Carol fought to catch her breath. "Just make it home. Hang in there. Just get home," she told herself.

Her tears and the rain on the windshield blurred the world around her as Carol struggled with each moment and each breath until she got home.

The rain pelted the roof and windows. It was coming down hard. Carol looked out the window to the dismal, depressing sky and exhaled heavily. It was just another cold, grey, gloomy, and grim day in St. Louis. Just like the day she was born, or so her mother had told her countless times.

Looking back at her imperfect life, Carol felt hopeless, meaningless, and lifeless. She had been nothing but a sickly failure from the start. Her life was full of pain, loss, betrayal, and devastation. The past 33-years had been so dreadful that she couldn't endure another moment of it.

Seventeen bottles of pills and a large glass of iced tea looked back at her from the coffee table. Carol tried to ignore their alluring stare, but she finally gave in. Carol glanced at first, then she looked, then she stared back. Since her competitors had no eyes, Carol eventually blinked and lost.

Slowly, Carol opened each and every bottle. There were so many pills, more than she had anticipated.

Carol took a deep breath. This was it. Carol poured as many pills, and as many different pills as she could, into her small hand. Nervously, she looked at the circles and ovals in the myriad of colors that rested in her palm.

Not allowing herself to have the opportunity to think, Carol tossed the hand full of medications in her mouth and drank some tea. She repeated the pattern rapidly until her glass was empty. She wanted this procedure to be over as quickly as possible. Finally, she finished the last little bit of pills and tea.

Carefully, Carol placed the glass back on the table. She stared at its emptiness and the reality of what she had just done. She looked to her left to see Sugar sleeping next to her, curled up in as tight a ball as a greyhound can be. Sugar yawned and stretched. Her head softly flopped onto Carol's lap. Carol then sighed as well, leaned back on the couch, closed her eyes and waited.

Her Blackberry began to vibrate in her pocket, but it went unnoticed. It kept vibrating...

More Great Books by Lauren Shiro

Impeccable

Carol – abandoned - waiting... for what, she couldn't know. She couldn't see that there was more life waiting for her. Carol is forced to face the demons of her past as well as begin to face life without Alex. Struggling to make sense of it all, Carol experiences her new life and all of the highs and lows that come with that life.

Unbreakable Hostage

Lareina Oliveira; she wants to share her passion for math. So it is back to school for Lareina... a tough Ph.D. program. A classmate is captivated by Lareina's beauty and intelligence, and despite her repeated refusals to his attentions, he kidnaps her! Only her determination and wits can save her...

Loving Her, Volume 1
by Lauren Shiro

In this series of stories, we meet a group of loving friends and couples. Each member of this group is diverse in personalities and abilities, but they are tied together by the common denominator - love.

from Chelle Cordero, Combining Passion & Suspense

This volume contains the first four stories in the Loving Her series. Each is also available as individual short stories. Loving Her, Volume 1 is coming soon in audio, and is available in print and all electronic editions.

Book 1
The Ballerina

A southern, redheaded, pickup driving lesbian ballerina? You bet!
Meet Liz: a southern belle with flair. Vivacious, eclectic and
graceful, she is unique to say the least. The first in the series of
Loving Her stories, Liz's story is the kind that stays with you long
after you've closed the book.

Book 2
The Cop

Donna White is one tough cop. Behind the badge, though, is a very
sweet, sad, sensitive soul. Truly a woman alone, Donna is simply
trying to navigate her way through life. Who is Donna? She is
dedicated, determined, distinctive and deep. Donna's rich and
touching story is second in the Loving Her series.

Book 3
The Mechanic

Linda - her name means beautiful... After facing rejection from her parents because she is a lesbian, Linda didn't feel beautiful... she felt lost and alone. As a skilled mechanic, Linda built her business... Her love life was a different matter. Until Katie... They survived the brutal beatings they received at the hands of Katie's ultra-religious father. Together they survived, and together would face their future, and find hope and a joy neither expected.

Book 4
The Model

She's exotic. She's beautiful. She's talented. She's unique. She's Stephania. A young successful model who started from nothing, she has experienced all the ups and downs of life. Never one to be kept down, she persists through life's trials and reaches for the fairytale ending she has always hoped for. Stephania's emotional journey is the fourth story in the Loving Her series.

Book 5
The Peace Officer

Brynn Racanelli - daughter, sister, friend, partner, police officer...
and so much more. Devoted to serving others through her police
work, and to helping her sister who battles chronic Lyme Disease,
she is the the poster child of selflessness. But she does have wants,
needs, hopes, and dreams. Will fate finally bring her the life and
love she's always dreamed of?

Book 6
The Shelter Director

Shy, quiet, humble – Jen is the kind of person that would give you
the shirt off her back and then ask you what else you need. She may
not be a movie star, but she'll treat you like one. She works
diligently to help save cats. She sacrifices her life and stability to
accommodate her partner. She gives until it hurts, and her reward is
a devastating diagnosis. What will her life become?

Book 7
The Writer

Everyone has that one friend; the mother of the group. Maria is that one friend; nurturing, wise, and with a spicy streak, Maria is the matriarch of the clan. Cerebral, emotional, and even sometimes comical, Maria's story is the seventh in the Loving Her series.

Book 8
The Vet Student

Determined to escape the small town and her religious, stifling parents,Katie works hard to get into veterinary school... in Philadelphia. Katie refused to let anything – or anyone – destroy her dream. Not even her own parents. She suffered many losses along the way, but she gained so much more. Tumultuous and tender, Katie's story closes the Loving Her series... for now.

Amnesie, a short story

What happens to love when life changes? Two women in love, one debilitating change...

Trajectory, a short story

Joe Davis has spent the last four years of his life behind a scope as a sniper for the Detroit PD's SWAT Team. A fateful call sends Joe and his team deep into the Detroit Ghetto; and reminds him that there is more to life than what's on the other end of his gun.

Lauren Shiro

Love without Boundaries

In celebration of her one year wedding anniversary and recent political changes that legalize her marriage, author Lauren E. Harvey (L. E. Harvey) and Vanilla Heart Publishing are excited to announce the re-releases of her books and a brand new series of Loving Her singles under her (legal) married name, Lauren Shiro.

Lauren Shiro was published nationally for the first time at age fourteen. Since then, her work has been published in newspapers, magazines, literary journals, and even textbooks.

In 2006, she began writing fiction and she hasn't stopped yet. From her set of intertwined short stories in *Loving Her*, to the powerhouse duo of *Imperfect* and *Impeccable*, Lauren has written stories that are sure to touch your heart. Lauren continues to write stories of love without boundaries.

When she's not writing, Lauren works as a licensed veterinary technician. In her spare time, she enjoys everything from wood working to roller derby. She resides in Rochester, New York with her wife and their menagerie of furry and feathered friends.

Visit with Lauren

Email AuthorLaurenShiro@gmail.com
Facebook Facebook.com/LaurenShiro77
Twitter twitter.com/AuthorLShiro @authorlshiro
Blog LaurenShiro.blogspot.com
Website LaurenShiro.com

www.ingramcontent.com/pod-product-compliance
Lightning Source LLC
Chambersburg PA
CBHW070612130626
46556CB00001B/337